Plus One

TRACY BROEMMER

Plus One

by

Tracy Broemmer

Contemporary Romance

Published by Tracy Broemmer

Edited by Lexie Broemmer

Cover Photos from Deposit Photos

Cover Design by Designed with Grace

Copyright © 2020

ISBN#: 978-1-951637-16-3

For my happily-ever-after guy, JB

I love you, and I love being in wine country with you

For my brother-in-law and his wife, who invited us to Napa Valley for our first trip to wine country—thanks Chris & Dena

For Jason & Julie Brendmoen, wine country friends we love to visit

CHAPTER 1

CAIT

The last time I flew across the country to California I was with my sister and her family. We were heading to Disneyland for my niece's birthday, because turning five is apparently a big deal nowadays. I think I got a new doll and my sister's hand-me-down bike for my fifth birthday, but whatever. The whole family enjoyed Stella's birthday, so there's that, I guess.

Anyway, back to the fact that I'm stuck in Row 17, on Southwest Flight 472, bound for wine country. Sounds perfect, right? I mean, given a choice, I'd rather be in like, *Row 6*, but still—wine country! If your destination is wine country, that makes up for any inconveniences on your flight, right?

Well, no. Not really.

The only thing worse than my current situation is that I could be sitting in the middle seat, stuck between my best friend Teagan and her guy, Derrick—lovey-dovey newlyweds—instead of in the window seat on the flight to my other bestie's destination wedding in wine country.

Well, I mean, I guess I could be flying to, like, Detroit for a destination wedding. Or anything, really, other than wine country.

I like my wine. Brynna, Teagan, and I all like our wine. Sure, we started our drinking career many years ago—maybe when we were underage, but I won't confirm that. Anyway, we started our careers with the cheap beer pretty much every high school—strike that—every young person starts with. Because first of all, it's cheap, and when you need to spend your money on jeans and shoes and cute tops, who has cash leftover for beer? Second? Well, none of us liked the taste of beer back then, so why would we want to pass up a new pair of gladiator sandals or Miss Me bootcuts for something we didn't even like?

From beer, we tiptoed into whiskey, but let me tell you, that stuff was way worse than beer. Then again, maybe some of that reflects on our mixologists. Show me a high school kid—I mean, a younger, inexperienced drinker— who can make a mean Old Fashioned, and I'm calling bullshit. We all took our turns doing the mixing, and yeah, we were all equally bad. Maybe part of that was because when you're young, the sole purpose of drinking is to get blitzed and be stupid, right? Not to enjoy the *taste* of something.

We didn't venture into wine until we were in our early twenties, definitely of age. And those first forays into the wine world were box wines and the two buck chuck stuff that tasted either like Kool-Aid or cough medicine. I'll never forget the first time Teagan killed a bottle of that stuff on her own. Teag loves to talk, and when you add alcohol, you seriously can't get her to stop talking. Pretty sure she recited the entire preamble to the Constitution that night. But she did it with a bunch of corny, badly done accents.

Teagan taps my arm now. I pause the music on my phone and take an ear bud out as I turn to her.

"You brought the stuff, right?"

"Yep."

She nods. "But. I mean. You brought everything. Right?"

"Got it," I promise her. By stuff, she's referring to the few gag gifts and bachelorette sorts of things she and I got for Brynna, our friend who would be a beautiful bride in just four days.

"Okay." She smiles and relaxes back into her seat.

The three of us met in first grade. Teagan was the chatterbox, the most outgoing of all of us, and the one who had to write *I will not talk in class* at least five times a year starting in fourth grade. In first grade, she had a bowl haircut, and her smile was missing a front tooth. Took forever for that tooth to grow in because it didn't come out naturally. She and her older brother—River's a year older than we are—were wrestling in their living room, and River knocked Teagan face first into the coffee table.

Knocked her tooth out. She's gorgeous now with short, spiky dark hair and a friendly smile, but if you know what you're looking for, you can see that that tooth didn't grow in as perfectly as the rest of them.

"But." She leans forward again and curls her fingers around my wrist. I eye her thick white gold wedding band and lift my eyes to hers. "Did you remember the body paint?"

"Teag." I tip my head at her. "It's all under control."

She studies my face to make sure she can trust me. Because normally, I am the forgetful one. I can make a long list of things to pack for a trip, and you better believe, I'm still going to forget something. Every. Time.

Not this time, though. I made sure to pack every last fun little gift we got for Brynna: from the slinky, sexy stuff to the kinky, funny stuff, to the actual real gifts we had picked out for our friend. I even have a gorgeous wine-colored gift bag that says *Bride to Be* in silver sparkles. The whole lot of it is the first thing I packed for the trip.

"'Kay." She smiles. Drags her front teeth—the right one is just a tiny bit shorter than the other one—over her lip. And then she snorts this cute little giggle that makes Brynna nuts. "She's gonna die."

Die of embarrassment, she means.

"Well, either that, or she'll kill us." I shrug.

Teagan closes her eyes, that smile still on her lips. I look past her to Derrick, who has his nose stuck in a Dean Koontz book. Like always. Not that I don't love a good

Dean Koontz book, too. Derrick must feel my eye roll—about their joined hands resting on Teag's leg, not because of the book—because he takes a quick peek at me.

Don't get me wrong. Love the guy. He's the perfect match for Teagan. He's the calm to her crazy. The quiet to her loud. The thought to her impulsiveness. They started dating when we were seniors in college. Brynna and I wondered if maybe they were shooting for a longest dating relationship before they got married last year.

So, yeah, okay. Boxed wine.

Well, I mean, thank God we graduated from that stuff. Some of us have experimented and found we actually like craft beers, and by some of us I mean Teagan and me. Give Brynna any kind of beer, and she'll just turn her nose up and go in search of good wine. Teag and I have taken to some mixed drinks, too, and an occasional shot of bourbon or whiskey.

But the three of us definitely love our wine.

Now that we're grownups, we've traded in the two buck chuck stuff for real-deal California wines. Brynna's aunt and uncle moved to wine country when we were first learning the ropes of drinking and sucking on pennies to get the alcohol off our breath so we could hide that we were breaking parental rules and real laws. The three of us have always been sort of family fluid, so on any given weekend, one of our houses could have all three of us there, leaving the other two families without their daughters.

Well, in my case, without their youngest daughter.

Don't take it the wrong way, but through the years, we were so close, that our parents were interchangeable. I was just as used to waking up in Brynna's or Teagan's room as mine. My mom did their laundry. Teag's mom helped Brynna and me with our science homework. Brynna's parents took us along on several family vacations. To the beach. To amusement parks.

And finally, to wine country. We were eighteen the first time we went. It was for Brynna's high school graduation, and even though we couldn't legally drink at the wineries, Brynna's aunt and uncle had quite a personal wine collection, and we were allowed to taste the good stuff under their watchful adult eyes.

And we might have pilfered a bottle or two through the years when we visited. Brynna's Uncle Tom marked the value on the bottom of each bottle with a silver pen. We were careful not to take anything we thought was too expensive. And we were careful tiptoeing down the steps of their house and sneaking out to the patio to sip wine and rehash old times and share our hopes and dreams.

Brynna was the most sentimental of the three of us. When we were twelve, she was in love with Henry Mason. I mean, it was almost comical the way her eyes bugged out of her head when he walked by us in the halls at school. She wrote his name on the inside of all of her notebooks in eighth grade. Drew hearts with his initials in them. Henry was clueless. He was kind of a dumb jock, though. Taller than most of the boys, and even then, he was almost twice as wide as most of them. Not fat wide, but football player wide.

Brynna loved a lot of guys through the years. Some of them loved her back. And one of them—Theo Garvey— really loved her back. They dated from the beginning of sophomore year until they went away for college. Theo found someone else before college freshmen orientation was over. He was a nice guy, but girl code clearly states that you never say that around the bestie that he dumped. So. Theo became the jerk that we didn't name. Brynna was broken-hearted. It took her a long time to date again.

Even then, she wanted us to find our guys. Or, as she started saying when we were older, our person. She's always been a flowery, sweet, feminine girl, and she loves romance, and she's always happy. She sees the good in everyone, and she wants happiness for everyone, so she tends to be a bit heavy-handed with dating advice and arranging for meet cutes for all of her friends.

Well, Teag doesn't have to deal with that anymore, right? We all thought Brynna would be the first down the aisle, but Teagan shocked us and did the *I dos* and so now, it's just me, fortunate enough to get all of my best friends' attention and set ups.

Really. It's just me.

Like, just before midnight last night, my boyfriend Ryan was supposed to hop a different flight this morning—he's been in Boston the past few days—to meet me in Sonoma for the wedding. And around midnight, about five hours before Derrick beeped the horn of their Honda Passport to let me know he and Teagan were waiting in the drive to head for the airport, Ryan called and let me know he couldn't make it.

Yep.

Just like that.

Hey, Cait, listen, I'm sorry. But I can't make the wedding. Give Brynn and Adam my best.

CHAPTER 2

Cait

It would be bad enough if it was just that Ryan had bailed on the wedding. But the thing is, he bailed on *me*. Like, Ryan Clarke is the first time I was dumped via a phone call at midnight the night before leaving on a fun, possibly romantic trip, to celebrate my best friend's wedding.

The thing is, it's not that big of a deal to me.

Well, it is. But not the way you might think.

Ryan and I have been seeing each other for six months, give or take. He's fun. Not drop dead gorgeous. Not smokin' hot. No bedroom eyes. But cute. And not puppy dog cute, but...fun cute. He's a big guy, like six five, or something crazy, and I'm average to short, so he towered over me. He works out a lot, and he plays in a recreational basketball league, but I'm not too sure he wouldn't have been better suited to football. He's just kind of massive, and he had sweet brown eyes, a goofy, crooked smile, and we hit it off pretty much right from the start.

We met at a work function. Well, maybe not a work function. It was an after-hour cocktail event for the downtown area. The cocktail hour is a biweekly event sponsored by the Chamber of Commerce to bolster interest and investment in the town square and greater downtown area. Ryan was there with two guys in the banking industry, and I was there with friends, and we found ourselves hanging out at the pool table, of all places.

Ironic for me, because I don't play pool. The closest I've ever come was just rolling a cue ball around on the old table my grandparents had stashed in the corner of their basement. I didn't play that night, either. Ryan actually shot a game, and he was so bad, I probably could have held my own if I had tried to compete with him. We laughed about it while we were talking to our friends, and we ended up wandering away to an empty two-top table where we parked and talked about the *Halloween* movie franchise and whether we liked it or hated it.

I like it, by the way.

Ryan hated it.

Maybe that should have been a sign.

Anyway, Ryan's phone call, being dumped—it didn't bother me except to annoy me. I mean, he knows my friends well by now. He knows the way Brynna, and now Teag, too, look at the world through rose-colored glasses and think that since they've found their HEA's, everyone else should, too. Especially their last unmarried bestie.

I don't love him. I'm not crushed. We had a lot of fun for a while, but never once did I look at him and envision walking down a church aisle or a white carpet runner on winery grounds to meet him at the altar. But I'm so annoyed that up until yesterday afternoon, up until *midnight*, I assumed my boyfriend would be my date for Brynna's wedding. I was so angry last night when he broke into all the reasons why things weren't working out, why he felt we needed to go our separate ways, that I had to bite down on my pillow to stifle a scream.

Maybe he met someone in Boston that turned his head. Maybe he's been interested in someone else for a while. Maybe he cheated, but I have no reason to jump to that conclusion, and because I wasn't terribly invested in our relationship, I wouldn't dream of accusing him.

But. Seriously.

This is my BEST FRIEND'S wedding. A destination wedding in wine country. At Divine Vineyards, one of our favorite wineries. The whole thing—the whole wedding weekend—screams romance and fairytale love, so of course, my true-love obsessed besties are going to notice when I show up for the ceremony alone.

I would be okay with that.

I truly would be okay with not having a date. I mean, other than my deep, everlasting love for Gale Hawethorne of *Hunger Games* fame, I don't think I've ever been in love.

Not sure I've ever even flirted with the possibility. I've dated. I've had some relationships that have lasted months, even one that lasted two years, and that whole most-precious gift of virginity has been gone for nearly ten years. But I've never been so into anyone, he's had the power to really hurt me.

Just piss me off on an incredibly grand scale, I guess.

So. In, like, three hours, we'll get off this plane in Oakland —maybe worse than Detroit, but at least I can rent a car there and program wine country into the GPS and escape —and traipse through the airport to baggage claim, hop a shuttle to pick up our rental, and pile in and drive about sixty miles north to Sonoma. It's going to be great. Teague and Derrick are staying in the same adorable little inn that I'm booked for—that *Ryan and I* were booked for, actually. Brynna's family is staying at the Divine Vineyards house on the estate, and no one knows where the newlyweds will stay after the wedding. We're supposed to meet Brynna and Adam tonight and join them and Brynna's brother and his girlfriend for dinner and a glass or two of wine.

The whole weekend is going to be incredible, because there's just seriously nowhere I'd rather be than wine country. Add in time well spent with the best of friends who are more like family and some fun planned events and whatever other shenanigans we find ourselves involved in—perfect. Abso-freaking-lutely perfect. I have been living for this weekend for the past several months, trudging through work and laundry and taxes and let's not forget a brutal Midwestern winter, and the best weekend of the year is finally here.

And I'm alone.

And annoyed beyond words for more than one reason. First of all, as I mentioned, this is Brynna's weekend, and the last thing I want to do is make it about me and my lack of a date for the wedding. Second, Brynna is the least selfish person I know, and no matter that this is the single most important weekend of her life, she will want to make it about me and my lack of a date, or more to the point, Ryan's absence.

I refuse to tell her that I got dumped the night before flying out to celebrate with her. Not because I care, but because she will. I don't want her focus to be on anything but having the time of her life, and because I know Brynna, I know she'll be devastated about Ryan ditching me, and she'll do her damndest to set me up with some long-lost cousin or a cousin's tag-a-long best friend. But not before she plies me with drinks to cheer me up, because she'll insist that Ryan was *the one*. That we were really going places and having fun and that all this time we've been dating, we've been inching that much closer to our own long aisle and forever vows.

All of this will be made that much more melodramatic because Teagan has her life figured out now, and she'll be that much more likely to join forces with the romance obsessed bride-to-be.

And the only reason I'll feel bad is because they feel bad.

That and the hangover I'm bound to have after they bring me comfort wine.

I know they mean well, but trust me; I've suffered through more than one hangover from emergency girls' nights they've called when I've casually mentioned that yet another casual relationship has ended.

CHAPTER 3

CAIT

Oakland International is big and busy, and Derrick, Teagan, and I head to baggage claim, making a pit stop at the restrooms on the way. Maybe I'm the only person alive to feel this way, but I hate using the lavatory on planes. It's not that I think they're dirty, not that I'm claustrophobic—the bathroom in my first apartment after college wasn't that much bigger than those on planes, and it had a shower stall in it, too—and I'm not terrified of flying.

But I don't *love* much about the whole flying experience, either. From the shuttles in the parking decks to checking bags and the security checks—the whole thing just shoots my anxiety level through the roof. So, once I get on a plane and find a seat, the last thing I want to do is get up and climb over people to get to the teeny, tiny lavatory and then climb back over people when I return to my seat. In case you don't believe me about not being afraid to fly, I also hate climbing over anyone and using public restrooms at concerts and sporting events. Even movies.

So, I normally don't drink anything during my flights. Just makes it easier and usually enables me to get off a flight without feeling miserably bloated. This wasn't just any flight, though. This was a vacation sort of flight with Teag and Derrick, and we were feeling festive and fun, and so, yeah, we had a beer on the plane.

One beer.

Teag's waiting for me when I step out of the stall and head to the line of sinks to wash my hands.

"Good grief, Cait," she says with a laugh. "You had one beer. That was almost a record pee."

In the mirror over the sinks, I aim an eye roll at her, but I laugh.

"That's why I don't drink on planes."

"Brynna texted."

"I saw that."

Hands washed, I snatch a paper towel and dry them.

Brynna and her parents have been out here since last weekend, kind of really doing the vacation thing big. She's a kindergarten teacher—hello, perfect job match for that girl—and since it's May, she took the last few weeks of school for personal time. Adam's in the corporate offices at one of our big local manufacturing companies, so he flew in late last night. I noticed Brynna's text when I turned off airplane mode.

Lots of gushing about the beautiful weather. She and her brother and his girlfriend had gone to the ocean on Sunday and walked the beach. They'd done some hiking the next day. She's sent me about a thousand pictures, including seven of the Golden Gate Bridge from their day spent in San Francisco.

Brynna's the girl to gush about flowers and blue skies and warm weather on any given day, but since it's been wedding week, she's gone a little nuts with the feel good vibes. I don't mind. In fact, I love her all the more for it, and I know Teag does, too.

"What about Ryan?" Teagan asks as we head back out of the ladies' room to find Derrick.

"What about him?" My stomach knots instantly. Remember how I said I'm the forgetful one? I'm also the one with the worst poker face. I can't lie to Brynna and Teagan. One look at my face when I'm talking, and they just know. I don't know what my tell is, so I have no idea how to learn to deceive them.

"Have you heard from him? When's he get in?"

We're standing just outside the women's room now, looking around for Derrick. I nudge Teag when I spot him across the way at a Hudson's News shop. He's flipping through a hardcover book, which interests me, because I know there's nothing new out there by Dean Koontz right now.

"Mmmm." Teagan groans appreciatively. For a second, I think she's happy that Derrick's looking at something other than a Dean Koontz book. I'm about to ask her what's wrong with his books, when she turns a grin and heavy hooded eyes my way. "Isn't he just beautiful?"

So, okay, Derrick's a nice-looking guy. He's a bit of an uptight, buttoned-up kind of guy. Always has at least two buttons on a polo shirt done. Perfect creases in his long-sleeved button-up shirts. If I were Teagan, I'd have insisted on some kind of prenup agreement stating that I would never be tasked with ironing his clothes. That he either visited the drycleaner often, changed his clothing style, or changed his fiancé.

Then again, I'm not in love with him and haven't slept with him, so maybe he's got something so fantastic that she doesn't mind.

"Yeah." I nod and smile, stomach still twisted up about telling my friends Ryan and I broke up. But this seems like a good distraction, so I'll go along with talking about how beautiful Derrick is.

"I bought him those shorts. Didn't tell him they cup his ass like that, because then he wouldn't wear them. He would think they're too small."

Derrick has a nice enough butt, I guess, but I tend to not look at the butts of the guys my friends are in love with. I give her a silent nod and look anywhere but at Teag's husband.

"The shirt's good, too," I say as we start walking just to make sure she doesn't remember that she asked me about Ryan. "That color." It's pink, so I have no idea what to follow that up with. "Kind of makes his eyes pop."

It doesn't. I mean, his eyes are fine, but they're green, and I don't think pink shirts and green eyes popping is a thing.

"You think so?" Teagan giggles. "God, I am the luckiest woman in the world to be married to that."

Mission accomplished. Teag throws her arms around Derrick from behind him and stretches to her tiptoes to kiss his neck. Meanwhile, I look around at the lovely airport souvenir fare—crew neck collared T-shirts that say Oakland. Ball caps. And of course, for those looking for a deal, the T-shirt and cap combo for just $19.95. Key chains. Coffee cups.

Not sure how long Derrick is going to peruse the books or how long Teag's going to stand behind him and feel him up, I mosey away from them to look at the bestsellers on the wall. Maybe I should get a book. Since I don't have a plus one at this wedding. Nothing too exciting going to be happening in my room at the inn, and I don't sleep well away from home.

"You ready, Cait?" Teag calls, and I nod without looking her way.

They hold hands as we walk on toward the baggage claim. Derricks fills us in on the book he was looking at, a new author who debuted on the bestseller list.

"Did you pack the candlesticks?" Teagan looks at me suddenly, eyes wide with alarm.

"Shipped them out last week."

"Really?"

"Yeah. I didn't want to worry about scratching them up when I packed them in my bag."

Along with the gag gifts and sexy gifts, Teagan and I also found silver candlesticks for Brynna and Adam. Not something I would ever want, and I honestly doubt Teag would use them. But Brynna lights candles when she and Adam have frozen pizza, so she'll love these for fancy dinners when they're celebrating birthdays or anniversaries.

Teagan laughs and flashes a little grimace.

"Sorry I keep doubting you," she says sweetly. "But you know you forgot something."

I didn't forget him, but yes, soon enough it's going to be very obvious just exactly what—who—I didn't bring for the wedding.

For now, though, I'll own the forgetful role. Instead of arguing that I know I packed every damned thing I could possibly need—tampons, panty shields (shouldn't need them, but ladies, haven't we all been surprised a time or two by that unwanted visitor), Tums, ibuprofen, at least eight pair of panties, three bras, several outfits (gotta have options), more shoes than outfits, two swimsuits, and as many cosmetics and jewelry items as I could fit in my bag.

And a hair dryer. Even though every hotel or inn has them now, I always bring my own.

And all of the fun things we have to give Brynna.

A jacket. My dress for the wedding.

Just no date.

Which means when we sit down for the wedding dinner, it will be glaringly obvious to everyone there, that I either forgot my date or forgot to mention to Brynna, that I don't have a plus one.

CHAPTER 4

CAIT

Our travel nights—no matter where we go—are always about Mexican food. In hindsight, I wonder if that's part of the reason Ryan ditched me. Not just because he didn't want to eat at La Casa with us tonight, but because as a group, we have things that we do. Period. No questions asked. Mexican food on travel nights. Sharing ice cream— no matter who gets what or if someone doesn't order anything, we pass spoons around like hot potatoes. Texting each other after midnight if there's something really, really important to share.

Like the time I woke up at 2:19 and had to text the girls to tell them about a dream I had. I mean, wouldn't you want to gush about a dream where you were dating Matthew McConaughey? Hmm. Maybe Ryan didn't love the whole dreaming about Matthew McConaughey thing—anyway, that's just the way Brynna, Teagan, and I roll. Derrick and Adam are on board, obviously. They've learned to fully embrace all of the crazy we generate. Maybe we're too much for Ryan.

Oh well. At least he paid for his airfare so I'm not out money for this. Rooms at the inn aren't cheap, but I will be sleeping in that room and showering there, so yeah, I'm going to have to pay for that.

We walk to La Casa from the inn. It'll be a little cool when we walk back but definitely bearable, considering we left a rainy fifty-degree day with a cold, raw wind when we flew out of Lambert in St. Louis.

I fell in love with Sonoma Plaza on our first trip to wine country when we were eighteen, even before I could legally walk into a winery and do a tasting. The square itself is a perfectly charming area that covers, like, eight acres of land. When we were eighteen and too young to order drinks, we studied the history of the town and the restaurants and shopping available. Well, okay, yeah, we were more interested in eating and shopping, but when we were drinking our iced coffees from Basque and ducking into one after another adorable little boutique wishing like hell we hadn't blown our money on the Natural Light beer the weekend before at Hayden Rooney's, we did read the plaques around town and browse through books on area history. We read enough to learn that the town of Sonoma is centered around the square, although to be fair, that seems pretty obvious. We also learned that the plaza is set up in the standard form of a Mexican town, and it's surrounded by some pretty cool historic buildings like the Sebastiani Theatre built in the early 1930s and the Toscano Hotel from the 1850s.

I love the feel of the area. Everyone is friendly—the tourists hanging out in the plaza and shopping in the boutiques to the people who work the touristy boutiques and restaurants. Almost everywhere you go, there are water bowls out for dogs, and it seems like every other person you pass on the sidewalks has a furry companion with them.

Teag asked me again about Ryan when we got to the car rental place. Like, we were next in line to get our vehicle, and she suddenly whipped her head around to look at me and said, "What about Ryan?" She sounded so dramatic and so worried, for a second, I was scared she had read my mind and knew about the phone call last night. Before I could say anything—my heart was pretty much crammed up into my throat—Derrick nodded at me as if to second her question.

Just then, we were called up to the counter, and the woman there asked if she could help us. The nametag pinned crookedly near the collar of her purple knit shirt said Wanda. Her face was twisted in a sour-looking frown, and she eyed us like we were hooligans from the wrong side of the tracks there to destroy their property. Let me tell you this. Teag's a badass cardiac nurse. I saw her in action once, although that was in the ER a few years back, and the woman has no fear. She's strong, and she's a professional, and she even looks like a grown-up when she's not in scrubs. And Derrick works in IT for the school district—see what I mean? A little buttoned-up, kind of nerdy cute. But definitely not a guy that should draw looks of judgement and suspicion like Wanda was currently giving him.

Her frosty blond hair dipped low on her forehead. I'm guessing it wasn't a fashion statement, so much as a late in the day, throw in the towel, maybe you need a haircut kind of thing. As Derrick tugged his wallet from his pocket—he would be the primary driver, though we had all planned to take our turns, and now we were down one with Ryan not coming—Wanda looked past him to me with a sneer. Apparently, though I was on the dean's list all four years in college and now held an official realtor's license, I didn't look too trustworthy, either.

It crossed my mind to suggest to Wanda that she drive north and grab a glass of wine and chill. But Teag glanced at me while Derrick was listening to Wanda's less than enthusiastic rundown of the rental agreement. She arched her brows again. My heart had moved out of my throat by that time, but it had kind of done a harsh drop to my stomach, and I stared at Teag silently, wondering how to get out of explaining about Ryan.

"Are we supposed to meet him here?" she asked when I didn't answer her right away.

Delighted to answer her truthfully, I gave her a big smile and glanced at Wanda to give her a dose of happiness, and then looked back at Teag. "No."

Because if he wasn't coming to the wedding, he wasn't flying into Oakland today. Therefore, no, we did not have to stand around and wait for him here.

She nodded absently, probably assuming she remembered that detail wrong or that his flight had been delayed or some such thing. Whatever, I whooshed a sigh of relief when she turned back to the counter and rested her elbows there while Derrick signed the rental contract. Wanda gave her one last withering look as she passed the keys to Derrick.

"That woman needs to get laid," Teagan mumbled as we walked away from the counter. Derrick's cheeks flushed a faint pink, and he threw his arm around her shoulders.

"We're looking for a Cadillac Escalade," he announced. "Black. California plates."

"Just tell us the spot number, babe."

I might have managed to avoid telling Teagan and Derrick the whole story, but I know the second we set foot in La Casa and Brynna sees me and not Ryan, she's going to ask where he's at. Maybe she'll be so caught up in wedding excitement that I can at least put her off for a while. At least until I can come up with a fib to get me through the weekend. Maybe I could tell her he had a family emergency. Nope. Can't do that. That would be cruel, because then she would spend her wedding weekend worrying about Ryan and his family. And God forbid, if there was some kind of emergency with someone in his family, I would feel like I somehow caused it, and I definitely don't want something bad to happen to anyone.

Maybe just for Ryan's flight to wherever he decided to go that was more important and more fun than being here with me is uber-late. That's not too mean, right? To wish someone a super delayed flight?

"You guys!"

Brynna's shriek carries from the dining area to the waiting area the second we step inside and the door closes behind us. Teag and Derrick are huddled together doing that sickening sweet lovey-dovey thing—which I actually think is pretty cute, but also, it makes me feel like a third wheel, and sometimes, they get a little carried away with their PDA, and I love her to death, but that gets a teensy bit awkward.

Since Teag and Derrick are doing their thing, I get Brynna's full-on, wedding excited, enthusiastic hug. Even knowing the hugs are coming, she still manages to catch me off-guard, and we stumble backwards a few steps, giggling like little girls all the way.

What would Wanda from the rental car agency think of us? She would probably ask us to leave because we're causing a scene.

"Cait!" Brynna squeals as she squeezes me so super tight, I can't breathe. If I were a squeaky toy, I would have just broken. "You're here! I'm so happy to see you guys!"

"Hey Brynn!" I squeeze her back just as tight, and she laughs and kisses my cheek as she pulls away. Her big brown eyes sparkle, and she glows, and her smile is so sweet and so sincere, I feel a little ache inside. I'm so happy for her and Adam, and for just a second, I wonder if it will ever be me in her shoes. Not the actual Birkenstocks she's wearing right now, but doing the whole bride-to-be, happily-ever-after thing. It's not that I don't believe in true love, not that I don't want to find someone to spend my life with. Just hasn't happened yet.

Pushing the thought aside before Brynna reads my mind, I slide my hands down her arms and take her hands in mine.

"I can't believe it's finally here!"

Her eyes shine a little too bright for a second—yes, being romantic and sensitive tends to mean Brynna cries a lot of happy *and* sad tears—but she gets herself under control and nods. She leans back in for another hug.

"This is all I've ever wanted," she whispers, and I know she means Adam and the life they're going to build together and the kids they're going to have. Both of them want at least five, which to me sounds a bit hard to swallow. But I'm excited for them, and I know they're going to be great parents.

"I know." I smooth my hand over her back, and my fingers tangle in her long, unruly blond curls.

"Love you," she whispers.

"Love you, too!"

She draws back and looks at Teag and Derrick over my shoulder. She draws her eyebrows down, clearly concerned, and I suck in a sharp, quick breath, knowing it just hit her that Ryan isn't with me. But thankfully, Teagan picks that moment to extricate herself from Derrick's arms and launch herself at Brynna.

They do the same squealing and giggling that Brynna and I just did, and thinking again about Wanda, I look around the waiting area in La Casa and see two older ladies sitting together and gabbing up a storm, paying no attention to any of us. A hostess appears from the dining area—probably to seat us—but when she sees Brynna and Teag, she stops at the hostess stand to watch and wait. From the look on her face, I would guess she's talked to Brynna and Adam at least enough to know it's their wedding weekend.

Derrick and I exchange a quick look. I'm hungry, but on the other hand, as long as Brynna is focused on Teag, she won't remember that Ryan isn't with us.

"Luz!" Brynna turns to the hostess with a grin so big it's wrapped around both her ears. "These are my maids of honor!"

Yep, Brynna has been gushing about the wedding. Luz offers us a warm smile and then leads us all back to the dining area where Adam is sitting with Brynna's brother Shane and his girlfriend Bailey. As we near the table, Adam stands to hug me and Teagan, and then he shakes Derrick's hand, but that turns into one of those bro hugs and backslaps. The guys didn't know each other before; their only connection is Brynna and Teagan. It's nice, though, that they've become good friends, I think, and again, I have kind of a fleeting wish that someday maybe I'll find somebody to love who feels just as at home with my group as they do.

We exchange hellos with Shane and Bailey, and then we sit down—Brynna by Adam, and Teagan by Brynna. Which puts me one empty chair removed from Derrick and seated next to Bailey. The empty chair sort of shouts for attention, and my stomach clenches so tight now I'm not sure I can eat.

Except that they already have chips and salsa on the table, and chips and salsa are my poison. Everyone's talking at once, and Bailey and Brynna are both reaching for chips, and Luz is lingering, talking to Adam, leaving me to assume they've been talking about wedding plans.

"Cait, where's Ryan?" Brynna's question kills the buzz of conversation around the table. Luz announces that our waiter will be back in a few minutes to get our drink orders, and now with all eyes on me, I'm dying for a margarita.

"Flight delayed?" Adam asks before I can think of a reasonable white lie.

"Are you kidding?" Brynna groans, and I still haven't had a chance to say anything. "I'm telling you, every flight I've heard of this year has been delayed."

"My parents' flew to Hawaii earlier this year," Adam reminds us of their anniversary trip. "Their flight was delayed three hours."

"Ours was actually on time," Teagan says as she crunches a chip loaded with salsa.

"Do you remember that time we went to Destin?" Brynna glances from Teagan to me, and I relax a bit because thankfully, I'm off the hook for the time being. I feel a little guilty letting the little lie slide by, but it beats dissecting the phone call from Ryan last night. And it's not like I'm lying to be mean or sly; I just don't want this to upset Brynna's wedding vibes.

Besides, of course I'll tell them. But maybe I can fib and say he had a work thing he couldn't get out of, and then after Brynna's wedding and maybe even after she and Adam get back from their honeymoon, I'll tell them what really happened and beg for forgiveness for keeping it from them.

"That was the flight from hell." Teagan looks up as our waiter approaches our table. He looks young, and he's kind of cute, and if the guys weren't with us, I would feel sorry for him. Because we girls are a bit ornery when we're out together having fun.

Hens' night, as my grandmother used to say.

Raising hell, my dad says. And we can't get into too much trouble with the guys here. The waiter seems like fun, though, and he heads away with our request for another pitcher of margaritas and three more glasses.

CHAPTER 5

CAIT

The Inn at Sonoma is such a pretty little place. It's homey, but it's super cute and inviting, and after the flight and the margaritas and the taco salad as big as my head, I'm beat. Between the seven of us—yeah, let's not forget how exhausting *that* is, lying by omission is difficult, especially when you're not a deceitful person—we killed three pitchers of margaritas. I feel like I personally consumed at least seven pounds of chips and salsa on top of the taco salad and the margs, and before we leave La Casa, I'm, like, five minutes away from face-planting in what remains of the taco shell bowl on my plate.

It's chilly when we make our way outside, gushing tipsy-to-drunk goodbyes and love yous, but it's not bad. We're all hugging and reiterating our plans for tomorrow, and once we split up—Teag, Derrick, and I heading to the Inn and the rest of the gang driving back to Divine—Shane drank one margarita and then switched to water—I figure the chill in the air might sober me up a bit.

Even at night, I love Sonoma Plaza. Maybe if I lived here, it would get old, or I'd identify a noise that makes me nuts every time I hear it, or I would find something to gripe about with a neighbor. Totally possible that being a tourist here—albeit one who visits often—makes the place seem idyllic. Not just Sonoma Plaza, really, but wine country, in general.

We talk about dinner as we walk down First Street toward the Inn, and though neither Teag nor I make a whole lot of sense while we ramble, it's a nice conversation. We hit the highlights, laughing about Bailey's hiccups and the way Shane almost climbed under the table when she tried to talk to the waiter and hiccupped so loud and harsh, she sounded blitzed. Teagan rambles about how good her burrito was, and I give into my earlier restaurant envy. The taco salad was great, but I love burritos. If I had Teag's lithe body with the curves in the right places and perfect boobs, I would order them more often. As it is, me being average to short tends to make burritos and stuff stick to my hips.

It's after ten when we get to the Inn. Derrick uses his room key to get us in the main doors, but the lobby and the reception area are dark. Yet another nice thing about a small inn compared to a big swanky hotel. This place closes down at night, and lights are turned low, and doors are locked. There's no one around to check you in at this hour.

We take the stairs, and though it's only two short switchback flights, I'm dragging by the time we reach the top. Our rooms are close together, so Derrick and Teag see me safely inside my room, and then I'm alone.

They asked about Ryan again—pretty sure each of them asked at some point during dinner, and Bailey and Shane don't even know him, only that he was my plus one for Brynn's wedding. I might have been tipsy, a bit looser after having a few drinks, but I was still careful what I said about him. In fact, I said very little. I mumbled *yeah* a few times in commiseration with the delayed flight thing, but I never did give anyone a direct answer.

I sag against the door once it's closed and take a deep breath. Made it through day one without telling my besties that I'm actually flying solo for the wedding. Only three and a half days to go.

Exhaustion consumes me, and I realize I'm actually kind of glad Ryan's not here. If we girls have a thing about our first night out of town being Mexican food and margaritas, Ryan had a thing about the first night out of town being a crazy sexcapade. Sort of ironic, really, considering he rarely made it past two times a night, and every now and then, he was passed out, sound asleep in postcoital bliss after one round.

Not what I would call crazy sexcapades in any shape or form, but on the other hand, the idea of spreading out in that queen-sized bed and taking up as much room as I want and not listening to him snore all night and not feeling guilty if I don't want to wake up to another round of crazy sex is pretty appealing.

With a yawn that I feel all the way to my toes, I turn to slide the chain lock in place and toss my purse over to the bed. First things first. Even though I used the ladies' room before we left La Casa, I have to go again now. I survey the room as I flip my dress up to sit down. Decorated in dark browns and grays, it gives off a craftsman vibe that I didn't think I was a fan of until seeing the room. I love the dark colors and the flecks of gold in the dark-colored tub tiles.

I make the mistake of looking in the oval mirror over the sink when I wash my hands, and I decide I look worse than I feel. Two rosy dimes sit high on my cheeks, and my eyeliner has smeared around my bloodshot eyes, racoon style. My hair—fine and hard to style at the best of times —hangs limp around my face. The look is courtesy of the drinking, sure, but this isn't far from what I look like on a normal travel day/night.

Ready to crash, I return to the living area of the room and dig my cosmetic bag and stuff from my suitcase. Because I am the forgetful one, I go through my nighttime routine assuming I did forget something, but I'm pleasantly surprised when I find everything I need from my cleanser to my moisturizer to all the items I'll need tomorrow morning.

I finish my routine with brushing my teeth, and then I duck out of the bathroom and go back to my suitcase, this time to dig my pajamas out. Except when I packed, I assumed I would be sleeping with Ryan.

"Great." I pull the silk nightgown out and stare at it with a frown. It's nothing kinky, not even that uncomfortable. A simple white silk gown. Spaghetti straps. There's a floral pattern in the silk, and the bottom flares out a bit over my hips and butt. Sexy, maybe, but not over the top. The tank and sleep shorts in the top drawer of my dresser at home would be a lot more comfortable since I'm sleeping alone.

Oh well. Not like I can just run back home and swap stuff out. I cast a glance around the room again and make sure the drapes on the sliding door to the cute little balcony are closed before I shimmy out of my peach T-shirt dress and let it slide to the bed. With a flick of my fingers behind my back, my bra is loose, and I shrug out of the straps.

Okay, so the girls would probably have liked a bit of attention at some point over this weekend, but they'll be good with some rest. Ryan has heavy hands, and he's a pincher, and it's never been my favorite move of his. I can be okay with resting this weekend. Partying with Brynna and Teagan and resting at night. I could pop into CVS and grab some Melatonin to attempt to guarantee a few nights of good sleep.

With that thought, I pull the gown over my head and snag my dress and bra from the bed and toss them over my now closed suitcase. Almost fidgety with excitement over such a big, comfy bed all to myself, I pull the bedspread and top sheet back, grab my phone and charger, and climb into bed.

The fireplace in the corner of the room calls my name. Which is dumb for so many reasons, the first being that it's May, and I'm actually a bit warm—which I have no doubt is due to the tequila. And also, yes, the fireplace adds a romantic touch to the room, but at no time have I ever been in a hotel room with a guy with a fireplace blazing while we get frisky.

I twist sideways to plug my phone in and then quickly scroll through social media sites I love to hate and hate to love. I'm too old, too busy for the drama, but sometimes, it's nice to catch up with friends via those same sites. Brynna's posted more pictures on Instagram, including some from dinner tonight. Teag and me mugging for the camera. Teag and Derrick hugging and looking almost as if there is no camera recording them. Teag, Brynna, and I—the original three musketeers.

I upload a few of my photos and hashtag them with things like weddinginwinecountry, maidsofhonor, and taylormade, and then I set my alarm for eight in the morning. We're meeting downstairs in the lobby to walk to Basque, an excellent little café on First Street. From there, we'll probably do a bit of shopping before we head out to meet Brynna and Adam and the gang at Divine.

I'm not afraid of the dark, but it's so quiet, so dark, when I turn the bedside lamp off, it's unnerving. I snuggle into the pillow and take a deep breath and remind myself that I'm thrilled to have this weekend to relax.

I don't miss Ryan. If he were here, he'd be hogging the sheet to his side of the bed, already flopped over on his back, arm thrown over his head, snoring louder than a high school band in a parade.

But the quiet bugs me.

I feel like I can hear bugs outside breathing it's so quiet in here.

With a groan, I stretch again to turn the lamp on and go in search of the TV remote. Maybe I can find some sitcom reruns to fall asleep to.

CHAPTER 6

Isaac

"Too soon." Jasmine Kline shakes her head at Josh's suggestion for our next vacation. Jasmine is the most likely to complain about any plans or decisions made, whether it's a vacation destination or toppings on a pizza.

"What do you mean too soon?" Logan Brink rolls his eyes. "We're planning for October."

"I don't wanna talk about skiing." Jasmine takes a sip of her coffee and turns her nose up. It's not the coffee; she's a coffee addict, and even if she had to suck it up from highway pavement with a used straw, she would do it, and shockingly, not complain. No, it's the ski trip she's griping about.

"You love to ski," Logan reminds her.

"I do." She nods so emphatically that her bobbed black hair swings in front of her face. "But it's May. We just got through seven years of winter. Let's skip ski talk."

Jasmine hates *Game of Thrones*. That whole seven years of winter thing is one of her favorite sayings, as a snub at GOT, because she knows us guys watched it.

"So, what do you wanna do? Surf?"

"In October?" Jasmine yelps. She puts her cup on the small table we're crowded around and looks at Logan like he grew horns overnight. "Seriously?"

Logan groans and leans in to engage Jasmine in an argument. If Jasmine loves to complain, Logan loves to argue. When you throw the two of them together, they can debate the correct pronunciation of the word *caramel* for hours. And for the record, Logan hates it, and Jasmine loves it, but never in coffee.

Bored with the ensuing debate, I glance at my buddy Josh, assuming he's equally tired of Jasmine and Logan throwing down every five minutes on topics that the rest of us couldn't care less about. But Josh and Kree have their heads together, bent over Kree's phone, whispering something.

That's new.

So new that I keep forgetting that it's a thing.

Restless, I pick up my cup—glad I had the foresight to ask for a to-go cup—and edge out from behind the table. I squeeze between Logan and the table, but Logan keeps talking about how you have to plan ahead, and if you want to ski in October in Colorado, you should probably start planning by May. Especially with the number of people we usually have on our trips. Josh glances up at me as I lift my foot extra high to get over Kree's crossed legs. Jasmine rails back at Logan, but now she's switched from raging on winter weather to griping about the lodge we were in the last time we took a ski trip.

"Where ya goin'?" Josh asks. He automatically reaches for his cup, like he's going to grab it and follow me out. So, maybe Kree's so new, he forgets they're a thing, too.

"Just outside." I answer quietly, because I don't want to interrupt Logan and Jasmine to the point that they feel the need to talk louder. I shake my head, trying to tell Josh that it's probably not a good idea for him to follow me outside and abandon his girlfriend.

His eyes grow wide when he realizes the misstep he almost made. He grins, because he knows I just saved his ass, and he turns back to Kree.

Basque Café is always busy. We've way overstayed our necessary time here. You go in, you grab your coffee and maybe a pastry, and if you're dining in, you eat and go. But no telling how long this stand-off between Logan and Jasmine will take. I look around the small café as I reach for the door. There's one vacant chair in here now, other than mine. The line is currently only three people deep, but as I pull the door open, another group hurries inside. There are five of them—two guys and three girls, and they're smiling and laughing, like they're having a good time.

We used to have a good time on our trips. I guess we still do sometimes, but the older we get and the more our real lives change, the more forced these trips seem to be. Too much pressure to measure up to times past when we were younger and maybe more carefree and still in tune with each other. We started doing these trips toward the end of our college career. Just a bunch of us—guys and girls— who were tight in school, and then each of us started adding friends to the mix, until we grew to twelve to fifteen people. Back in those days, we were all in the same place. College or trade school. Working two or three jobs to make ends meet. Paying off tuition. Living with a roommate or three to cut the cost of rent to something more feasible.

None of us were seriously involved back in the beginning, so if we could scrape enough cash together, we were in the clear to take our party on the road and paint Nashville or Vail or Destin or Monterey or wherever we wanted. Things changed gradually, which is normal, I know. Pierce got a job first. He worked at a bank for a few years as a loan officer. You've probably heard the jokes about bankers' hours, but really, Pierce worked a good forty-hour week, and sometimes, he even worked on the weekend.

Adrienne went to medical school, so we rarely saw her for that stretch of time. And then she got a job in an ED in a hospital in a decent size town in Ohio. So, we still don't see much of her. She was pretty good about staying in touch with us via phone calls or FaceTime and texts for a while, but I haven't talked to her in several months.

Skye went to Europe for an extended stay and came home with a French guy she married. Logan got married and divorced in between Adrienne's phone calls.

And now Josh has a girlfriend, and Jasmine is driving me batshit crazy, and we're only a few days into this vacation. Used to be Josh and I commiserated about the group. You know how it is when a friendship reaches the point that you find yourself annoyed with someone almost more often than you enjoy being around them. You start making smartass comments to one friend about another. It sucks, but we all do it.

Which doesn't mean anything. Jasmine is a pain in the ass, but I would do anything for her. Short of taking a bullet, maybe. Our friend Jarod is a cop, and he got shot on a routine pullover two years ago. The guy's a big, tough-as-nails badass, but that bullet tore a big hole in his shoulder, and he's had a couple of surgeries since. I'm not a pushover, but I'm not built like a Mac truck, either. I would rather not have the experience of a bullet tearing through my flesh and bones.

Anyway, what's that saying? Familiarity breeds contempt? Maybe that's what I've been feeling now for a while. And now that Josh is with Kree, being around my friends like this is a bit too much to handle. Josh and I have been tight since we were ten or twelve. My family moved into his neighborhood when we were in fifth grade, I think. I saw him outside two houses down from ours. He was shooting baskets, and I watched him bang six shots off the rim—sloppy and loud enough to wake the dead. Basketball was my game even then, so after watching him for a while and both of my parents urging me to go outside and shoot with him, I did.

I banged a few shots of my own off the backboard. The first few I did just so he wouldn't think I was some dickhead who wanted to show off a sweet, smooth jump shot. The next few I actually wanted to make, but maybe it was the whole new kid nerve thing, because I sucked it up for a little while. When I finally started hitting the shots, the ball swishing through nothing but net, Josh had snatched a rebound and hit me hard with a chest past. Face screwed into a frown.

"You hustlin' me?"

It might have sounded like a threat, but we were two scrawny kids with pipsqueak voices and about a pound of muscle between us. I don't even think I answered him. Just dribbled and put the ball up for a lefthanded layup that missed the entire backboard.

The last girl into Basque gives me a quick smile. She's pretty in a soft, natural way. Her lips shine with a colorless gloss, and when she slides her shades off, I can tell she has a touch of eye make up on. Her dark blond hair is pulled back in some sort of messy twist, but a few curls have pulled free to frame her heart-shaped face.

"Thank you." Her voice is soft but lower in pitch than I anticipated.

"You're welcome."

So, I'm not a saint. I'm not above ogling a pretty woman when I see one. Not even opposed to checking out said pretty woman's ass, so I stand for a moment and watch her join her friends in line. Two of them—a guy and girl—are hanging on each other, head to head whispering about something. Makes me think of Josh and Kree. They've been seeing each other for a few weeks, I think, but they were friends before they decided to try dating. Josh works in radio, and Kree worked at his station in marketing. They got pretty tight. Every conversation any of the rest of us had with Josh included some kind of mention of Kree. The next thing we knew, she left to work for the local newspaper conglomerate, and they started dating.

The girl I'm watching is wearing those shorts that are in style now where the waistband is stretchy and kind of looks like a bag. I must admit until seeing them on her, I wasn't a fan. Hers are ivory with a pale pink flower pattern, and she wears a pale pink sleeveless blouse with them. She's not tall, but in that outfit, her legs seem to go on forever—all smooth, bronzed skin over taut-looking muscle.

The third girl with them leans in to say something to her, and I watch my girl's face light up with delight. Yep, pretty much an over-the-top word I am sure I've never used in real life, but there it is. Her green eyes—yes, I noticed the grayish-green when she took her shades off—are wide, and she's laughing. A full-blown hearty, feel good laugh, not a nasally snort that some of the women I've dated do.

I love the real, deep, honest laugh. So much so that I feel a weird urge to step back up in line to order something more. Just so I can be close to my girl again.

My girl.

Wow. Yeah, time to walk outside and take a break, Isaac.

As I turn to go outside for real this time, I catch Josh's eye. He arches his eyebrows and nods his head at *the* girl, not *my* girl. I notice the slight shrug of his shoulders, but I only shake my head and step outside into a nice, sunny day. I'm guessing the temperature is in the 70s today. The air is warm, without being sticky, and there's a nice, slow breeze that tosses the leaves of the trees across the street in Sonoma Plaza.

Coffee cup in hand, I wander down to the corner and then cross over to the Square. While Basque has good coffee and even better pastries and breakfast sandwiches, it's much too nice a day to be inside. As soon as Jasmine and Logan call a truce on winter weather, skiing, and the hotel we stayed in on our last skiing trip, we'll all be piling into the van and heading to our first winery. For now, I'm fine with just being outside.

I'm an architect, so I'm indoors most of the time. I try to make up for that on weekends—still like to get out and shoot baskets. In fact, Josh and I play in a recreational league, and we play summer league games on outdoor courts. I like to golf, and I fiddle around with tennis, although Josh can kick my ass on a tennis court.

Even so, I don't take these trips for granted. Don't get me wrong. I know I complain from time to time about Jasmine or Logan or Pierce or whoever, but these guys are my people. If I needed a kidney, I'm pretty sure one of the gang would cough one up for me. And honestly? I would take a bullet for Jasmine. I just hope that I never have to prove that.

But I like the outdoors as much as I like hanging out with friends. We ski, and we do beach trips. Not everybody surfs, but everybody's good with the beach in general. We do winery trips, and we've toured breweries and distilleries. We've gone snowmobiling and hiking. We've even done some casinos and some shopping.

Not going to lie, though. As happy as I am for Josh—because he seems pretty into Kree and she seems to be equally into him—this might be one change too many for me.

Eyes on the buildings across the street, I wander down the sidewalk. I don't want to just not do vacations anymore, but on the other hand, I'm thirty-one, and maybe it's time to grow up. Not that I'm one of those guys who has been known to climb on the bar with a girl and dance. Or play Quarters until someone passes out. It's been a good ten years since I've been involved in drinking games like that.

But maybe it's time to tune into life at home. I'm paying rent for a decent-size loft, and I like my job. Have some coworkers I consider friends, although none that I'm particularly close to. And there's the basketball thing. Golf on the weekends, when I can.

Realizing how bleak that sounds, I sit on a park bench and sip my now lukewarm coffee. As always, my eyes are drawn to the architectural detail on the Sebastiani Theatre building. I love the Italian Renaissance style, but I'm just as intrigued by the history of the building. Well, all buildings, actually. The Sebastiani Theatre was built in 1933 by August Sebastiani, of the Sebastiani wine growing family.

How the hell has my life become so boring, so empty, that I've come to rely on my friends to provide entertainment? That I've actually grown bored with those friends? Josh has already started hinting that I need a woman, that he can set me up with someone. My guess is Kree has a friend she wants to set up, but I could be way off the mark there.

I'm not against dating. Not a cynic when it comes to love. In fact, I was seeing a woman a few months ago, but it wasn't really going anywhere, and we kind of just agreed to let it go. We still see each other, and we're still friendly, I guess. But no. I'm not into the setups. I don't want to do a blind date. I don't want to do a double date with Josh and Kree, even though I like her, too.

Setups feel too immature to me. I mean, if Josh said hey, I want you to meet someone and we all happened to be at the same cocktail party or Super Bowl party or something, that's one thing. But no. I draw the line at actually being setup on a date.

Adrienne and I used to be a thing. Sort of. We were really tight in school. The best of friends. She was wicked smart, and maybe by extension, she had a wickedly smartass mouth. Well, actually, she's still smart, and she still has a smartass mouth. She's also very athletic and competitive. We started out with the friends thing, and I think we were both fine with that. We even kind of did the wingman thing for each other a few times when we were in school.

And then one day, I was watching her when she was studying, and it hit me that she wasn't just smart. She was pretty. Really pretty. And fun. Everything we did together was fun. So I kissed her. Talk about a gamble. I was more nervous about that kiss than if I'd been in Vegas betting my last dollar at a Black Jack table.

She kissed me back, and we fell into bed together and had a relationship for a while. We never said I love you, but I did love her. Adrienne is the only woman I've ever imagined a future with. But I knew she had bigger and better dreams, so I never told her how I felt. The last thing I wanted to do was drag her down and hold her back from med school. Well, actually, that's not true. I knew nothing I had could compete with her dreams of med school, so the last thing I wanted to do was sully our relationship and kill our friendship by telling her I loved her and making things ugly before she left.

Josh knows. Well, I suppose all of our friends know we were involved back then. But only Josh knows how I felt about her.

"Let me guess."

I look up when I hear that voice again. The girl from Basque is standing a few feet away from the bench where I'm sitting. Curious by what she's going to guess, I tip my head at her and wait for her to go on.

"You're with the bunch at the table right up by the door."

She's right. But then I think there were two or three older couples and a young family in there with us, so it's not like rocket science.

I nod, but before I can say anything, she continues.

"Feeling like a fifth wheel?" she asked with a small smile. "Because I sure am."

Ah. Okay. I see what she means. She must be the fifth wheel in her group. And she assumes Logan and Jasmine are a couple—they probably come off that way as much as they argue—and Josh and Kree are obviously a couple, still in the flirty, sweet stages of their relationship.

"Sort of." I shrug. And it hits me, I do kind of feel like a fifth wheel. And no, I don't think there's a thing in the world going on between Logan and Jasmine, and if there was, one of them would kill the other before they celebrated an anniversary. But on the other hand, yeah. The dimensions, the boundaries of our group in some ways have become more fluid—always changing—but also more set in stone, with people pairing off or finding someone outside the group and bringing them in.

I don't fit in with Josh and Kree, and I wouldn't want to come between them. I could fit in with Jaz and Logan, but I don't want to.

The thought flies at me and smacks me between the eyes so hard, I almost duck like a bird is flying low enough to get me.

"Teagan and Derrick are just out of the newlywed first year," the girl says and rolls her eyes. She softens the sarcastic move with a grin. "And Brynna and Adam are getting married Saturday."

"Oh." I nod. She's kind of got a double-whammy going on. "Here? They're getting married in Sonoma?"

"Divine Vineyards," she answers. She takes a step toward the bench and glances at me in askance. I nod and scoot over a bit to give her room. "Have you been there?"

"Yeah." I nod. My friends and I have been to several of the wineries in Sonoma and Napa Valley, both, although I'm not sure a person could hit them all and do them justice if he tried.

"Okay, so you know it's gonna be so beautiful and perfect." She groans and then huffs out a sigh. "I'm sorry. I'm really not mean. And I love them all to death."

"But." Sensing there's a but coming, I go on and throw it out there for her.

She turns her face the slightest bit toward me and shakes her head.

"Here for a wedding?"

"No." I lean over to rest my elbows on my knees. "Just a vacation with some friends."

She sips from an iced drink, drawing my attention to her hand. Her fingers tipped with a pastel lavender polish. A small ring that might be a birthstone on her middle finger. Nothing on her ring finger.

I'm dying to ask if she's got a date for the wedding, but I don't. Because I'm not cheesy, and I'm not desperate, and I'm never going to see her again anyway.

But seriously, sitting there with her eyes on the buildings across the street and the breeze teasing the loose curls around her face, I think she's the best thing I've seen in wine country. Ever.

"You ever see a movie there?" she asks suddenly. Her eyes are fiery and intense when she looks at me. "The Sebastiani?"

"No."

"Do you come here a lot? Sonoma?"

"Been here a few times, yeah." I nod.

"Never been in there, but it's such a cool building." She shrugs and shoots me a lopsided smile. "I'd just love to see the inside of it."

"I've heard the interior is all original to the 1933 structure."

She giggles and turns again to quirk an eyebrow at me.

"You know the history of the building?"

I answer with a sheepish grin. Way to ensure you'll never see her again, Isaac, I think. You can't show a woman your nerd card in the first five minutes of conversation with her and expect her to stick around.

"I'm an architect. I love historical buildings."

"No way." She draws back like I've actually told her I'm the crown prince of some middle eastern country.

I catch myself before answering *way*. *That* might send her hauling her cute little ass back across the street. She doesn't strike me as a *Wayne's World* fan.

"How about the El Dorado Hotel?"

The question pops out of my mouth before I can stop myself. Not sure hammering her with the history of architectural design is any better than a Wayne's World reference. *Nerd much, Isaac?*

CHAPTER 7

Cait

Brynna and Teag are probably wondering where I am. They'll be out here looking for me any minute. However, they'll be searching the boutiques, because that's where I would normally go. And let's face it. They'll do a little browsing, too, so I know I have a few minutes before I have to get back across the street and play innocent.

When this guy walked out of the café after holding the door for us, I was just kind of drawn out to follow him. I mean, he's really good-looking—tousled, sandy blond hair, a little bit curly and long on top, the hint of the same color of scruff on his lean face. Cheek bones that could cut glass. Blue eyes the color of the ocean under the rising sun.

It was more than that, though. Something about his magnetic smile. Friendly, but not calculated. Charming, but not over-the-top.

Teag had grabbed a hold of me in line to gush about the carbs she planned to order and devour, and okay, yes, I love Basque's pastries and coffee. But my mind had wandered out of the place after this guy. I can't tell you what she ended up ordering. In fact, I'm not sure what I ordered, other than this iced latte, and the only reason I remember that is because I'm still drinking it.

"Built in 1843," I answer him, although he didn't ask a specific question about the El Dorado Hotel. "Built for the brother of the founder of Sonoma Valley? Is that right?"

His eyebrows kind of slide up slowly. Not sure if I've surprised him or impressed him. Or if he was asking if I've stayed there or dined in their restaurant, and now he thinks I'm a history geek or something.

But when he nods—slowly, almost carefully—my mouth starts moving again.

"It's been a school and a church and…" The words gush out in rush, but then I remember that he probably thinks I'm weird, and I finish what I'm saying hesitantly. "A wine-making facility? I think."

"How do you know that?" He tips his head at me. "Why? Do you know that?"

"Well." I clear my throat and look around the square. Dappled sunlight falls through the trees above us and creates shadows on the grass near our feet. Eyes on my toes, I remind myself it doesn't matter if this guy thinks I'm weird or cute, because we're hanging out in a very touristy place and in about five minutes or less, we'll part company, and I'll never see him again. "The first time I learned about the history of Sonoma Square, I was eighteen. My girlfriends and I were too young to legally taste anything, so we made sure to learn the history of the town and to…" I look up at him now with a sheepish grin. "Shop. Lots of boutiques here."

The guy chuckles like he's amused, but his smile is friendly rather than impatient or cruel.

"And the next time?"

I stare at him for a second and then with a shrug, I explain.

"I'm a real estate agent. I notice buildings. And even though I'm currently doing more with rural areas and farm acreage back home, my interest is historical buildings."

He nods and stares at me like I just told him I designed the Taj Mahal.

"Rehabbing or acquiring them to tear them down and put up parking lots?"

I almost choke on my latte. Hand to my throat, I cough and sputter a bit and tip my head at him.

"Seriously? You said you like historic buildings." I narrow my eyes at him. "You're not one of those guys who researches all the reasons why those buildings should be paved, are you? All the businesses you could build to bring in more money? Do you build parking garages?"

"No." He holds up his hands in surrender, one of them still holds a to-go coffee cup. "No, I'm not. And I love that song."

"Cheers to that," I say with a nod and reach out to tap my plastic cup against his paper cup. Haven't met too many guys who like Joni Mitchell and "Yellow Taxi." Guys I date are usually either all in for Metallica or George Strait. "Thought that was going to be a deal breaker, dude."

"So, you're into rehabbing?"

"Well, if I had the money and time and expertise, I would love to buy half of my downtown back home and rehab all of those gorgeous buildings. A lot of them have been redone already, and they're incredible."

"Where's home?"

"Quincy, Illinois. Right on the Mississippi—"

"River," he says with me and he nods. "I know where it is."

"Right." I roll my eyes, a little disappointed that he's going to start playing games now. This has been a fun conversation. No need to ruin it with cheese.

"A couple of hours north and west of St. Louis, Missouri," he tells me. "Home of the St. Louis Arch. And the Cardinals. The Blues. Lam—"

"I know where St. Louis is." Another eye roll. "I'm in St. Louis a lot."

"Seriously?"

"Cardinal games. Blues games. Lambert is the closest international airport. Excellent dining and shopping. And a good bar scene."

"Laclede's Landing."

"Yeah." I stretch my legs out in front of me and flex my feet. I wonder if I've been reported lost or stolen by now. "But there are a lot of great places there. Like some really cool places on Delmar."

"The Loop?" he asks and nods at the same time. "Have you been to HopCat?"

"I have."

"You like craft beer?"

"I do."

"But you're in wine country," he reminds me.

"Can't a girl like craft beer and wine?" I narrow my eyes at him.

He grins and nods again.

"How about the Bissell Mansion?"

"I've been there," I say quietly.

The guy takes a drink of his coffee and makes a face like he's swallowing motor oil. He looks around again, and it occurs to me that maybe his friends are looking for him. Maybe he's looking around, trying to find a graceful way out of this conversation.

While he's taking in the sights, I steal that chance to study him. Folded over with his elbows on his knees again, he's tall and long-limbed. A summer tan already colors his skin and up close, I see tawny gold streaks in his hair. He's wearing one of those super soft looking T-shirts. Gray. Fits his shoulders and biceps like a second skin, though I seem to recall it hanging a bit looser around his waistline. Navy shorts that are hiked up a bit now to reveal a bit of hard, muscular thighs above his knees, though they were totally a cool length when he was standing at the door of Basque.

Because yes, I most certainly did look. Closely.

He's wearing grey Sperry's, but they look old and worn, not like he ran out and bought cool new shoes to come to wine country. There's a watch on his left wrist, and I'm kind of impressed that it's not an Apple watch. Even though, yes, I have one, and no, I wouldn't hold it against him if his was an Apple watch.

The whole picture is casual and comfortable and smoking hot without trying too hard.

Naturally this is a guy I bump into on a trip across the country. Why can't I find a guy like this at home? Then again, I remember thinking something along those lines with Ryan. He wasn't movie star hot. Didn't have a gym body. No bedroom eyes. But he was cute and funny and nice, and I thought that was supposed to be better than ticking all the physical attraction boxes.

What's a girl supposed to want? Good-looking? Drop dread gorgeous? Money? Charming personality?

Trustworthy? Responsible? Faithful? Seems like all of the above, but it's pretty rare to find all of that in one person. And let's talk about the fact that I gave up looking for all of the above back in school. I'm not superficial. I mean, I'm not going to *not* look at guys that look like this one, but I'm totally fine with looking beneath the surface, seeing past a pretty face to find a real person. A nice guy. A big heart.

Failed at all of the above. And yet, I know it's possible to find the right guy. Look at Teagan and Derrick and Brynna and Adam. Nope, not ready to just give up on finding my own Mr. Right. But I am wondering if I should take out an ad. Maybe a mail-order groom?

"Red or white?"

I swing my eyes from the guy walking a dog so giant he looks like a small giraffe and see that this guy appears to be looking at Mary's Pizza Shack, on the north side of the square. Excellent pizza, but I'm not sure what he's asking me. The interior is a lot of red and white checkered, old school stuff. Again, I love it, but I'm not sure what he means.

"What?"

He looks back at me with a smile.

"Sorry. Just watching that guy with the little girl and the dog."

I look over his shoulder and see a guy I assume is a dad, holding a dog's leash in one hand and the back of a little girl's bike in the other. He's not even super tall, but he's hunching way over and trotting behind the bike as the girl pumps the pedals. The dog—looks like a wiener dog—is flying, ears out like wings, tugging hard at the leash.

Adorable.

This guy was watching that, and now he's looking at me with what I can only describe as a wistful look on his face, and my ovaries are weeping.

Are you kidding me? Fate? God? Mother Nature? Whoever is in charge up there, how, *HOW* is this fair?

"Do you like red or white wine better?"

I snicker, because *duh*. We're in wine country. What else could that question possibly mean when you're in wine country?

"Mmm." I shake my head slowly and consider his question. "Normally red. Dry reds."

"Pinots? Zins?"

"And cabs, oh my." I nod, and we share a laugh. "But there's also nothing better than a chilled chardonnay or rosé on a warm summer day."

He's staring at me with so much intensity now, I feel like he's reading my mind, and he's already back through a few years' worth of stuff to know about me. I feel a blush tingle in my cheeks thinking about some of those things he could learn if he read my mind.

"Might be something better." He speaks so quietly I have to think hard and wonder if I heard him right, and then when I decide I did, I have to wonder what he meant. My phone buzzes in my purse, which is pushed up against my thigh.

I groan. "I think my girls just noticed I'm missing," I tell him. I hate that this is going to be goodbye. And I hate that I feel like I'm going to leave a vital part of myself here on the bench with him.

We both stand and sort of nod, and it almost feels like the end of a first date with someone new when you're both wading through those awkward thoughts of *should we kiss goodnight? Is that weird? Was it a good time? Should we go out again?*

He grins again and reaches toward me to tap my cup with his.

"Enjoy the wedding," he says, and his smile is so ridiculously sweet, my teeth hurt. "I hope your friends have good weather."

CHAPTER 8

Cait

Don't look back. Do. Not. Look. Back.

At the corner of 1st and Napa on the east side of the square, I do it. I glance over my shoulder and see that the guy is still standing near the bench where we were sitting. And, of course, he catches me looking back at him. He holds a hand up in a wave—or maybe it's a hand out to ward me off so I don't come bounding back to him like a stray dog looking for more attention—so I toss him a casual wave and turn around and pretend like my heart is not in my throat and my fingers are not a little shaky.

I don't even know his name.

Once I'm across the street, I pull my phone from my purse and read the text from Teag.

Where are you?

I don't want to tell her I was just flexing my nerd muscles with some totally random hot guy. I mean, I don't want to admit to yakking about historical buildings to someone who looks like he probably drove up the coast from Hollywood. No doubt, Teag would point out that might be part of the reason I'm single again—after she probes further and gives me crap about flirting with someone, only for me to tell her Ryan ditched me, and therefore, I am single again.

Took a walk. Where are you guys?

I stroll down the block toward Basque, all the while feeling like I have my finger jabbed into an electrical outlet. The hair on the back of my neck is standing straight up, and there's a warm hum low in my belly. Wondering if he's watching me. If he wishes we could have continued our conversation.

Perlé. Brynn's buying something for her mom and her aunt.

I love boutique shopping, and I know it would be stupid to mope for the rest of the day over a guy I talked to for less than a quarter of an hour. So, I turn around and head back across the street, past the square and over to the cute little shop on West Napa. Brynna steps out of a dressing room just as I step inside the boutique. She's got a cute little pink dress on, and she slinks over to me as I join Teagan by a jewelry display.

"Like it?" she asks us.

Teagan rolls her eyes and looks at me. The dress is adorable and would be adorable on anyone, but also,

Brynna could wear gunny sacks or coveralls and somehow make them trendy.

"Yep."

"Honeymoon yes?" Brynna tips her chin down to examine the dress on herself.

"Definitely."

She nods and looks up at us with a grin and then disappears into the dressing room again.

"Where were you?" Teag studies a pair of earrings, but I know she's very capable of paying close attention to more than one thing at a time, so I have to be careful with my answer.

"Just took a walk," I tell her again. "It's so nice out there."

"It is," she agrees with an enthusiastic nod. "Were you talking to that guy?"

"What guy?"

Yeah, so we've covered the fact that I can't lie. Worse than that, I can't act to save my life. I spoke too quickly just now, and even I heard how my voice jumped a couple of octaves trying to sound innocent.

"That guy from Basque. You guys had a moment there in the doorway. It looked like you were talking to him in the square when we walked by."

"A moment?"

Don't have to act this time, because I am baffled by her comment.

"All hearty eyes like a cartoon," Teag continues. "I heard something knocking. Wasn't sure if it was your knees or your heart."

Oh no. I feel a rush of heat heading straight to my cheeks. Good grief, was my reaction to him that obvious?

"Or maybe it was the sound of his chin hitting the ground and all of his teeth breaking while he checked you out."

"Did you spike your coffee?" I tip my head at her. The blush barely reached my cheeks and then eased away, thankfully. "The only guy I saw in there held the door open for us. I thanked him, and he said you're welcome."

"Mm-hmm." She nods and picks up a thin silver bracelet.

"That's courtesy, Teag, not a having a moment."

"Were you talking to him?"

"I ran into him in the square, yeah," I mumble. When she looks up at me with a cool, curious stare, I shrug and turn away from her. Feeling her heavy stare on my back, I busy myself with studying the clutch purses and find myself seriously considering buying one. I don't need it, but this is vacation, and they're really cute.

And I did get ditched this weekend. Didn't break my heart, but it did break my pride, and I haven't even told my friends yet what happened. That's going to suck, and maybe I deserve a little pick-me-up.

"That's cute." Teag nudges me, shoulder to shoulder. "Which of these do you like?"

She holds out two necklaces for me to choose one.

"This one." I tap a delicate chain with a ruby charm.

"Me, too."

She points at one of the purses—it's a little beaded clutch —and tells me to get it.

"It'll be cute with your sandals." She points at the flat leather sandals on my feet.

"Oh. Yeah." I study my sandals and decide she's right. Definitely need the clutch.

"What were you talking to that guy about?" Teagan curls her fingers around my wrist and tugs me over to a shoe display. "Love or hate?" She taps a snake print mule.

"Love!" I pick one up and turn it this way and that, as if I'm going to change my mind. "Did you try them on?"

"Yep."

"You should get them."

"Who is he?"

"I don't know. We were just talking about the Sebastiani Theatre."

"Like, what? I mean, did he ask you to see a movie with him?"

I snort as if going out with him is the craziest thing I've ever heard, when if he would have asked, I might have ditched my girls for a night and gone to a movie or anything he might have suggested. Well, no. Probably not. But I wouldn't have been opposed to giving him my name. Maybe swapping phone numbers.

Odds are I'll never see him again, but then again, life is short. Take chances, right?

"Buy the shoes," I tell her. "Life's short. And no, he did not ask me out. We were just talking about the cool building. You know. With the big marquee sign. I think I read somewhere that it's the only theater in the United States that still has its original marquee."

Teag stares at me blankly, and for a second, I wonder if I've put her to sleep. I'm not dull, not boring. I love to laugh and dance, and at times, I am like Teagan and I talk way too much. But Brynn and Teag don't share my love for history and buildings. And the *Halloween* franchise. And frisbee golf.

"You're hopeless." She shrugs. "You know that, right? Thank God, you have Ryan, because you have got no game."

"Ouch." I swat at her playfully.

"Seriously, Cait. You're the most adorable girl I know, but somehow, you manage to say some of the most bizarre things."

"It's a cool theater," I argue. "And he's an architect. It was something said between two strangers admiring the town."

"Where's Ryan?" she asks so suddenly I almost gasp out loud.

"Got hung up with a work thing," I answer. I'm so proud of how nonchalant I sound that I almost blow it with a self-congratulatory squeal.

"Seriously?" she groans and gives me a sympathetic eye roll.

I hate lying to her, so I just shrug and nod and clear my throat.

"I'm gonna go pay for this."

"Yeah, good idea," she agrees and follows me to the register. "I'm ready for wine."

"Where's Derrick?"

"I think they went in that kitchen store around the corner. The Bear? Sign of the Bear."

"Oh."

"Derrick's got this incredible recipe for ribs." She fishes her billfold out of her purse and slides her credit card out.

Brynna appears with two dresses draped over her arm—the pink one and one that's longer with a flower print. She's also carrying two scarves, and I assume those are the gifts she's buying for her mom and her aunt.

Once we pay for our finds, we head back down Napa to find the guys. Brynna texts Adam, and we meet up with them on the northwest corner of the square. Teag and Derrick hold hands as they walk, and then Adam wraps his arm around Brynna, and I think of that dad who was running along behind the bike, holding his little girl up.

And the look on that guy's face when he pointed them out to me.

Maybe he has a wife back home. And a kid. Or maybe he's divorced and doesn't get to see his kid enough.

Whatever the case, it's pointless to think about it, but I do.

I even look toward the bench when we pass that spot in the square on the way to the rental. Of course, he's gone. I knew he would be, but I guess I was hoping for one last look.

CHAPTER 9

Isaac

I prefer red wine, although as I sip this St. Francis zin now, I can't help but agree with the nameless girl. That sounds terrible, thinking of her that way, but on the other hand, I can't keep thinking of her as *my* girl. Not that I have a problem with that, but if it slipped out in conversation somewhere, it would draw a ton of curious frowns and a shit-ton of questions.

And if you're wondering, yes, it *could* probably slip out in conversation—mention of the nameless girl, *my girl*—because she's all I've been able to think about since my friends and I piled into the minivan we rented and headed out on CA-12. You should've heard Jasmine gripe about the minivan. She went off on a tangent about how she doesn't even want to be a mom, so how did she get stuck driving a soccer mom van on vacation. I think it needs to be noted that she hasn't driven yet.

Logan's driving today, and Jasmine is copiloting. And complaining that Logan hugs the center line when he drives—totally doesn't—and drives like a bat out of hell. Yep, he does kind of do that. So, anyway, they're in front; they've already had three or four arguments over which way he's supposed to turn and whether or not he should have taken this road or that road.

Josh and Kree are in the backseat. So, my eyes have been trained forward every time we climb into the van. Not that they're screwing around back there. I do think we've all outgrown that phase, at least. Not to say they haven't done any kissing or whispering, but none of us is so immature anymore that we have to cop a feel at every chance we get.

Still, they're in the first stages of their relationship, and I respect that. So, I'm trying to give them time to talk and share and laugh and all that stuff new couples do without me butting in. Keeping my head straight and eyes forward has allowed me to notice the tick in Logan's jaw every time Jasmine opens her mouth to talk. He gets red in the face when she criticizes his driving. They can talk civilly to each other, but now and then I wonder if they really even like each other.

The girl from the plaza—she said she likes red wine, but that there's nothing better than a chilled chardonnay or rosé on a warm day. Maybe. Not a big white wine drinker, but the thought of sitting outside on Viszlay Vineyard's patio and sipping a cold chardonnay or sauvignon blanc isn't a bad thought. Well, if I were sitting there having that wine with her for company, that is.

When she said that earlier about nothing better, my mouth almost got away from me. Because there's definitely one thing that I would enjoy more than chilled wine. And that's sitting in Sonoma Plaza with her, drinking lukewarm coffee, and talking about architecture and Joni Mitchell songs. She's not my go-to artist, but my mom and my aunts listened to her often when I was younger, so I'm very familiar with her work. And who doesn't share her thoughts in her song "Yellow Taxi"?

Well, maybe cold-hearted professionals who would rather raze historic buildings and put up parking garages or convention centers or even shopping areas to increase cash flow to an area. Definitely not me, although I do design some of those sorts of buildings. But I've never been part of a project that involves demolishing any buildings on the historic register.

Demolition can be fun, though.

"Isaac?" Josh nudges my foot with his hard enough to knock it off my knee. I sigh and sit up straight. He and Kree are both watching me carefully which tells me I've missed something.

"What?"

"Did you find that girl?"

"What girl?" I sip more wine.

Why didn't I at least get her name? People did that now. She and I could have exchanged names and numbers and just talked to each other. We could have texted. As much as I like my friends, I would much rather sit here and text that girl than listen to Logan and Jasmine argue who was the better quarterback—Manning or Brady—and Josh and Kree make plans for Christmas. I mean, *c'mon, guys. It's May.*

"The one at Basque."

I stare at Josh and wonder if he watched me cross the street earlier this morning. If he saw that girl leave the café and follow me over there.

"I wasn't looking for her." I hope my answer puts him off.

When we left Basque, our first stop was Sebastiani Vineyard. Logan had asked me as we walked in where I disappeared to earlier. I didn't tell him I was talking to anyone. Logan is the last person I would say that to. If any of us are still a bit immature about women or anything, really, it's Logan. I told him I just needed to get some air, which he took as me slamming Jasmine. He nodded along with me and rolled his eyes, and I just said something neutral about how nice it was outside, and that I would rather get the fresh air than loiter in a small café.

"But did you see her? She walked out almost right behind you."

Head on Josh's shoulder, Kree watches me. I like her. As much as it kind of sucks that my best friend might already be pussy-whipped, I like Kree, and I think they're a good match. She's tall and willowy thin. Not skinny. Dear God, do not call a woman *skinny* around Jasmine. Apparently, that's as bad as the opposite. She's strong or lean, not skinny, according to Jasmine. She wears her strawberry blond hair long. Sometimes loose and curly and sometimes, like now, she pulls it into a ponytail high on her head.

"Yeah."

I can't put Josh off, and more than that, I don't want to. I want to talk about her; I just don't want to feel like an idiot talking about some girl I talked to for ten minutes and will probably never see again.

"She was pretty," Kree says, and I like her that much more. She wears a small smile, her eyes sincere, not teasing.

I nod my agreement.

"She was into you."

That makes me roll my eyes. How can you look at someone and know in a space of five seconds if she was into someone?

Well. I mean, I did that, didn't I? I looked at her for five seconds in the doorway, and I was totally into her. But still, that feels stupid, like something a guy would tell his buddy in high school.

"I don't know about that." I shrug. What else is there to say?

"What's her name?"

"I don't know." I lean forward again and prop my elbows on my knees. "We were talking about some of the buildings around the plaza."

"Oh, no." Josh groans and drops his head back to stare at the sky in disgust. "You didn't."

"What?" Kree sits up and stares at Josh like he's having a heart attack. "What does that mean?"

"Sounds like Isaac let his inner nerd out and gushed to the pretty girl about arcades and cantilevers instead of getting her name and number."

"Arcades?" Kree turns to me with a frown.

"Covered walkways," I tell her.

"Dude." Josh narrows his eyes at me.

"Actually, we talked about other stuff, too. She's here for a wedding."

"Hers?" Josh asks quickly.

"Right. That's why she bailed on the café crew and came out to talk to me."

"She came out to talk to you because she was into you," Josh repeats.

"Or maybe she wanted to be outside."

Kree shakes her head. "Nope. She was definitely looking for you."

Damn. My heart just kind of did a funky gallop thing. Totally not cool to let Kree see that, even if she is my best friend's girlfriend. Instead, I pass it off as heartburn and press my fist to my chest.

I feel like that means something. I think it's different when women notice things. Like, I think Josh noticed the girl, but maybe Kree noticed who the girl was noticing? Or is that just wishful thinking?

"You didn't get her name?"

"No." I toss my hands up in defeat, careful not to spill my wine. "She said she was here for a wedding. And we talked about the Sebastiani Theatre. And the El Dorado Hotel."

"You could call around and see where the wedding is."

I give Josh what I hope is a don't-be-ridiculous stare.

"First of all, odds are high that there'll be more than one wedding here this weekend. And I don't know the bride or groom's name. Second, yeah, let me just whip out my cell and call over a couple hundred wineries and hotels to see if any of them are hosting weddings this weekend."

"Yeah, that's a bit much, huh?" Josh shrugs the corner of his lips.

"It was just…" I shake my head. "A nice…visit. A nice interlude."

"What?" Josh snorts. "Did you say *interlude*?"

Logan and Jasmine wander back to our table on the patio behind St. Francis. I glance at them, surprised that they walk close enough their elbows are rubbing. Me reading too much into nothing? Or is hell freezing over as we speak?

Damn. Maybe I will feel like the fifth wheel before this week is over.

"Who said interlude?" Jasmine asks, and I turn my head to stare at Josh. If looks could kill, I'd take him down right now.

"You guys kill that zin yet?" Logan picks up the empty bottle from the table and holds it above his head so he can see it better.

"Logan, you don't kill a bottle of wine," Jasmine corrects him. "You sip it. You savor it."

"It's my experience that if you sip and savor enough of it, you will eventually kill the bottle."

Jasmine rolls her eyes.

"You're gross."

"What?" Logan draws away from her as if she slapped him.

I drink the last of my wine, all the while wondering what would happen if I backed out of the next group vacation. What if I begged off for work reasons? It happens, of course. All of us have had to cancel from time to time, which is why our group numbers can vary from three to fifteen. Just depends.

Still, I've never just bailed because I need a vacation from the vacation dynamics and drama. Sitting here at St. Francis Winery & Vineyards with Josh and Kree for a while was nice, but now that Jasmine and Logan are back, I remember how weary I am of their back and forth.

And suddenly, watching them elbow each other and trade insults back and forth, I feel like an extra on this trip. Like none of them would have noticed if I had stayed home this time.

CHAPTER 10

CAIT

It's perfect. Well, I knew it would be perfect. I've visited this winery several times before, and I knew it was the perfect place for Brynna and Adam to begin their life together. But seeing it again, sitting here on the patio with my friends and Brynna and Adam's families, it feels real now. I can envision twinkling lights out here on the patio around the pool. More people will be flying out to attend the wedding—my parents included—but Brynna and Adam wanted to keep the guest list relatively small. The patio and the winery grounds will be perfect for wedding guests to mill about and take in the gorgeous view.

Including my best friend, who is going to be a beautiful bride. Teag and I got a peek at her dress again when we first arrived at the winery a while ago. We did the dress shopping with her, though I have to say it didn't take long for Brynna to find the one. She tried on four, I think, but that fifth one—that was it. Teagan had been stunned, because she is the least fashion-conscience of all of us, and Teag had spent two different Saturdays roaming four different bridal boutiques and tried on, like, twenty-eight dresses before falling for one.

"Are you listening?" Brynna elbows me out of my thoughts. The guys are in the tasting room right now talking to some of the guys from the winery, so it's just us girls and Shane's girlfriend Bailey here now.

"Sorry." I give her a quick smile. "I was just thinking about how your magic number was five. And Teag's was—what? Twenty-eight? Thirty?"

"Magic number for what?" Bailey's drinking a glass of Pinot, one of the wines Divine is well known for. I love it, but I decided I wanted something lighter. Something chilled, because it's a bit warm out here in the sun.

And also, drinking the rosé—a wine that sells out fast here —makes me think about that guy. The one I shouldn't be mooning over, because I'll never see him again.

Can't help it though. Sitting here with a glass of rosé makes me wonder what he was thinking when he said he could think of better things than chilled chardonnay or rosé on a warm summer day.

"Well, if the magic number is orgasms, you're totally lowballing it on my side," Teag says as she tips her head and blinks at me. "Because I am so far past thirty."

"Um, if my magic number is five, I can promise you she's not talking about orgasms." Brynna talks into her glass and then gulps a big swallow of rosé. "I think that happened last night."

"Do tell!" Teagan sits up straight and licks her lips in anticipation of good girl talk.

"Seriously?" I cringe at the thought, and a heavy shiver rolls over my upper body. "You guys had sex in that house last night?"

"Yes?" Brynna frowns, confused by my question. "Why? Are you suggesting we're supposed to wait until after the wedding?"

"Well, I know that ship's sailed." I shake my head. "But aren't your parents and Shane and Bailey staying there, too?"

"Well, yeah, but there is more than one bedroom." Brynna rolls her eyes. "It's not like we're all in a one-room bunkhouse."

"Still." I sip more wine hoping it'll erase thoughts of having sex in the same house as my parents or my sister and her husband. Doesn't help, though. Still kind of need some mind bleach.

"Did you hear us?" Brynna glances at Bailey, but Bailey snorts and ducks her head.

"Is that a yes?" Teag's laugh is bold and loud.

From the corner of my eye, I see people walking toward the entrance to the building and a couple other vehicles pulling into park.

"Nope." Bailey lifts her eyes and grins at us. "We were too busy. To hear…anything."

"Oh." Brynna sort of flinches and nods.

"Damn!" Teagan takes another drink and glances at me. "Maybe Yvonne and Michael were busy, too."

"Okay. No." Brynna shakes her head and points a finger at Teagan. "Nope. Not going there."

"So, it's okay for all of us to have a fun night, but not your parents? Or Adam's parents?"

I know from the look on Brynna's face she's trying to come up with a reasonable argument. Something that suggests sure, it's great for her parents, for Adam's parents to have fun, but not under the same roof as them. She can't pose her comeback in those exact terms, though, because she thinks I'll call her a hypocrite.

We're all teasing, things we've joked and laughed about many times before when we're drinking and even when we aren't, and yes, sometimes, Yvonne has been involved in these discussions. I think she gets more of a kick out of them than we do.

Right now, though, my heart isn't in it. Because I'm guessing from what Teagan said—that it was okay for all of them to have fun—that she and Derrick had some fun at the inn. Which is awesome. I'm all about good sex, but I'm really feeling like the odd girl out right now.

"Hey." Brynna leans into me this time and grabs my arm. This is it. I feel it coming; she's about to ask about Ryan. I fight the urge to cross my fingers and hope she's just tipsy enough to believe the lie I'm about to feed her. Either that or maybe I should cross my fingers just as a sorry for telling these little lies to my friends.

"What?" Okay, that was good. I sound normal. My voice was totally level, no yelping. No nerves blaring in that one word.

"Where's Ryan? I thought he was supposed to meet you guys at the airport yesterday and drive up with you."

I think I'm okay with lying right now, because yes, Brynna's eyes are already a teensy bit glassy. Her cheeks are a bit pink, and though some of that might be from the sun, I'm pretty sure a lot of it is the wine.

"Are we having lunch here?" I look around and notice Teagan watching me. Not like a friend who's involved in a conversation with other friends. But like a bad cop. Complete with a deep frown. She's not as tipsy as I would like. "Don't you think we should eat something again?" I'm looking right at Teag, but I nod my head toward Brynna.

"Cait." Brynna slides her hand down my arm to link her fingers with mine. "Where is he?"

"Um." I shake my head and pull on a face that I'm thinking a girl might make when her boyfriend screws up a fun weekend schedule because he has to work longer than he planned. "He got caught up. In a work thing."

"A work thing?" Teagan repeats.

"Yeah." I nod. "Where's your mom, Brynn? She said something about having a light lunch out here, right? I think you need to eat something."

"But—"

"It's early. We've got a lot of drinking to do!" I remind her. She laughs and pats my hand and then nods and looks around the patio.

"I know, I know. Yes, Mom's got some kind of light luncheon thing planned. I'm sure the guys are gonna love the cute little sandwiches. Speaking of guys." She fixes me with a firm stare, like she's willing herself not to be tipsy. So I know she means business. "Is Ryan coming still? Like is he flying in today?"

"Not today, no." I clear my throat and empty my glass.

"But he'll be here?" Brynna says. "For the wedding, right?"

Okay, so saying yes to that question is one lie I'm just not ready to tell. My stomach feels a little funny, like I've got some bees buzzing around. My mom would tell me it's guilt for being dishonest. But the thought of telling Brynna now that Ryan and I aren't a thing anymore makes me feel worse. It seems cruel to dump something like that on her two days before her wedding.

"Yeah." I say it quietly, as if that makes it less of a lie. Uncomfortable under Teag's suspicious stare, I extricate my hand and arm from Brynna's grip and climb to my feet. "I need to go to the bathroom. I'll be right back."

Bailey asks Brynna something about where the priest will stand as I walk away. We went over the basics when we first arrived. The guys hung around a bit while Brynna and Yvonne and Marilyn—Adam's mom—walked all of us through the ceremony. The event coordinator for the winery was out here with us, too, so we know everything planned is kosher. Allie was just as excited about the details as we are, but then again, that's why Brynna's family loves Divine. They're like part of their family.

It's a good thing we went over that stuff right away, since Brynna's already tipsy. She'll sober up if she slows down and eats some lunch. But, still, I'm glad we did the wedding business talk first. There will be a short rehearsal tomorrow night, too, and then we'll hang out here on the patio for drinks, which I guess could be a rehearsal for the reception.

Not that any of us need to rehearse how to have fun.

I wasn't lying when I said I had to use the restroom, so I duck inside and take care of business, slipping by the few people at the bar. I hear them talking about the Eastside Pinot and give them a silent nod of approval as I close and lock the door.

This sucks.

Not so much that I'm here without Ryan. We've covered that. I didn't love him. But I did like him, and we did have fun, and now I'm stuck at my best friend's wedding. Alone. It sucks that I'm at my best friend's wedding alone. My pride has, like, a big-ass dent in it, and I'm just kind of pissed because if he didn't want to come to the wedding, he could have just said so to begin with. If he wasn't happy dating me, wasn't into me, I wish he just would have said so long before he did.

I'm not going to wallow in self-pity. I didn't cry myself to sleep last night. In fact, I slept really well and woke up feeling great. But, on the other hand, who can deny that it's just more fun when you're at a wedding and reception, when you're on a trip like this with other couples, to be with someone. To have a date.

A plus one.

If Ryan had told me up front that he didn't want to come out with me, I could have asked someone else. A friend. I have guy friends.

No. That probably wouldn't have worked, either.

First of all, it would have been weird for me to ask someone else to go as a plus one, if Ryan and I were still dating. Even if I asked a friend. Because I'm thinking Ryan wouldn't have appreciated that. And also, there's always the possibility that a guy friend might expect something in return for coming along.

While I don't necessarily balk at casual sex, I don't want to go there with any of my guy friends. So that could have been a disaster.

The only thing that would have worked is if Ryan had ditched me several months ago, so I had a chance of meeting someone else. Which sounds callous, but then again, that midnight phone call wasn't particularly thoughtful, either.

Oh well. I'll make the most of it.

I wash and dry my hands and then pull the door open and run smack into Teag.

"You okay?" She backs up to let me out, and to my frustration, she doesn't go around me to get in, but follows me when I walk away from the restroom.

"Yeah, I'm fine." I lead her outside, noticing more people on the patio.

"Cait." She catches my hand in hers and spins me around to look at her. "Ryan's not coming."

I fight to hold eye contact with her, but I can't do that and lie at the same time.

"Is he?" She tips her head and arches her eyebrows. Already I can see the concern in the tight line of her mouth.

"Yeah." I shrug and look away. "Yeah. He's just—"

"Cait Pendleton." She lets go of my hand and crosses her arms over her chest.

"No." This time I look right at her. Drawing in a deep breath, I scramble for something to say. But she beats me to it.

"Oh, man." She groans. "He really does have a work thing? Did they keep him out of town longer?"

Well, freakity freak freak freak. She's handing me an excuse. A way out of this for the weekend anyway. And then next week, I could come clean with her and finally tell Brynn what happened when she and Adam get back from their honeymoon.

"Um."

I can't do it. Now that she's called me out on the first lie, I can't throw down another one.

"No?"

Her eyes get big and wide, and there we go. They look glassy, like she's going to cry.

For me.

And I don't need that. I don't want her to get upset for me. Because then Brynna will get upset.

"Ryan called at midnight the night before we left," I confess. I can't see Brynna and Bailey, so I don't know if they're watching us. If they know something is up, or if that's just my guilty conscience speaking.

"And?" Teag nods and shrugs dramatically.

"Told me he changed his mind."

Teagan licks her lips and frowns again. "About the wedding."

"About the wedding," I agree. She slumps with relief. "And about us."

"Cait!" Teagan yelps. "Are you serious? You guys broke up?"

"Shhh!" I step closer to her and reach out to rest my hands on her arms, still folded over her chest. "Shh. I don't wanna talk about it."

"But you broke up!" she wails loud enough for everyone on the patio to hear her. "Cait, why didn't you tell me and Brynna?"

"I don't want Brynn to know."

"But, we're your best friends!" she insists. "You should have told us. We could have done shots last night or something. I mean, this sucks."

"Yes, it does." I squeeze her arm and meet her eyes. "The timing sucks. I'm fine, but I don't want Brynna to find out."

"Why not?"

"What do you mean why not?" I straighten and let my hands fly up to make my point. "Because she'll be a basket case, and she's getting married in two days."

"Well, she would be a basket case because she loves you. And Ryan pulled a dick move."

"Yeah, I know. He did. And I know she does. But I'm fine. I'm pissed, Teag, but I'm fine. I don't wanna drag Brynn down now."

"So, you're just gonna lie to her?"

"I don't know. I hate lying, but I don't want to make her feel bad. This week is about her and Adam. I don't want to make it about me."

"But you need girlfriends," Teag reminds me.

"I know. I have them." I throw my arms around her and give her a big squeeze. "Please trust me. I'm fine."

"You guys okay?" Bailey asks as she passes us, most likely on her way to the bathroom.

"Yep." I nod and look at Bailey over Teag's shoulder. "All good."

"Are you sure?" Teagan whispers. "You guys were together for a long time."

"Six months." I wave her concern away.

"Well, that's a long time for you to be in a relationship."

We both laugh, but Teag still looks like she's going to cry.

"Maybe, but I'm fine. Ryan and I…" I shrug helplessly. "We had fun. But it wasn't love. Not by a long shot."

"How do you know? Maybe it was. Maybe you loved him, and he ditched you. You've never been in love—"

"Are you trying to make me feel bad?" I narrow my eyes at her.

"No!" She laughs and dabs at her eyes. "No. I'm sorry. I'm just shocked."

"Yeah, me too." I can admit that much. Never saw this coming. "But it's fine. I don't wanna rain on Brynna's parade. And I'm pissed because I kinda hate being the fifth wheel, but I'm fine."

"Fifth wheel? What?"

"Never mind." I shake my head. "Please? Promise me you'll keep this a secret?"

"You know I will." She sighs and nods at the patio. "Looks like Yvonne's got lunch under control. Let's go feed the bride."

CHAPTER 11

Isaac

Josh and Kree lead the way up toward the Divine building. Josh, Logan, and I have all been here, but Kree and Jasmine haven't tried their wines. I'd rather buy a bottle and go sit out back on the patio than go inside and taste a bunch of wines. It's great to try the new vintages and stuff, but it's also a good way to end up drunk on your ass before the day's even half over.

Some guys—Logan included—will claim men don't get drunk on wine. He's called me a pussy to my face on more than one occasion because I've had too much wine. Never enough to deck him when he gives me shit about it, but yes, men can get drunk on wine. Here's how it happens: you drink too much of it.

And it's easy to do. You might not think so. A standard pour for a tasting is two to three ounces. Okay, but multiply that by the number of wines you're tasting at a particular winery. Anywhere between three and five, maybe. And if you happen to be members of any winery clubs—Pierce was on one of our trips out here—the sommeliers might open a high-dollar super fancy wine to sneak you a taste. Or they might let you choose another couple to taste. Or you can revisit something you're already had. Once you taste their wines, if you like something, you can buy a bottle and uncork it and sit outside to drink it.

And then you're probably going to pack up and head to another winery.

Repeat.

Yes. I've been drunk on wine.

"I'm gonna syphon the python," Logan announces to me as we near the building.

Yeah. I'm ready for this week to be over. I suppose we can all pull a pissy mood now and then, but I've had it with Logan and Jasmine. And God love Josh and Kree, but I'm just done. I could be at home getting something done on vacation. I bought a new light fixture for my bathroom I could have installed. I could be painting the kitchen. Had a can of cola explode about a year ago and no matter how many times I've wiped down the wall by the refrigerator, I can still see the cola drips and streaks.

Or, I could have gone to Seattle. Or Boston. Or the beach. I don't usually vacation alone, but right about now, it seems like a better idea than the rest of this week with my friends.

"You comin' in?" Josh turns to look at me. Jasmine and Kree stand arm in arm now, looking back at the vineyards. They turn their backs to the vines, and Kree lifts her phone to take a selfie. I'm good about pictures. I like having the memories after good times. But girls in selfies with the duckfaces or their tongues out make me irrationally angry.

Thankfully, neither Kree nor Jasmine makes a weird face.

"No. Just buy something," I say when I look back at Josh. "I like it all. I'm gonna sit out here on the patio."

"You okay, man?" Josh speaks quietly and steps toward me. So, we've been buddies for years, and we've gone through some things together. Josh's older brother joined the military when he was eighteen. He was stationed in Afghanistan. He died in Afghanistan. He and another guy were driving the lead Jeep in a convoy. They drove over an IED. Killed them both. Josh took his brother's death really hard.

I was around. Did whatever I could for him, for his family. We talked some, sure, but guys don't have to sit around and discuss their feelings to be in tune with how shitty we feel. Or how shitty our friends feel.

So, no, I'm not going to stand out here with Josh now and tell him about this sudden restlessness.

"Yep. I'll find us a spot out here."

He nods and then waits for Kree and Jasmine to join him, and he holds the door open for them. I head on back to the patio to find a spot to hang out for a while. It's busy today, just like St. Francis was, and Sebastiani, too. It's perfect outside, so I'm guessing everywhere we go will be packed.

There's an open table on the far side of the patio, so I make my way past the pool to grab it. It's just after noon now, and the sun is unrelenting. Even with sunglasses on, it's bright. I shield my eyes with my hand for a second as I reach for a chair. The table is clean, so I assume no one has claimed it, but I look around to be sure.

A table of women catches my eye. Probably eight or ten ladies in varying ages, all of them enjoying the day. Drinking wine, obviously, and nibbling on those tiny little sandwiches that look bite size to me. They're all talking at once and laughing, and it's fun to see. I sink down in the chair and wonder if they're family or friends. Here for an afternoon outing.

Or a tea party. Well, a *wine* party, I guess.

The Divine Vineyard grounds are pretty, rolling green and vines as far as the eye can see. The view is kind of soothing, actually. I force Logan out of my head. Logan and Jasmine, who snipped at each other the entire drive here from St. Francis. Logan actually took a shot at Jasmine's hair style, which to me, is kind of over-the-top. Jasmine's pretty, but even if I didn't think so, I wouldn't insult her.

Several conversations buzzing around me draw my attention back to the patio and pool. And that brings back memories. I'm being too hard on my friends. We've always had a great time when we're together, whether we're in Colorado or Chicago or back at home. The pool makes me think of a trip we took when we were just out of college. We were at a hotel in Florida, pretty close to the beach. I don't even remember now if we were in Clearwater or Destin—doesn't matter. Pierce was drunk before noon that day. He walked into the hotel pool—fully clothed—climbed on a raft and floated there the rest of the afternoon. Because he passed out. He had a wicked-looking burn. From his knees down to his feet. His flip-flops fell off his feet at some point and sank to the bottom. And just above his elbows to his hands. He had big white circles around his eyes for days from his sunglasses.

I don't think he spoke to any of us for the rest of that trip, because we were all so busy drinking and playing volleyball that we didn't think about him frying to a crisp there in the pool. Then again, he ended up marrying the nurse he met when he went to a dermatologist when we got back in town. He doesn't drink like that anymore, and he wears sunscreen.

Which Logan thinks makes him a pussy.

I look back toward the building, wondering how long the gang's going to be. At the table where the ladies are still having a good time, I notice one of them is wearing a ball cap with a tiny little white veil attached to it. So, it must be a wedding shower or bachelorette party of some sort. Ignoring the little twinge in my chest, I look past them, determined not to think about Adrienne again, either.

Adrienne who went to medical school and moved away. Adrienne who didn't want marriage and family, but a career. Adrienne who is now married to a guy at least fifteen years older than she is. So, as it turns out, she didn't have kids, but she has three stepchildren, and the last I heard, she's got a grandkid on the way.

I'm happy for her. Adrienne and I are still friends. Just sometimes when that stuff happens, when a girl leaves a guy for her education and career, adamantly opposed to marriage and family life and then meets someone else and gets married, it messes with the guy's head.

Still no sign of the gang. I remind myself that the girls have never had Divine's wines, so of course, they're going to want to taste everything they can. I could walk inside and buy a bottle and get started, but then I risk losing the table.

When I see her—the coffee girl, *my* girl—my heart sort of beats so hard, it feels like it might break out of my chest. What are the odds?

I tell myself I'm being ridiculous. Yes, she's here for a wedding, but wine country is a huge area, and there are probably a lot of weddings going on at tons of wineries, and I'm conjuring the girl up from my memory just because I want to see her.

But then I hear her voice, and my heart does a little shift thing, kind of expands and dips a bit, and I look back, and there she is.

It's really her. I'm kind of too stunned to move for a second. I'm sort of a little bit star struck. She's really pretty. Sitting on the arm of a chair by the bride-to-be, she's holding a glass of red and kind of leaning into the girl in the chair, the one with the veil on her hat. That girl's pretty, too, but not like my girl. My girl is smiling, and she's laughing, and she looks so sincerely happy it takes my breath away.

I'm also just blown away that she's here. That fate is giving me a second chance to talk to her. Get her name. Maybe a phone number. Not likely it would go anywhere, but on the other hand, what's wrong with talking to her again? With exchanging numbers? This day and age, people connect through texts and social media, so it's not out of the question.

I push my chair back so I can get up and approach her, but my movement or the sound of the chair on the deck draws her attention. She looks up with her glass at her lips, and then she sees me, and her eyes open wide in surprise. Her smile lights up her face, and I feel a punch in the gut. She's stunning, sitting there with her friends and smiling at me.

"Oh my God!" She climbs to her feet as I do, and she laughs as she crosses the patio to stand by me. "This is amazing!"

She steps closer to me, and I feel that gut punch again when I realize she's going to hug me.

"Long time no see," she says as she presses against me and slips her arms around my back.

"I don't think we were finished with our conversation," I tell her. Of course, I'm going to hug her. If she's willing to press that beautiful body against me, I'm going to hold on for a second. It's a real hug, not a quick hug for appearances. Her breasts are pressed against my chest, and I remind myself touching her ass would be a really bad idea. I keep my hands firmly pressed at her sides, which is probably just as dangerous, because if I move them up another inch or two, I would feel the under curves of her breasts.

"I'm Cait," she says as she draws away.

I hate to let her go, so I hold on just for another second. Her eyes are on mine, and if anything, she's smiling bigger.

"Isaac."

She leans in again for another hug, and this time I wrap her up tight in my arms and breathe in her citrusy fresh scent.

"Hi, Isaac." She laughs when we draw away from each other. "God, I can't believe you're here."

It feels like we've known each other forever, like we're friends who haven't seen each other in ages, instead of strangers who had a ten-minute conversation about architecture during a chance meeting in the town square.

"I was kicking myself for not getting your name."

"Mmm." She nodded and sipped her wine. "Me, too. Where's your wine?" She looks around now and then back at me. "Where're your friends?"

"They're inside doing a tasting. The girls have never been here."

"But you have?" She tips her head to study me. The move seems natural but still flirty, and my eyes get hung up on her parted lips. I wouldn't need wine if I could just kiss her. And no, not because I could taste the wine on her mouth, but because I just *want* to kiss her. One touch of her lips on mine would send me over the top. What is that? Love-drunk? Can't be, just met her.

Something, though.

"Been here a few times," I answer when I remember she asked me a question.

"So, are they getting you wine?" She looks back over her shoulder toward the entrance to the tasting room.

"Eventually." I shrug, not concerned with wine or my friends now that she's here.

"You can share mine." She offers me her glass, and suddenly, I'm in high school again, and all I can think is that she's offering to share a glass with me. Which means my lips are going to touch the glass where her lips did.

Apparently, I need to get laid, because all the blood in my body rushes south as I think it. I hope she doesn't notice, because I'm not a perv, and I'm pretty sure I haven't reacted this way to a woman since I was in high school. Maybe my first time, when I didn't have a snowball's chance in hell of controlling myself.

"Thank you." I take a sip. "Mmm. It's a Pinot."

"It is." She takes her glass back, and we stare at each other silently. It's not awkward, though. I have no idea what she's thinking, but I have this crazy urge to take her hand so we can take a walk. Alone. I love the sound of her voice, and the conversation we had earlier was refreshing and fun, and it blows my mind that I met someone like her, someone pretty, someone with common interests, when I'm so far from home.

What the hell?

I take her hand and tug gently. She follows me without hesitation to the back rail of the patio where we stand side by side to take in the view.

"It's beautiful, isn't it?" Her voice is full of wonder.

I glance at her, and when she looks up at me, I nod. "Yes, it is." Because the view is really incredible, and she's beautiful.

"This is where Brynna's getting married," she tells me.

"Today?" I look over my shoulder. The bride-to-be is still sitting, still talking with the rest of her friends. She looks up suddenly and catches me watching her. She peeks at Cait, her smile a little uncertain, and then she looks back at me and lifts her hand in a sort of half wave.

"No." Cait shakes her head. "No, the wedding's Saturday. We're kind of having a shower...I guess? The guys are around here somewhere."

Guys.

Wait. What?

Didn't she say something about being a fifth wheel earlier? At the square? Pretty sure she did. And there were two guys with the girls at Basque earlier.

Still.

Maybe I should ask if she has a boyfriend. Maybe she does, but he's not here yet, and that's why she feels like a fifth wheel.

"And what guys are around here somewhere?" I hope I sound casual. Cait eyes me for a second, and I think maybe I didn't sound so casual at all. She doesn't answer me right away. Instead, she presses her lips together and looks back at the rolling hills and vines.

"Teag's husband, Derrick. Brynna's brother. Her dad and uncle. Her fiancé, Adam."

I feel a little better, but there's still the possibility that she has someone stuck at home, too busy with work to come with her to her best friend's wedding. If that's the case, he sounds like a dick. A dumbass dick, if you ask me. If Cait were my girlfriend, I would be right here at her side. For one thing, wine country with someone special is just fun.

And also, I wouldn't want her out here roaming around, looking so pretty and alone.

"But you don't have a plus one?" I ask quietly, eyes on the vines. I feel her eyes on me, but I don't look at her.

"I told you I feel like a fifth wheel," she reminds me. "Because I'm here with my besties and their guys, and I have no date."

"And…" I lean into her and press my arm against hers. "Do you really expect me to believe a girl like you doesn't have a boyfriend?"

Her laugh is bittersweet and small, and she leans back against me and passes her glass to me.

"A girl like me," she mumbles. "I'll bite, Isaac. What does that mean?"

I drink from her glass, a little giddy again at the thought of my lips touching her glass and more than a little hung-up on what she just said.

I'll bite, Isaac.

With a glance at her, I see that she's looking up at me with wide eyes, lips slightly parted again. For just a second, I consider leaning over to kiss her. Just a brush of my mouth over hers. My dick springs to high alert, and my heart does something weird again. I give myself a mental shake and remind myself that there's a big group of women behind us who know her. I don't want to embarrass her in front of her friends.

To say nothing of how I would feel if I kissed her and she hauled off and popped me in the nose. She's smaller than me, but that doesn't mean anything, and I like my face and teeth as they are.

"You're gorgeous," I say quietly, but her eyes light up when she hears me. She stares at me silently for a moment and finally ducks her chin and grins. Her cheeks flush with a touch of pink, which only makes her prettier.

"Mmm." She takes a deep breath and turns to look at the vines again. "Thank you. You didn't have to say that, but you just made my week." She drinks again. "Month." A shrug before she swallows again. "Year?"

"Is he at home?"

"Is who at home?" she asks still avoiding my eyes.

"Your boyfriend?"

"Who says I have a boyfriend?"

"Do you?"

"I had one," she says softly. She glances at me again. "He called me at midnight the night before I flew out here."

"Something came up?"

"No." She licks her lips. "He was in Boston on business. And he decided he didn't want to come out here."

Oh, he's not just a dick. He's a first-class dick.

"Or home to me." She adds the last words with a casual shrug.

"Wait." I turn to her at the railing and study her face, though she doesn't look at me. "Your boyfriend ditched you? By phone? At the midnight hour?"

"Sshh!" She touches my hand and looks over at her friends. The bride-to-be happens to glance at her again. I see the look that passes between them, and I wonder what it means.

"What?"

She pushes her glass at me again, so I take another drink.

"Brynn doesn't know," she mumbles.

"And…" Eyes back on Cait, I feel her friends watching us. She's either playing me with the getting ditched story or she's trying to keep it from her friends. I don't know her well enough to call it here, but there's something vulnerable and real about her that makes me think she's trying to keep a secret.

Which doesn't make sense to me because I thought girls shared everything.

"Brynn is the bride?" I'm careful to speak softly so my voice doesn't carry.

"Yeah."

"But she's your best friend?"

"Mm-hmm."

"And you don't want her to know? That your boyfriend ditched you."

"I don't want her to know." She nods.

"I thought girls shared all that stuff. The good and the bad."

She empties her glass and sets it on the rail.

We need wine. I'm not sure if Cait would stand around and talk to me if we didn't have wine to share, but I don't want to find out. I look past her girlfriends to the building, but there's still no sign of my gang.

"What if I get a bottle of Pinot?" I suggest. "Want to share it with me?"

I actually stand up straighter, square my shoulders to her, and take a deep breath. I guess I'm worried she'll say no, that she needs to get back to her friends.

There's a slight blush high in her cheeks again, and I wonder if it's me, talking to me, that has her flustered. Or if she's had more wine than just this glass we shared.

"Yeah." Her grin is quick but so sweet, it almost drives me to my knees.

"I'll be right back."

CHAPTER 12

Cait

When Isaac goes inside to get the wine, I linger at the rail of the patio for a few seconds to marvel over running into this guy again. If I believed in fate, I might think we were meant to see each other again. He's even sexier than I thought. Maybe it's because standing at his side, looking up at him while we talked gave me a new angle. I got an eyeful of the dark blond scruff on his firm jawline. The column of his neck. Looked just right for nibbling, so I tried not to stare.

Then again, maybe it was hugging him. Man, he had a hard, lean body that felt much too good pressed up against mine. What made it better was that he acted like he didn't want to let me go.

Okay, but now I know Brynna's watching me and wondering what the heck I'm doing. I take a deep breath, grab my glass, and wander back over to the girls. I owe her some kind of explanation, even if I still don't want to tell her the truth. Teag stares at me with wide eyes as I perch on the arm of Brynna's chair again.

I have no idea what Teag's thinking, and I'm dying to gush about Isaac. But I can't. Instead, I look down at Brynna with a big smile, my brain scrambling to think of something to say.

"What are you doing?" she asks as she scooches around in the chair. She turns her back to the group, so no one else will hear her read me the riot act for flirting with another guy when Ryan isn't here.

"Nothing." I shrug and fight the urge to glance at Teagan. Surely, she understands, right? I'm not doing anything wrong.

"Cait, do you know that guy?"

I'm not sure how to answer her. I could go all in with a whopper lie and tell her yes, that I've known Isaac for a while. That we're friends. But then she would want to know how long I've known him, where we met, and why I never told her and Teagan about meeting a hottie like him. I'm still a little floaty over hugging this guy and talking to him—sharing my wine with him, hello? His lips were on my glass. Is it wrong that I kind of want to lick it? —so I'm not sure I can think on my feet here, or my butt as is the case, and come up with a good story.

"I bumped into him in the square earlier." I decide to go for the truth. Okay, partial truth, anyway.

"And now you're hugging him? What?" Brynna leans forward to grab her bottle of water from the glass-topped table. She twists the cap off and takes a quick drink. She looks much too sober for me to feed her much of a story, let alone a whopper lie. I don't want her to feel like roadkill later or tomorrow, but if she were at least a little bit tipsy, it would be easier to fool her.

"He's a nice guy," I say quietly.

"And you already have a nice guy," Brynna reminds me.

"Brynna, I'm just talking to him."

"You hugged him."

"Like I hug you and Teag. Not a big deal."

"You sure?"

"Mmm." I nod. "He's an architect. We were talking about the historic buildings around the square."

Brynna's whole body relaxes.

"Oh." She nods and sort of laughs. "What was I thinking? Nerdy Cait doesn't flirt with guys. She talks buildings and business."

She doesn't mean it as an insult, but the words hit me wrong and make my stomach hurt. Maybe she's right. Maybe I've never found my own Mr. Right because I don't know how. I talk about nerdy things like buildings and business, and most other girls probably talk about clubs and music. Then again, Ryan and I clicked. We had fun together. We laughed together a lot, and we were pretty good together in bed. So, why wasn't that enough for him?

Because other than the sex, we have the same relationship that I have with Brynna and Teagan. We're friends. We were friends with benefits, and apparently, Ryan is tired of the particular benefits I offer.

Brynna clears her throat and looks up over her shoulder. A million bees are in my stomach now, flying and stinging, and I wonder why Isaac wants to share a bottle of wine with me. So we can talk about the square footage of the barrel room?

"Eastside Pinot okay?"

I jump when I hear his voice. It teases over my skin like shockwaves, and I have to fight not to shiver. It's not even that I don't want Isaac to see how he affects me. Right now, I don't want Brynna to notice.

"Yeah." I swallow a mouthful of doubt and nerves as I stand. "Brynn, this is my friend Isaac." I hope he doesn't mind that I've called him my friend. "Isaac, this is Brynna, the bride-to-be."

"Congratulations." He doesn't appear to be upset at all. In fact, he flashes Brynna a warm smile and tries to shift the bottle and his glass around so he can shake her hand. Without thinking, I reach for his glass, and he passes it to me without looking, and it has the feel of something two people who have been together forever do naturally. Brynna sizes him up curiously. I know her well enough to know she thinks he's drop dead gorgeous. I hold my breath as she smiles and takes his offered hand, but apparently, she remembers that her nerdy friend Cait has already put the skids to any naughty thing he might have been thinking with her riveting conversation about appraisals and porticos.

"Thank you."

"I'm going to go grab that table," Isaac says, and as he turns to his right to nod toward the table, he rubs his right arm over mine—again, a completely natural movement that sends my heartbeat sky high. I nod and watch him mosey toward the table, afraid to look back at Brynna.

"He's beautiful," she mumbles, and that gets my attention. I swing my gaze back around to meet hers. She arches her eyebrows in question, expecting me to respond. Normally, I would agree. Even if Ryan were really just running late and still planning to be here for the wedding, I would agree, and she and I would engage in some whispered words about his ass or his shoulders or his eyes.

But I can't make myself do it right now. Maybe because I feel so guilty. And not guilty about Ryan. But for lying to Brynna.

"He's cute." I clear my throat and go to wipe my hands on my shorts. I'm fidgety, and if I don't get away from her ASAP, she'll notice that. Problem is, I'm now holding both mine and Isaac's glasses.

Brynna tips her head to study me. It's an intense stare, like Superman's heat vision. Only she's not trying to burn anything down. Except maybe my walls. She's trying to read my mind. And when I ask if she minds if I hang out with him for a while, her suspicions are going to multiply by the thousands.

"Care if I sit with him for a while?" I go for casual, but my voice is an octave higher than it should be. She knows I'm keeping something from her, and I know she's going to be hurt when I do finally tell her the truth.

"No." She glances at him and shrugs. "Cait?"

She catches me before I can take a step away. Teagan climbs from her seat between Bailey and Yvonne. She catches her foot and hops a few steps to catch her balance. Brynna twists around to look at her as she approaches her.

"Come with me," she says to Brynna.

"Where?"

"To the bathroom."

"What? Seriously?" Brynna frowns up at her. "Are you drunk already?"

"No. I wanna ask you something."

"So, ask me."

"Not here. It's about your wedding night."

Brynna snorts as she looks at me and rolls her eyes. But when she stands, Teag peeks at me. She's giving me an out, knowing that Brynna was about to ask about Ryan again.

"I know how the wedding night's supposed to go, Teag," Brynna says with a giggle. "We've been practicing."

"New position." Teagan grabs her hand and tugs her away from me. For just a second, I watch them slip away. I know Teagan won't tell her about Ryan. And odds are, anything she's about to say to Brynna about sex, we've all talked about five hundred times or more. But I feel a twinge in my chest, just a little pinprick of pain.

Worse than that fifth wheel feeling when they're both with their guys, I feel out of the loop with my girlfriends. Not because Teag's dragging Brynna off to the bathroom. Not because they're whispering and giggling about sex.

But because they're about to have something in common that I don't have.

The words *wedding night* flash through my brain as I make my way back to Isaac. He stands as I approach, and the gesture takes my breath away. Not sure when that last happened, if ever.

"Everything okay?" he asks and reaches for my glass first.

"Yeah."

"She's cute." He splashes red wine into my glass, and when he hands it back to me, his fingers brush mine. "I like the hat with the veil."

"Her aunt did that." I sit as he pours his own wine and then sits down with me.

"Is she going to be angry with you for bailing on the shower and talking to me?"

"I don't think so." I hope not. Probably not. After all, it's not like I left the winery. I moved a few feet away just to talk to someone else for a bit.

"Why don't you want her to know about what's his name?"

I feel a pang of regret that we're not sharing a glass anymore.

"What is his name?" His grin zaps me, and those tingles race up and down my arms again.

"Ryan."

"Ryan. Why don't you want Brynna to know about Ryan?"

"Because it's her wedding weekend." With my elbow propped on the chair, I rest my chin in my hand and stare at him. He really is beautiful.

"And? You don't want to upset her?"

"Exactly."

"I can't believe he broke up with you over a midnight phone call."

I purse my lips and then take another drink. But when I put my glass on the table again, I see a look of sympathy on his face. That makes me panic. Because I don't want Brynna to get wind of it, sure, but mostly, I don't want Isaac to think Ryan broke my heart.

Because even though I'm newly single, I'm not bouncing around looking for a rebound relationship. Because anything that happens now is fair game. Could be the beginning of a long friendship. Could be a weekend fling, rated family fun to sexy, private fun. Could be more.

"I'm okay," I tell him, but it's not enough. It doesn't begin to cover what I feel, what I'm thinking, and I'm afraid if I try to do that, I'll sound desperate. Which might make it sound like I am upset over Ryan.

"How long were you together?"

"Six months. Give or take." I sigh and nibble on my lip, trying to decide how to explain myself. "Ryan and I were…friends. I guess. I mean, we dated." I nod my head back and forth, hoping he gets that I'm saying we were sleeping together so I don't have to come out and say it. "But it was never serious. We were exclusive, but I don't think either one of us ever thought we were forever."

"But you don't want Brynna to know?"

I laugh softly. "Long story."

"Bottle's at least half full." He nods to the bottle on the table.

"Brynna's a romantic. She's always believed in fairytale love, and she wants everyone to have it. She's got her prince, and she's determined that her friends find the same. Doesn't matter who I date, she reads love and commitment into every smile or every word exchanged."

"So, she'll be more upset about your breakup than you are."

"Yes. And I don't want her to waste a second thinking about me and Ryan when this weekend should totally be about her."

"And you're not upset with him? At all?"

"I'm frustrated that he left me high and dry for a date for my best friend's wedding. But the only thing he hurt was my pride."

"I get that."

"Teag's just about as bad now." I sigh and close my eyes. "She and Derrick got married last year, and so, now, she's on the relationship train, and she thinks everyone has that one great love."

"You don't think that?"

I shrug. "I don't know."

"Oh, no. You accuse me of being the type of guy to tear down beautiful buildings in the name of progress, but you don't believe in true love?"

Eyes on my wine, I feel the blush climb my neck and flood my face. Is he flirting with me? Or are we just having some deep, philosophical conversation because we're strangers sharing a bottle of wine in a beautiful setting?

"I do," I argue, but he pins me in place with an intense stare. "I do. My parents have a good marriage. My sister is happily married. Brynna's parents. Even my best friends are happy and in love."

"But?" He tips his head. "It's not for you?"

"I just haven't found it," I mumble.

"Are you looking for it?"

I start to say yes, because I like being out. I like dating. I enjoy hanging out with—well, with Ryan, last. But no, I wasn't looking for love when we started seeing each other. I never once looked at him and thought we were going to end up here. With rings and vows and honeymoon plans.

I can't say I've ever felt that way about anyone I've dated.

But that's not because I don't want to feel that way about someone, with someone.

"I don't know." I press my lips together and shrug. "I don't know. Maybe I've been lazy. Thinking if it's meant to be, it'll find me."

"That's not lazy," he argues. "That's just natural."

He pours more wine for both of us.

"For the record, I think Ryan must have a rock for a brain." Before I can react to that, Isaac narrows his eyes and finally shrugs, as if he's having a silent mental debate. "Or maybe a rock for a—"

"Shhh!" I snort and gush and duck my face behind my hand to hide the furious blush heating my face.

"I was going to say heart, Cait." His playful tone tells me he was most definitely not going to say heart.

"Okay." I nod and sneak a quick peek at his face. His wicked smile wrecks me. I squirm in my chair at the flash of heat low in my belly.

"And that, too." He looks away as he says it, but he's still smiling. I laugh, but the heat threatens to melt things now. For instance, my panties. When he glances back at me, I hide my face in my glass this time and take a big gulp. "Then again, maybe that's a good place to have some stone."

"Oh my god!" I lean forward to set my glass down and cover my face with both hands. "Stop it!"

"Okay." He agrees too readily. "Let's talk about size."

"Isaac."

"How many square feet do you think their barrel room is?"

I hold my breath for a second and then give myself a mental shake.

"Have you been to the castle?"

Assuming he's talking about Castello di Amarosa, I nod.

"The one in Italy?" He looks surprised.

"What?"

"The one they own. The family who owns Divine," he says and nods back at the tasting room.

"Oh. No. I haven't."

"Have you been to Italy?"

"No. You?"

He nods. "Yeah. We went about six years ago."

"We?"

"The usual suspects."

I assume he means his friends, but I was hoping for a more specific answer. Like, if he ever takes a girlfriend when he travels with his friends.

"Did you go to the castle?"

"No. We did The Vatican."

"That's cool."

"If you could go anywhere right now, where would you go?"

Tough to answer. If I were at home and someone asked me that, I would say wine country. And by wine country, I would mean Sonoma County. Maybe Windsor, California. Most likely, right here on this patio. There's a reason Brynn's having her wedding here. We love the setting, the wine, and the people.

All of the above holds true. But right now, it's even better, because I'm sitting next to a beautiful man who seems to enjoy talking to me.

"It's not a hard question." He nudges me with his elbow. His skin is warm on mine, and I swallow hard before I can moan my appreciation.

"Well, normally when people ask me that, I would say here."

"Here."

"Yeah. Right here."

"Okay, but somewhere out of the country."

"Greece."

"Have you been?"

"No."

"Why Greece?"

"Why not Greece?"

"Fair enough." He pours the last of the wine into our glasses, and I take the moment to look around. The guys have reappeared behind us, and that yawning empty feeling is back in full force. Worse now, because I am the only one here with my group of people without a date. "Wanna go for a walk?"

I do. A minute ago, I wanted to go for a walk and get this guy somewhere private and get my hands on him and steal a few kisses. Now I just want to go for a walk to get away from all of the love mojo.

"Yeah." I nod. "Did you see your friends inside?"

We stand and head back over the patio. Brynna and Adam are head to head, sneaking kisses, and my face heats with the thoughts I just had about kissing Isaac. Teagan catches my eye as Isaac and I slip past them.

She looks at Isaac and wags her eyebrows.

"Going for a walk."

She nods, but she reaches for my hand and tugs me away from Isaac.

"Be careful."

"It's fine," I promise her, though I really have no idea if it's fine, do I? He's a stranger. Just because he's a beautiful stranger doesn't mean he's not dangerous. I glance at him as he sidles up beside me with a warm smile on his face.

However, I think the only thing I really have to fear is that he could break my heart. And I've only known him for an hour. I mean, that right there is a problem.

"Teagan, this is Isaac." I want to fidget again, but I make myself stand still and behave. "Isaac, this is my other best friend, Teagan."

"Hi Teagan." Isaac's voice is pleasant and friendly, and Teagan grins and greets him like she's known him forever.

"It's nice to meet you," she says, and they shake hands.

"What's the plan?" I ask her, as our group disperses around the patio.

"Well, I think the couple of the hour wants to take a nap."

I can't help the snort, but I duck my head and look away from Teagan and Isaac.

"Well, to be fair," Teag adds with an innocent shrug, "Brynna needs to pace herself."

True. But I'm sure a nap entails a bit more than sleeping.

"What about you and Derrick?"

"Whatever you wanna do," she answers me, and I feel bad, because probably, they would like to go back to the room and take a nap. I hope their newlywed status hasn't already faded away, anyway.

"You okay with me taking a walk?"

"Of course," she answers. "Derrick just bought another bottle."

"What do you drink?" Isaac asks her.

She tips her head at him, happy that he's asked her something, happy that he seems to want to be part of the conversation.

"I like cabs, but he bought a pinot."

Isaac lifts his glass as if in a toast. "Good man."

"We'll be back soon."

"Okay." Teagan nods. "Just remember you're wearing pastels. They grass stain easily."

"Teagan Jones." My face burns with embarrassment. I refuse to look at Isaac, directing what I hope is a blistering gaze at my friend.

"Happens to the best of us," she reminds me with a wink. With that, she moves away from us, and I peek at Isaac, wondering what he's thinking. Good grief, I don't even know if he has a girlfriend tucked away somewhere, and she's suggesting we're going off to make out.

CHAPTER 13

Isaac

I love the pink in her cheeks when she blushes. It's adorable. She's sexy in a sweet, natural way, and I fight the urge to throw my arms around her and pull her tight. We have limited time together, and I can't decide if I want to say funny things to her to make her laugh, to tease her to make her blush, or devour her mouth in a greedy, hungry kiss.

I hold the patio gate open for her and follow her out. As soon as the gate closes behind us, we move closer together and fall into step.

"I'm sorry," she mumbles.

"For what?"

"Teagan." She glances at me and rolls her eyes.

"The grass stain warning?"

"Stop it!" She laughs and rubs her hand over her face, I'm guessing wishing she could rub the blush away.

"Don't do that." I reach for her hand.

"What?"

"Don't hide your face," I tell her. "You're beautiful. I have to look at you."

"You're a smooth talker, Isaac—"

"Stratton."

"Isaac Stratton." She nods.

"If all we have is today, I have to look at you so I can memorize your face."

"Wow."

I laugh, but when I realize I'm still holding her hand and she hasn't tried to tug it away from me, a bolt of heat hits me. Straight down my throat to my toes, scorching everything in between. It's not a bad feeling.

I move my hand around so I can slide my fingers through hers. She curls her fingers up around my hand, content to hold on.

"Does Teagan know about Ryan?"

She nods as we walk, but she won't look at me.

"And you told her because it's not her wedding weekend?"

With a sound between a groan and a laugh, she finally turns to look up at me.

"I told her because she saw me notice you in Basque. She knows I followed you out to the square to talk to you."

Her admission makes me feel the way a swallow of good bourbon does. Warm in all the right places. A pleasant taste in my mouth. The desire for more.

"Wait." I grin when she rolls her eyes, clearly embarrassed again. "You? You noticed me. And you followed me out to talk to me?"

"Yeah." She shrugs and finally nods. "Yeah. I did. I followed you out hoping to talk to you. And then I drop the nerd talk, and there it went, right?"

"Wait, what?"

We're walking down the narrow drive now, the winery building and the estate house out of sight behind us. A breeze stirs the air and the curls that have slipped free from her messy twist. She's laughing a little, though she still wears her sweet blush.

When she doesn't seem inclined to say more, I take a big breath and dive in.

Because, why not?

"I noticed you, too," I admit. "And I'm glad you followed me out."

"Yeah?"

"But what about nerd talk?"

She shakes her head dismissively. "Brynna thinks I can't keep a guy because I'm nerdy."

"What about you is nerdy?" I narrow my eyes at her and let them roam down over her shoulders and her breasts. I want to linger there, but my dick is already stirring from holding her hand and the thought of laying her down to grass stain her shorts. Cait bites her lip when I keep my gaze moving, slowing over her hips, and then swing it back up to her eyes. "Sweet. Feminine. Pretty. Sexy as hell. I don't see anything nerdy."

She throws her head back to cut loose with a hearty laugh exposing her long, graceful neck. I wonder what she would taste like if I pressed my lips to the hollow of her throat? Flicked my tongue over her skin?

"I told her we were talking about the historic buildings on the square," Cait says quietly. "She thinks I talk about work too much."

"You're in real estate," I say as much to remind her as to remind myself.

"Yeah. I've been handling farm and acreage sales lately."

"Okay. We weren't talking about farms. Although I have nothing against cows."

She laughs and starts to pull her hand away from mine.

"What're you doing?" I tug back. "I'm not going to let you cover your face."

"But we were talking about the buildings. And history."

"And buildings and history interest me, so I still see nothing nerdy."

"Do you need to tell your friends where you are?"

I shrug. "Probably."

"Tell me about them."

"Um. Okay." We're still walking, still holding hands. "Josh and I grew up together. And he recently started dating Kree. They're a good fit."

"They were the ones all cozy at the coffee shop?"

"Yes."

"And the other ones?"

"Logan and Jasmine. Logan's kind of a pain in the ass. Likes to argue. Jasmine likes to complain. Maybe they're a good fit, too."

Cait sips her wine. "She's pretty."

"Jasmine?"

She nods, but she looks up at me. "Well, both of them are, but I meant Jasmine."

"We're not dating."

"Do you have a girlfriend tucked away somewhere? In this country or another?"

"No."

"And you expect me to believe that?" She loves that she's throwing that back at me.

I don't know what comes over me, but I tug her so close we're rubbing arms, and I lean over to kiss the top of her head. Her hair is warm from the sunshine, and it smells like oranges. Heart in my throat, I wait for her to pull away or give me hell for the familiar gesture. But Cait only laughs and squeezes my hand tighter.

"No girlfriend. Not for quite a while."

"And, Mr. Stratton, what do you think about true love?"

"You're enjoying this, aren't you?"

"I'm just making conversation." She's the picture of innocence.

"I think it's out there." Because I know she's watching me, I keep my gaze on my shoes now. "Haven't found it yet, but maybe someday."

"Never been in love?"

Adrienne's face comes to mind, but if I have a limited amount of time with Cait, I don't want to spend it talking about exes and what went wrong.

"I shared about Ryan," she reminds me when I've hesitated too long to *not* answer without appearing to be lying to her.

"I dated someone in school. We were pretty into each other, but I knew it wasn't going to last."

"Why did you know that?"

"Adrienne wanted to go to med school. She made it clear from the beginning we were never going to be anything but friends with benefits."

"Mmm." Cait kind of winces, like she feels bad for me. "And is she a doctor now?"

"She is. We stayed friends when she went to medical school. I still talk to her. But she's also married now."

"Ouch."

"Obviously, I've dated since that ended. But I haven't been interested in more."

"Why do you say obviously?" She leans into me this time, the soft swell of her breast presses to my arm. "Because you're smoking hot with a beautiful face?"

Well, that gets me.

"Oh my god!" She squeals, clearly delighted that she made me blush. "That's freaking adorable."

"That's the kiss of death," I argue, but we're laughing and pushing at each other now as we walk.

"That you're adorable?"

"It's not a compliment when a pretty woman like you calls a guy adorable."

"Why? I meant it as a compliment."

"It's a little bit like being cute." I shrug and give her a little smile. The sun catches the little green stones in her ears when she tilts her head. "Friend-zoned."

"Oh." She nods. "Well. I wasn't trying to friend-zone you. I just loved that I made you blush."

My heart does that weird little seizure thing again. My dick perks up, and I have to grind my teeth together and think about the vines and the grapes and the fermenting and winemaking process to will it back down.

"So, you said you have a sister."

"Lesa's thirty-two. Married for seven years. Has a little girl who turned five recently."

"And you?"

"No kids." She ducks away with a laugh when I reach over to grab her and wrestle her again.

"How old are you? You have to be legal to drink wine, right?"

"Twenty-nine," she answers. "That was the equivalent of adorable," she adds.

"What?"

"Women my age don't want to be taken for kids."

"I thought women always wanted to look younger."

"I'm good with who and where I am," she says honestly. "Gimme a few years, and that comment would be a compliment."

"I didn't mean to offend you."

We've reached the end of the drive and turned right, and now we're walking on Limerick Lane.

"So, you were fishing for my age." She squeezes my hand again. Busted, all I can do is nod. "Because you're wondering about a single woman who got dumped the night before leaving town for her best friend's wedding?"

"Because sometimes it's good to know a woman I find attractive is of age."

She stops walking and stares at me boldly. I think she might be embarrassed, but the color in her cheeks now seems to be something different.

"Do you think we should get back?" she finally asks.

We probably should. My friends have no idea where I am. Her friends might think I've whisked her away to hurt her. I have no desire to turn around and take her back to her friends and walk away.

But we do. Turn around to head back.

We're quiet now, as if we both realize this is it. As soon as we get back to the top of the drive at the winery, we'll part ways and most likely never see each other again. Cait still holds my hand, and the closer we get to the drive, the slower we walk.

Finally, we're on the drive, and I can't take another step.

Not yet.

She looks at our fingers, still linked, and then lifts her chin to look me in the eyes.

"I'm sorry." I force a smile. "I dread having to take you back to your friends. I dread having to go back to my friends."

She nods. "I know what you mean."

Her eyes roam over my face and linger for a moment on my lips. God, I want to kiss her.

"Will you…" I blow out a long breath. Do I do this? If I ask to see her again out here, am I just setting myself up to get shot down? "Will you have any down time? Before the wedding?"

Her eyes go wide, and she looks a little like she swallowed her tongue. I wonder if it was too much, asking to see her again. But then she smiles and raises her eyebrows.

"Like when my couple friends need to take naps?"

"Something like that."

"Yeah. I might."

"We could...swap numbers. And if you find yourself bored, you could text me."

She stares silently for another long few seconds, her eyes moving over my lips again. Does she want me to kiss her?

"I'd like that." She nods. "But my phone is up on the patio in my purse."

"You could give me your number," I suggest. She hugs herself as I let go of her hand and pull my phone from my pocket. I hand it to her and take her glass as she enters her name—Cait Pendleton—and number. "You can put everything in there if you want."

"My address?"

"Why not?"

"You get to the Midwest a lot?" She shoots me a grin and then dips her chin toward my phone. "My friends would warn me not to give you my address." She considers what we want versus what her friends would advise her. "You could be an ax murderer."

"I didn't pack my ax." I hold my hands up, but I'm still holding the glasses.

She laughs softly. "What are we doing?"

"It's okay." I mean it. I want her address. I want every single piece of information she could give me, but I can wait. "But you can put your favorite color and flower and animal in the notes section."

"Why?" She snorts, but she starts tapping away on my phone.

"Because I would like to know everything about you."

"Okay. Well, my favorite color is blue. My favorite flowers are tulips. And I love dogs."

"Do you have one?"

"No, not right now."

"We have to go back, don't we?"

She takes her glass back from me and hands me my phone. I glance at it long enough to see she did enter her address. And her favorite color, flower, and animal in the notes section.

"Cait Elizabeth." I read from my screen.

She nods as I slip my phone back into my pocket.

"Not Catherine?"

"No. Just Cait."

"Good. I like that." I take a step closer to her. "It fits you."

I'm going to kiss her. I have her number, but just in case, ya know? Life's uncertain. Eat dessert first. If you get the opportunity, you kiss the pretty girl. And then you hope you get to see her again. But you don't wait to get that kiss.

She tips her head back when I lift my hand to touch her face. Her skin is warm, soft, under my fingertips. Our eyes meet when I trace my fingers over her parted lips. She swallows hard, and then we're leaning toward each other. Her soft, warm lips taste like the wine we're drinking, and this beats the hell out of getting excited because she shared her glass with me.

"Isaac."

She says my name on a sigh as I start to pull away from her. I want more. I want to taste her. I want my tongue on hers, inside her mouth. I want my hands on her hips, on her back, and her arms up around my shoulders.

I want to pull her in close and grind my damned dick into her. I can't, though. I'm so hard for her right now, there would be no hiding it. And if she moved just right against me, I could possibly embarrass myself.

Her hand's on my face now. She's stroking her fingers over my cheek, her eyes on my lips, and what the hell? Maybe she wants that other kind of kiss as badly as I do? Maybe she wants to taste me, too?

This time, we linger. Draw the kiss out, slow and deep and wet. I taste her wine again on her tongue, and she presses her soft body to mine. Even though I don't yank her in close, she has to feel what she's doing to me.

Without a word, we pull away hesitantly. And that quickly, my favorite memory of a day at the winery is over. We walk up the drive, and Cait slips her fingers back in mine.

"I don't wanna take you from your friend's wedding weekend," I tell her. Because I don't. It's obvious she's close to her friends, and this should be a special time for all of them. "But I would love to see you again. Take you to dinner tonight. Coffee tomorrow morning."

When she doesn't answer, I glance at her. She appears to be lost in thought, and I immediately panic. I took that kiss too far. Maybe it was too soon? Too deep? Maybe she felt my hard-on, and it offended her? Maybe she has no interest in ever seeing me again.

"So." She finally huffs out a quick breath like she's nervous. "Um. I have a question for you."

"Okay."

We're at the top of the drive now in front of the estate house. People are milling about, but we're only standing together. Holding hands, yes, but it's a far cry from that lip lock I sure as hell want to do again.

Cait clears her throat. I wonder what she wants to ask me. What would make her so nervous?

"How long are you and your friends here?"

"I fly out Monday afternoon."

She nods and huffs out another breath.

"Do you have...like...stuff planned? Are you free Saturday?"

"Nothing planned. We kind of did all of that stuff earlier in the week."

She rubs her lips together and looks at me, a little bit wistful.

"Would you want to go with me? To Brynna's wedding?"

CHAPTER 14

Cait

Oh shit. I asked him. I said those words, didn't I?

I hold my breath, cussing myself for being so dumb. Of course, he doesn't want to spend a perfectly good Saturday hanging out with me at my best friend's wedding. He hardly knows me, and he doesn't know any of my friends or the family who will be there. Talk about putting him in an awkward position.

"I'm sorry." I shake my head. "I don't know where that came from."

Well, I mean, actually, the thought hit me out there on Limerick Lane. Before we turned around to walk back, and I thought I would die if he didn't kiss me right then and there.

Isaac starts to answer me, but I shake my head again, almost violently this time. I feel, like, all cringy, and I don't even want him to have to make excuses to get out of my dumb idea. He starts to answer again, but I lean into him and press my hand holding the glass to his chest and put my other hand over his lips to shush him.

"I'm sorry. That was ridiculous. Never mind."

"Are you shushing me?" He laughs and grabs my fingers in his hand. "Seriously? You're shushing me?"

"I'm sorry, Isaac. I didn't mean to put you on the spot like that."

"So, are you uninviting me now?" He tips his head. Before I can answer him, he kisses my fingers. His breath on my skin makes me weak in the knees. Wow. I have never swooned before, but I'm thinking this must be what it is. How it feels.

I like it.

I want more of it. And now I've gone and scared him off.

"Um." I swallow hard and shake my head. "No?"

Because he sort of sounds bummed now. I think.

"I would love to be your date for Brynna's wedding."

I blink at him. Waiting for a but. Or for him to laugh. Or for the sky to fall. Or something.

"You—? Really?"

"But what about Brynna? And Ryan?"

He's right. This isn't the best way to handle this with Brynna. But at the moment, she's the last person on my mind. I wanted to put her first for the weekend, but now that I'm here, now that I've met Isaac Stratton, I feel pretty selfish.

I want to be with Brynna and Adam for their big day, but I'd rather be with Isaac. And if I can bring those two worlds together for a short time, I'll figure out how to deal with telling my best friend I lied to her about Ryan.

"Did you just say yes?" I ask him. I can't help the big smile on my face that tells him just how excited I am that he said he wanted to be with me Saturday.

"Do you think I would pass up an opportunity to spend more time with you? It sounds like fun."

It does. Because it hits me that even though Brynna and Adam's ceremony will be small, even though the reception will be small, there *will be* a reception. With toasts and cake and dancing. I've just gone from sitting alone or being a pity dance partner to all of the men in Brynna's life to having a partner of my own. All night. To dancing with Isaac. All night.

The words give me a jolt.

Okay, maybe not all night.

Not that that doesn't sound like an incredibly awesome idea, but this is moving fast enough.

"I'll figure out a way to tell Brynna."

"She won't be angry?"

"That I lied about Ryan? Yes." I nod. "That I've asked you to be my date? No."

"Okay." He kisses my fingers again, and that light-headed feeling sweeps over me.

"What about your friends? Will they mind?"

"No." He doesn't seem concerned. Instead, he links his fingers through mine, and we walk back to the patio together. Brynna and Adam are nowhere to be seen. I wonder if they are napping. Because there's no way I could be in the estate house having sex when my family and friends and other winery guests are milling about out here.

"Stratton."

Isaac looks up when someone calls his name. I follow his gaze to find that his friends are gathered at the table he and I were sitting at earlier.

"Do you want to meet them? Because we can go hang out—"

"Of course, I do." I give his fingers a squeeze. "I just invited you to a wedding. You're gonna be mobbed with female attention."

"I can handle it."

I glance up at him. He was teasing, but something tells me he's used to the attention.

"Oh, I'm sure you can."

He leads me to the table, though, and it hits me that we're still holding hands as Teagan turns around at the railing and see us. She smiles and waves, but her eyes pop wide open when she sees our hands.

"Josh. Kree. This is Cait."

Josh is kind of cute. Like a little kid face on a nice body. Friendly brown eyes. Thin lips that smile with ease. He's no Isaac, though.

"Cait, this is my best friend, Josh. And his girlfriend, Kree."

Josh stands to shake my hand. Kree scoots her chair over and looks around, as if she's going to pull up a chair for me.

"What the what?" The other girl says from the other side of the table. "Leave you alone for fifteen minutes, and you're trolling to pick up women?"

"Jaz." Isaac grinds her name out, like just the sound of her voice irritates him. But she turns back to me and flashes me a big, friendly smile. "This is Cait. Cait, Logan and Jasmine."

"I love your shorts," Jasmine tells me.

"Thank you."

Teagan and Derrick mosey over, and my stomach pinches because I know I need to go. If they're ready to leave, I have to go, too. I'm here with my friends, and I can't bail on them. Nor can I expect Isaac to bail on his buddies. Except for when he already said he would on Saturday.

"Brynna and Adam go inside?" I ask Teag. Derrick slides a couple of chairs up for Teagan and me to sit. Maybe they're not ready to leave yet.

"They did, but I think Brynn really is tired," she says so that only I hear her. We both look behind us at the chairs Derrick's dragged over, and then we look at each other. Teag shoots a grin in Isaac's direction, and we both drop to sit down.

"What're you drinking?" I reach for her glass and take a sip when she passes it to me. "What is that? It's not a pinot, is it?"

"It's a cab," she tells me.

"It's good, but I'm going to need some water."

"Me, too." She looks up at Derrick when he leans over her to shake Isaac's hand.

Oops. I feel a pang of guilt for not introducing Isaac to him.

"So." Teagan looks back at me. "Must have been a nice walk."

Not sure that I'm ready to share how nice it was, I only nod. Across the table, Jasmine gets up, and Isaac's other friend Logan shoots her a curious look.

"I don't see any grass stains," Teag continues, glass at her lips.

My face three shades of red again, I shake my head and glare at Teagan. "Shut. Up."

"Hey, ladies." Jasmine drags her chair over by me, Teag, and Kree. "Sorry. So much testosterone over there, I can't taste my wine."

Teagan snorts. "I'm Teagan."

"Jasmine. And the guy in the ballcap thinks he's God's gift. Don't be fooled."

Logan snaps his intense gaze to her, as if he knows she said something about him. He eyes her for a moment and then tunes back into the guys' conversation.

"Are you guys here with the wedding people that were out here earlier?"

"We are," I tell Jasmine. "Wedding's Saturday."

"Oh, that's so perfect." She swings her head around to take in the surroundings. "What a beautiful spot for a wedding."

"So, Derrick and I tied the knot in a traditional church wedding. Brynna and Adam are doing the winery thing. What's yours gonna be, Cait?"

"Well, currently, it's going to be a stag ceremony, I guess." I'm not offended by Teagan's question. When we were younger, we spent a lot of time planning our weddings and how many children we were going to have, and where our houses would be. "Maybe if I find a groom, we'll run off and have a circus wedding."

"You could recite your vows from the trapezes."

Kree swats at Jasmine, but I can't help the laugh that pops out of my mouth.

"Be nice," Kree tells Jasmine, and then she turns to me and Teagan. "Jaz's anti-wedding. Well. Maybe you're anti-relationship?"

"I am not," Jasmine groans. "It's just not the most important thing in my life."

"Cheers to that." I tap my glass to hers. The longer I sit here talking about weddings, surrounded by happy couples, and the beautiful venue, the more I want to wallow in self-pity. Again, not because of Ryan. But because I'm alone. Still. Still haven't been madly in love.

I have swooned, though. And damned if that wasn't a pretty incredible feeling.

I eye Isaac on the sly, because the last thing I need is for his friends to see me checking him out while we're discussing my wedding plans.

"Where are you guys staying?" Teagan asks them, and I figure she's going to put on her Sherlock Holmes coat and start investigating Isaac since she saw us holding hands.

"We're in a bed and breakfast outside of Sonoma," Jasmine answers. "You guys?"

Teagan sighs. "The three of us are at the Inn at Sonoma. It's a really cute place. But Brynna and Adam and her family are staying here. In the estate house."

"Nice." Kree nods.

"Derrick and I made the reservations in Sonoma thinking we would want to travel all over. Visit other wineries. We usually do. But we should've just booked something in Windsor, because I have the feeling the rest of the weekend is going to be spent up this way."

"At least it's not a long drive." Jasmine picks at her fingernail. "Although I guess it is, if you're drinking."

"You could change hotels," Kree suggests. "Move up this way."

"We could." Teagan shrugs. "Windsor is such a pretty town. But. I think we're probably tied in on reservations now in Sonoma. Might gain a night without having to pay for the room."

"Well, we can run around tomorrow," I remind Teagan. "Even if Brynna and Adam are busy here or with family."

"Do you want to?" Teag glances at me and tips her head. She's fishing about Isaac.

"Yeah, of course." And I do. We're in wine country. I love that we'll be back here at Divine for the wedding in two days, but we have all of tomorrow to roam around on our own.

"Need anything?" Isaac brushes my shoulder with his fingers. The gesture is so sweet, it takes my breath away for a second. Of course, I want to venture out to other wineries while we're here. But I also want to be stuck like glue to this guy, because I have a very limited amount of time with him. "I'm going to grab some water. Do you want any?"

"Thank you." I nod and watch him walk away.

"So." Jasmine clears her throat. "That's Isaac."

Dammit all, if a stupid, sappy grin doesn't slap itself over my face.

"We've met."

"I've known Isaac since we were sixteen," she says, and I wonder where she's going with this. Is she about to ask my intentions? Warn me not to hurt him? Chase me away and claim him?

"We met in the square," I tell her, because I don't know what else to say. "We were talking about the historical buildings there."

"Mmm." Jasmine considers this. She swallows a big drink of wine. "He does love his historical buildings."

"Cait's in real estate," Teagan tells Jasmine.

"Oh, my god, you were speaking his love language." Jasmine squeals with delight.

Isaac returns with water, and the conversation continues for quite a while before Teagan tells Derrick she's hungry. I look around for my purse and see it hanging on the back of Logan's chair. Derrick sees me panicking, so he hands it to me. I pull my phone out to see that it's almost five.

No wonder we're starting to feel hungry again. Little cucumber sandwiches don't stick to the ribs when you're drinking.

"Wanna get some dinner?" Derrick asks Teagan.

"I do." She nods. I do, too, but the thought of walking away from Isaac, even with him having my phone number, even after he agreed to be my date Saturday, feels a bit like cutting my heart out and leaving it at the table when we leave. "Do you guys wanna go, too?"

God love Teagan. I barely refrain from throwing myself into her lap to thank her for being the one to suggest it. Part of that is this crazy, wild attraction I feel toward Isaac. I'm sure part of it is the amount I've had to drink, too.

"You hungry, babe?" Kree tugs on Josh's shirt.

"Starved."

"Are you?" Jasmine twists around to look at Logan. He flashes her a grin, and for the first time, I see that he's kind of cute. She rolls her eyes, apparently unaffected by the dimple under his lips.

"Where should we go?" Josh asks.

"Do you guys like Mexican food?" Teagan stands and pushes her chair out of the way. There's a general chorus of yeses, and suddenly, we're all shoving chairs back under tables and grabbing belongings and heading over the patio and out the gate.

We just had La Casa, but I can eat Mexican food every day of the week. I haven't met anyone who feels differently.

Except Ryan.

"There's a place on McClelland Drive. Called Lupe's," Derrick says to Josh and Isaac. Logan and Jasmine are bringing up the rear as we head to our respective vehicles. They bicker back and forth and head past the rest of us when we slow to agree on a place.

"I know where that is." Isaac nods. "We'll see you there?"

I follow Teag and Derrick, but when I look back over my shoulder thinking that another kiss from Isaac would be perfect right about now, he's still standing there watching me.

He smiles.

And my knees go weak.

I'm in trouble.

CHAPTER 15

Isaac

I like food probably more than alcohol, though maybe not always. I like just about all kinds of food, and yes, I can eat Mexican food a couple times a week. And Lupe's Diner has good food. But the waiter could serve me a piece of cardboard greased up with some sour cream and cheese, and I would be happy. I'm just thrilled to be sitting next to Cait. Thrilled to have a date with her on Saturday. No clue what Sunday will bring, but I'm going to spend Saturday with *my girl*, and nothing makes me happier.

Our friends are talking, having such a good time over chips and salsa and margaritas, that they don't seem to notice Cait and I are in our own little world. We're at the end of a rectangular patio table, chairs turned slightly toward each other, heads together, talking. She's sipping a margarita, but she's also drinking water. I like that she's being smart about drinking, making sure to hydrate. It tells me that she doesn't want to lose control, and it suggests that she's got some experience in wine country.

On the drive into Windsor from the winery, Kree curled up against Josh and dozed off. Jasmine drove, which unfortunately left me wide open for conversation with Logan. I expected him to comment about Cait, and I figured it would be something offensive, something that would piss me off. But he didn't even mention her. Instead, he brought up a 5K he wants us all to do to raise money for autism awareness. It was a welcome surprise, but sitting next to Cait and talking about the Eagles versus CCR is a lot more fun.

"So, are you a Glenn Fry fan?" she asks now. Cait is into both groups, though she favors CCR. She's referred to someone she dated once who didn't care for either groups, and she leaves me wondering if she's talking about the last ex that dumped her.

"Yeah." I nod and relax back in my chair. "You know, there's not a lot of music I don't like. Especially if it's live."

"Me, too!" she agrees enthusiastically, and I wonder, maybe if that ex didn't care for live music. "Favorite show?"

"Oh boy." I groan and drop my head back to stare up at the sky. The blue is so crisp and thick up there, it looks fake, like a painted canvas. Even the few clouds look a little 3D, like they're made of string and added as an afterthought. The weather here is perfect.

Everything about this trip is suddenly perfect, and I have this insane wish that it could last for another week or two.

Or a month. It's ridiculous, because no vacation can last forever. I have to return to work next week, and I'm sure once the wedding is over, Cait will be going back home to the Midwest.

The thing is, I'm from the Midwest, too. I know exactly where her town is; I've driven through it a time or two. It's right on the western tip of the state on the bluffs of the Mississippi River, about two hours north and west of St. Louis, Missouri. I grew up in Indianapolis, and I live in St. Louis now. So, it's not exactly that much of a long shot that she and I could see each other after this weekend.

For a long-distance relationship, it would totally be doable.

But what if Cait gets back home, and all the wedding stuff is over, and she realizes she was in love with that guy? The one who dumped her over the phone? I get that she's frustrated about it. I get that she's angry that he put her in this position with her best friend. But what if it's easy for her to hold onto that anger right now and not feel the hurt, and then when the rush from the weekend is over and she goes home, the heartbreak catches up with her?

I'm not sure I'm ready to throw myself that far out there just yet. Maybe it's better to just live in the moment, have fun with her while I can—not gonna lie, the thought of dancing with her makes my stomach flip—and see what happens. Maybe we'll walk away friends.

And maybe someday, once she's settled back home and has a chance to really process the breakup with this guy, maybe then the time will be right for a little something more.

"C'mon." She nudges my leg with her knee. "It's not that hard. Mine's Shinedown."

"Shinedown?" I don't know why that surprises me, but it does. The waiter is back at our table, but he's at the other end setting platters out in front of our friends. Nothing about Cait says she wouldn't like a hard band like Shinedown, but I guess I was expecting Rob Thomas or Maroon 5 for an answer. "Really?"

"Yes. They put on an excellent show."

"Hmm." I nod and consider this. I've seen several concerts, though I don't go to them as often now as I did when I was in college. Never seen Shinedown, though. Maybe I need to look at their tour schedule. "I'd have to say Bon Jovi."

"Ooh." Cait raises her eyebrows. The waiter leans around me to put my plate on the table, but Cait's eyes stay fixed on me. "Okay, first concert you ever saw."

I was ten at my first concert. 1999. My uncle took me to see the Foo Fighters. Pretty good one to claim as my first concert.

"Foo Fighters. I was ten."

"Never seen them." She leans forward and scoots her chair closer to the table. Down two seats, Josh and Derrick are talking about geothermal heating. And Cait's friend Brynna thinks she's a nerd for talking about interesting buildings? "Like them?"

"Yeah. Great show."

"Matchbox Twenty," she tells me, and I laugh and point my finger at her like a gun.

"Gotcha!"

"Wait!" She drops a forkful of rice and rests her fingertips on the back of my hand. Her gentle touch makes me think of kissing her, and my eyes are drawn to her lips—parted now in surprise and curiosity, maybe. "What? What does that mean?"

"Well, you got me with Shinedown." I shrug. "I figured you would say Matchbox Twenty or something."

She grins and rolls her eyes.

"Do you play an instrument?" I ask her. I stare at my tacos and wonder what in the world I was thinking ordering them when I'm sitting with her. No way to be neat about eating giant tacos.

"Nope." She sighs. "I was the athlete. My sister is a musician."

Because I want to know about both things and the first of my tacos is now in my mouth, I hold up my little finger as I chew. Cait's eyes lock on mine, and I feel like we're the only two people in the world right now.

"What's your sport?"

"Played basketball and softball in high school." She scoops a bite of black beans, but she doesn't eat it right away. "Started softball in college, but it wasn't what I wanted."

"What do you mean?"

She tugs at her lower lip with her teeth as she thinks. "I was hardcore when I was younger. Very competitive. Played for travel teams. Loved it. I grew up with a ball in my hands. I don't know. I hit college, and I met new people, and I wanted different things."

"Were you on scholarship?"

"For academics, yeah." She nods. "I played ball my freshman year, but I decided I wanted to focus on school. I shadowed professionals in real estate and law, and I interned at a few different jobs."

"And were you happy with that decision?"

"I was." She nods. "I am. I loved the years I played ball, but I learned a lot in school. And I met some good people. I mean, it's all about networking, right? Hanging out here with you now—who knows? One day, we might meet on some historical building project, trying to save a museum on the preserves or something. Can't hurt to make connections."

"So." My first taco is halfway gone now. "You're saying you're using me in case of a hypothetical historical building being torn down in our future."

"Of course not!"

I start to tell her I'm teasing, but I notice the smirk on her face and the laughter in her eyes.

"I'm using you for your dance skills Saturday." She sips her margarita again. "You can dance, right?"

"I love to dance," I tell her. And I do. "When's the last time you did the Foxtrot?"

Her face goes slack. "Are you serious?"

"I am. My mom taught me all kinds of dances, Cait Pendleton. We're gonna wow your friends Saturday."

She shakes her head. "I have two left feet."

"Well, maybe we should practice before then." I'm joking again, because I'm not sure where or when we could practice. But Cait's face lights up, this time with happiness.

"That'd be great."

"So." I wipe my mouth off with my napkin and toss it down. I've had enough food. I want more Cait. She pushes her plate away, too and then covers a yawn with her fist. "Wanna go for a walk? While they're still finishing?"

"Yeah, that sounds good."

As we stand, I fish my wallet from my pocket and toss cash out toward Josh. It's enough to cover both Cait's and mine. Josh glances at me and takes the money with a nod.

"You didn't have to do that." Cait leans into me and grabs my arm as we cross the street.

"I wanted to," I tell her. I lift my arm to curl it around her neck. Apparently, it feels as natural to her as it does to me, because she doesn't bat an eye.

"Well, thank you."

"You're welcome." Across the street, we head to the right to walk along the square. I find myself studying the buildings here, the same way we did in Sonoma Plaza. I don't know much about Windsor, but I have a sudden wish to drag Cait along to the library so we can research the history of the town together.

Maybe her friend Brynna is right; maybe Cait and I are both nerds.

"So, you were the athlete. And your sister was the musician?"

"Lesa played the flute. And the guitar. And the piano." She groans, but she's laughing. "Lesa was in the school choir. She gave piano lessons when she was in high school. She sings at church now."

"Do you sing?"

"Not out loud."

"Me neither."

"My niece loves to sing. She's so funny. She loves that old Beatles song. 'From Me to You.' Lesa and Tim get her to sing it all the time."

"Your niece sings Beatles songs?"

"My brother-in-law loves the Beatles."

Cait's pressed to my side, and my body can't help but notice how soft and warm she is. I smell oranges again and assume it's her shampoo or lotion. Whatever it is, pretty sure oranges may be my new favorite fruit.

"You don't like the Beatles?"

"Of course I do!"

"Okay, gotta ask." She points at a life size statue of a rainbow-colored Snoopy on the sidewalk as we pass it. "What's the deal there?"

"I actually know the answer to that one," I tell her and mentally thank Jasmine for that. "Charles Schulz is from Sonoma County. He refused statues of himself, but he was okay with statues of his characters. So, Santa Rosa started sponsoring an art parade thing. You can find statues of Charlie Brown, Snoopy, Lucy, and Woodstock. They raised a ton of money for art scholarships."

Cait simply stares at me for a few seconds, the hint of a smirk on her lips.

Maybe I should cuss Jasmine for my knowledge on Charles Schulz and the Peanuts Gang out here. Maybe I just threw down a big nerd card that'll end up revoking my dancing rights.

Finally, she nods. She turns away from me, but her lips curve up in a big smile as she does.

"Okay."

"What?"

She chuckles a little, and I feel her shoulders shrug under my arm.

"I love that." Her voice is soft, almost filled with wonder, as if I just introduced her to Charles Schulz or Snoopy, rather than relaying information that Jasmine read.

"You love…what?"

"That you knew that. I don't know anything about Windsor, but yes, I want to now. And as much as I liked watching *The Great Pumpkin* when I was a kid, I don't know much about Peanuts, either."

When she looks up at me, she looks happy. No hint of sarcasm. No signs that she thinks I'm a loser for knowing something about a cartoon.

"Jasmine is a Peanuts fan," I confess. "She actually did the research."

"Still." Cait wags her eyebrows. "You remembered it."

"I bet they do a farmer's market here on the square," I say as we turn the corner and keep walking. "That would be cool."

"I love going to the farmer's market back home."

"Do you like to cook?"

"I do." She nods. "Sometimes, I cook a lot. Freeze stuff. And sometimes, I get stuck in a rut of eating out, grabbing something quick."

"I think we all do that."

She looks up at me with interest. "Do you cook?"

"Some."

"Can you really do the Foxtrot?"

"Yep."

"Hokey Pokey?"

I laugh and nod as we continue around the square. What would it be like if we left here, if we left California, and stayed in contact? Sure, we could text and even do video calls, but would we get together? Would she come to St. Louis, or would I drive up to see her?

"Um." I tip my head from side to side. "It's been years since I did the Hokey Pokey, but I suppose I still could."

"With skills like that, you could be a professional plus one." She leans into me and wraps her arm around my waist for a second. It's a quick squeeze, and she's laughing, but my chest feels tight, and my dick stirs again. "Think about it. You could move out here. Live in wine country all year. Buy yourself a little house and hang a shingle for plus-one services for hire. I can't even imagine how many weddings there are out here every year. Spring and fall, both."

"Sounds like the life."

"Right?" She laughs. "I mean, you've got a movie star face. And you like music. You can dance. You appreciate good wine."

"I'm not bad on speeches."

"Nope." She shakes her head. "Plus-ones don't usually give speeches. I suppose if you were, like, playing the part of best man or something, that would be a good skill."

"So, I would just need to show up and look pretty."

"And drink wine and dance." She nods. "You could charge for your services. You'd have access to good wine and food. Music."

"I'd only want to work for the pretty girls."

I'm still joking with her, but then again, I'm not. It's not like I'd ever hang such a shingle out anywhere, but if I did, I would only want to be her plus one anyway. Our eyes meet when she looks up at me, but we've made the full square now, so we check for traffic and then cross McClelland back to Luper's Diner, where our friends climb to their feet as we approach.

"This guy!" Derrick points at Josh, and the rest of them laugh, and obviously, Cait and I missed something, but when we look at each and share a private smile, it's just as obvious we don't care. "Seriously."

I have no idea what the guy might be talking about, and Josh is my best friend. The only thing I can think right now is that we're leaving, and I'm not going to see Cait for a while.

"So," Jasmine announces. Logan shoves his hands in his pockets and eyes Jasmine belligerently, which makes me wonder what they've argued about while Cait and I were walking. "We thought we'd meet back here in Windsor tomorrow morning. Grab breakfast at KC's and maybe explore some together."

Right about now, if I were going to choose a team—Logan or Jasmine—I'd be all about Team Jasmine. Any excuse to meet back up with Cait and her friends is perfect to me. I'm not sure how we're going to work out the wedding thing, since my friends won't be a part of that. But I'm pretty sure that if I have to go rent my own vehicle just for Saturday, I'll do it.

"Are you…" Teagan turns to Cait and then flicks her eyes my way. "Ready? To go?"

"Yeah."

"Because we can…" She offers us a dramatic shrug, but when Cait laughs and rolls her eyes, Teagan snorts and blushes. "Well, this is new, Cait. I'm not sure what the rules are here."

"No rules. We're just hanging out," Cait assures her. "And um…Isaac is going to be my date for Brynn's wedding."

She said *date*. Not *plus one*.

Maybe it doesn't mean anything, but it feels like it might.

Okay, to me, it does.

"Oh." Teagan bites her lip, but she's smiling, and she doesn't appear to be angry or even, too surprised. "Well, this is going to be interesting."

"Is Brynna gonna be pissed?" Cait asks softly.

"Of course," Teagan reaches out to take Cait's hand, "but she'll get over it fast."

There's a flurry of goodbyes then, and Cait and I are left alone on the sidewalk. Our minivan is parked to the left; her friends walked off to the right.

"So." I take a deep breath and decide kissing her again might be too pushy. Especially if any of our friends are watching. "I'll see you tomorrow."

"Goodnight, Isaac." She stretches to her tiptoes and brushes her lips over my cheek. This is the part in a romantic movie where, if I were a girl, I would swoon and tell my best friend I'll never wash my face again.

I watch Cait walk away and wonder what guys do if girls swoon. Sure, my dick's all pumped up and ready to get to work. But it's more than that. I'm free-falling. My stomach is up where my heart should be and my heart and lungs are pushing around in my head and my brain's just gone, I guess.

No other reason to want this to be something. No such thing as magic, no fated lovers, no love at first sight stuff for me.

But damned if I don't feel a little bit of every damned thing for Cait Pendleton after spending one day with her.

CHAPTER 16

Cait

Breakfast at KC's American Grill is excellent. And the food isn't bad, either. I mean, if I weren't so stuck on everything about Isaac, I think I would marvel at how well our groups are hitting it off. It's kind of unheard of, really. Even when you have a few girlfriends and then add in another who is new to all but one person in the group, it's rarely seamless. Real relationships—the kind where you meet and get to know someone over time and then maybe fall in, well, *something* and then try to mix families and friends—can be challenging.

But I couldn't have written this better myself, the way things have played out for Isaac and me. Teagan thinks Kree is awesome, and she's pretty into Jasmine's smartassery, too. And from what I can see as we sit around the tables on the patio outside the restaurant, it looks like Logan thinks Derrick is a comedian. I know, right? Love Derrick to bits and pieces, but I'm not sure I've ever laughed myself to tears over anything he's said.

As for this thing with Isaac and me? I laid awake way too long last night thinking about him. The kissing. I like kissing and cuddling and sex as much as the next girl, but I don't usually obsess over it. Last night, I kind of did. Didn't help assuming Brynna and Adam were enjoying each other's company in the estate house at the winery, that probably Shane and Bailey were, too—maybe her parents and aunt and uncle, but nope! So wasn't going there!—and worse yet, in the same inn as me, just down the hall, I had to assume Teagan and Derrick were having some fun.

Still, I didn't just think about *that*. About kissing Isaac. I kept running through our conversations. The way he'd assumed I would say Rob Thomas was my favorite performer. The amused smirk on his face when I admitted my first concert was Matchbox Twenty. The whole information dump about Charles Schulz and the Snoopy statue on the square in Windsor. That had been so freaking adorable—not even sorry, because since when is *adorable* not a compliment?—that I stared up at the ceiling in my dark room with a ridiculously goofy grin on my face for longer than I care to admit.

I like him.

Yes, I really liked kissing him. Not even sure when my heart had last fluttered in my throat and pounded in my ears like when he kissed me. Definitely hadn't been that kind of fluttery stuff with Ryan. Or the guy before him.

I sip my water now, eyes on Jasmine as she and Logan bicker over a bowling night from some time in the past. They're arguing, yes, but it's obviously not a real argument. It's that sort of flirty kind of bickering. You know, the kind when maybe there's something more just below the surface, but neither person wants to dig too deep?

It hits me suddenly. I haven't felt the fluttery stuff, the tingles in my skin and weak in the knees with anyone, really, since my first kiss. And that was at least fifteen years ago. As first kisses go, it ranked right up there, totally over the top, obviously setting the bar way too high since no one has reached that level since then. Until now.

I sit my glass down a bit forcefully, drawing Isaac's attention. The heat in my face is all about the way he looks at me—a mix of embarrassment and lust—and my hands itch to cover the blush. He arches a thick, dark blond eyebrow at me as if he knows exactly what I'm thinking.

My first kiss. Fifteen. I was an angular tomboy with a teenage girl heart and a ridiculously painful crush on Emmett Cassidy. Eighteen. Senior. Starting quarterback who set a record for touchdown passes thrown his senior year. He had eyes like whiskey, and his muscles had muscles, and the craziest thing?

He was nice. Charming and good-looking, but seriously nice. We didn't go out. Nothing like that. And it wasn't really a hookup. It was a kiss.

I wrote for the school paper. Emmett came to Mrs. Goodman's classroom one day to do a picture for an article about something to do with football and his letter of intent. It was after school, and there were a few of us working. Normally we would have been in the computer lab, but as luck would have it, the IT guy was running some kind of major update to the system, so there were a few of us hashing out stories in her classroom, the photographer was arguing about something with the yearbook photographer, and Emmett stuck around for a while, talking to Mrs. Goodman. She wasn't a favorite teacher, by any means, but he seemed to really like her.

I'd finished a rough draft—like heavy-duty grit sandpaper rough—of my article about one of the math teachers retiring, so I packed my stuff up and headed out. I was out of season at the time, so my plan was to walk home and get my homework done. Emmett followed me out and offered me a ride home. Before that day we hadn't ever really talked, but he was always friendly, always nice to everyone, including underclassmen.

On the drive home, we talked a lot, though. About his college plans and about my plans. He asked if I planned to play ball in college, and I realized he knew who I was. That was a pretty heady feeling for a fifteen-year-old girl. He told me his little sister was a gymnast, that she had potential to go far, maybe even the Olympics. What I loved most was the awe in his voice when he talked about her.

Brynna and Teagan had nearly fallen over in shock the next day when I told them he kissed me. Teagan had been infuriated, as if a senior guy had rudely taken advantage of me and treated me horribly and copped a feel and then gone home to send out a group text about how easy I was. Totally not the case. He had parked in front of my house, and we talked for the better part of an hour, and even though I was no different than any other girl at school, even though Emmett was the hottest guy I had ever laid eyes on, I didn't think it was the start of something. I didn't sit there in the front seat of his old Bronco thinking he was going to ask me out and take me to prom.

I was totally into the conversation, interested in his sister —who did actually compete at the national level—and the football stories he shared, and I told him about a basketball game we had battled down to the last second and lost in the finals of the state junior high tournament when I was thirteen. We commiserated. We actually talked about how losing heartbreaking games like that builds character, and he shared a few of his own stories about losing and learning to see the losses as an opportunity to improve.

When he kissed me, his approach was easy and comfortable. The way he leaned toward me and cupped my chin in his hand and brushed his lips over mine. Nothing familiar about the things that kiss did to my body.

I remember now the way my heartbeat hammered in my fingertips and toes and my throat and ears. The way my mind was shrieking EMMETT CASSIDY IS KISSING ME!!! The way he tasted like root beer—I later learned root beer barrels were his favorite candy—and the way his tongue on mine chased electric tingles down my throat and into the girl parts I didn't really understand at the time.

The next day in the halls—after Teagan came unglued and Brynna started planning my wedding to him—he saw me passing by his locker on my way to chemistry. He hollered at me and waved. We're still good friends. I've never seen him as anything but a good friend who happens to be a genuinely good-hearted, drop dead gorgeous guy.

I feel that same sort of comfortable with Isaac.

The conversations we've had, the easy touches. Hand holding. No, I didn't confess deep dark secrets to him, although that's because I really don't have any deep dark secrets. I feel like if I had something big going on, I could tell him. Confide in him.

The same way I would listen to him.

I feel like I've known Isaac forever. The same way I felt with Emmett that day in his car. The day we started a really good, strong friendship.

With a kiss.

While I love having Emmett as a friend, while I want to have that same thing with Isaac, I feel a tiny little prick of disappointment, of sadness, at the thought of only being Isaac's friend.

I want more.

Of all the ridiculous, crazy, impulsive things to feel, I want. More.

More of everything.

With Isaac.

A guy I met yesterday.

I feel a groan inside, and I must make some kind of noise, because Isaac looks at me again. Now the gang is talking about the Armstrong Redwoods Reserve in Guerneville. Teagan, Brynna, and I have hiked there a lot, mostly back before we were of age to enjoy the wineries. It's beautiful, and I'd love to do it again, but none of us girls are dressed for it today. We're all wearing dresses and sandals; our first planned stop after breakfast is Albini Family Vineyards.

Realizing Isaac is still watching me, I take a quick breath of courage, shove those unwelcome feelings back down my throat, and turn to him.

"What?"

"You okay?"

"I'm good."

He stares at me suspiciously for a moment, the trace of a smile on his lips. Finally, he nudges my fork into the bit of pancakes still left on my plate.

"Was it good?"

I had some kind of potato and vegetable thing with cheese and sour cream, and not realizing the serving sizes would fill giants, I asked for a short stack of pancakes, too. It was all delicious, but I'm so stuffed right now, I'd be willing to bet I could wait until Monday when I'm home to eat again.

"It was delicious." I flop back in my seat and rub my hand over my stomach. "But I'm so full."

He grins. "Are you gonna finish those?"

"Do you want me to explode?" I whisper with a quick frown.

"No, I want your pancakes," he tells me. Shocked—he ate an omelet the size of a small country and a side order of bacon, and he has room for more?—I snort out loud and push my plate toward him. "You sure?"

"Have at it." I nod.

"My mom makes the best pancakes." He picks up my fork and digs in.

"Your mom makes the best everything," Josh reminds him.

"True." Isaac nods and says around a mouthful, "I love pancakes."

When he flashes his blue eyes at me, I'm still stuck on him using my fork, and yep, I'm acting more like a teenager with a crush than I did when I was a teenager in the car with Emmett. I laugh, though, and sit up because guilt flashes over his face, like he's going to apologize for stealing my breakfast.

"Aren't they cold?"

He shrugs. "Pancakes. Syrup."

Our eyes meet, and I have no idea what he's thinking. But the word syrup has my mind going places it has no business going. Another stupid blush broadcasts my thoughts, though, and his smile is all heterosexual male.

"I'm gonna go to the restroom," Teagan announces. "Go with me?"

Isaac turns to Kree as I get up to follow Teagan to the restroom.

"You're into him." Teagan just announces it as soon as we walk away from the table. Since it's not a question, I don't say anything. I mean, look at him. Of course, I'm into him. And of course, I know there's nowhere for it to go.

So, what's the harm in having a fun weekend?

"What if he's an ax murderer?"

"He promised he isn't," I answer her. The restroom is only for one person of either sex or even an alien, according to a sticker on the door, but Teag grabs my arm and tugs me into the room with her. She flips the lock and then stares at me. "Go ahead," I tell her.

"I don't have to go." She shakes her head as if she can't believe I fell for that line.

"Oh. Okay, so this was what? He's finishing my pancakes, and so you felt a sudden urge to warn me he might be a serial killer?"

If either of my friends is going to lecture me on what I'm doing, on the possibilities of what could happen this weekend, it's Teagan. Brynna would probably already be contacting caterers for our engagement party. At the moment, I'm not sure which I'd prefer. I need a go-with-the-flow friend.

"Cait." She tosses her hands up, and then we're both laughing.

"Look, we took a walk yesterday. We had dinner together. We're hanging around them today. Tomorrow, he's going to be my plus one at a wedding where otherwise, I would probably be the only one there without a date. How is this dangerous? No matter who he is, I don't think he's going to poison the punch tomorrow."

"Wine," Teag corrects me.

"What?"

"We aren't in wine country to drink punch at a wedding reception."

I roll my eyes but laugh at her comment.

"Maybe he's not a serial killer or an ax murderer, but what if he's a heartbreaker?"

"What if he is?" I shrug. "I just met him. We're having fun. He likes wine. He likes live music. And he knows how to do the Foxtrot. How's that gonna break my heart?"

"He knows how to do the Foxtrot?" Teagan draws back and looks at me with a curious frown. "Why?"

"I think he said his mom taught him to dance."

"Oh God." She drops her head back and groans.

"What?"

She pivots on one foot and paces away from me.

"I can see it now."

"See what?"

I assume she's still in lecture mode, so what she says surprises me.

"You guys are gonna put on a show. Aren't you?" She turns back to me and groans. "You're gonna be like that gum commercial."

"What?"

"You're gonna, like, come fox-trotting onto the patio, and then the music's gonna jump to something hip hoppy, and you're gonna do some sort of dance that's gonna go viral on social media."

The thought of dancing like that with Isaac makes me so giddy, I feel like the teenager with a crush again. I'm not so much into being a social media splash, but really, being that in tune with him and finding a rhythm like that would be so much fun.

"And when would we choreograph that?" I tip my head at her.

"I dunno. Tonight?" She props her hands on her hips. "After we all say goodnight, you guys could get together and plot it out."

"Teag, if I see Isaac tonight after we all say goodnight, I can think of other things I'd rather do with him."

"So, you do wanna do some horizontal dancing with him!" She shrieks like an ah-ha!

"Horizontal." I shrug. "Vertical. I mean, my bed's great, but I'm good with up against the door as we push it closed."

Teagan snorts and shakes her head.

"Cait."

"What?"

"Use condoms."

CHAPTER 17

Isaac

Vacation is supposed to be a fun break from everyday life. Somewhere over the last few years, that fun has felt a little too planned or forced, making it harder to relax and enjoy whatever it is I'm doing. Maybe part of that is natural; we were all good friends, but we've become adults. Not necessarily even adult versions of ourselves, because a lot of us have changed too much to fit together the same way anymore. And maybe we've exhausted the possibilities of the good times, and now each time we venture out together, we're just rerunning old scripts, and the pressure to outdo each last time is just too much.

I don't know. Is that another way of saying familiarity breeds contempt? Or maybe it's just another way of saying I'm restless and bored with the status quo, and I'm ready to find more for my life now. Not ditch the gang, but maybe I need more in my personal life.

Like a girlfriend. Well, no, not a girlfriend. *Commitment.* A wife. A family. If that's what I want.

Seeing Josh and Kree together kind of stirred that part of my brain—not the biological clock thing, but just the need to step back and take stock of my life. Who knows if they're in it for the long haul? Right now, they seem happy, and seeing that has really made me aware of what's missing in my life.

And no, I'm not talking specifically about Adrienne.

Just someone special.

Cait and I orbit each other and our friend groups effortlessly all day as we do tastings at more boutique wineries. We're not clingy, but even when I'm ten feet down the bar from her, standing with Josh and tasting a Malbec or across a barrel room from her, watching her and Teagan whispering and snorting, I feel a connection. The way I sometimes catch her watching me tells me she feels it, too. I'm not sure I would call it love at first sight, because how can you commit to love someone until you're in the day-in, day-out trenches with that person? When you wake up next to the same person day after day and you see sleep lines in her skin, and you have seven arguments a day over the proper way to put the tie on the bread bag?

Sure, there's some sort of spark of instantaneous attraction that draws people together. No denying that. Whether it's two people who've known each other for years and suddenly see something in each other that explodes into more or two strangers who share a conversation over coffee in the town square and find themselves drawn to each other—there's always a spark of awareness.

Takes real life to see if that spark can burn for the long haul.

Damn. Long haul. Those words again.

Before I can stop myself, my eyes dart to the picnic table to the right of where we're sitting. Cait and Teagan are sharing an order of sweet potato fries—I mean, that right there could be a deal breaker. I like sweet potato fries now and then, but seriously? What if Cait's not into real French fries?—sitting backwards at the table, legs stretched out in front of them.

Cait doesn't catch me looking this time, but Josh does.

"Dude." He laughs and shakes his head. "You've got it bad."

"I like her."

No reason to deny it or play games.

"She seems pretty cool," he agrees, but I know there's a but coming. "But how well do you know her?"

"Obviously not well, Josh."

"She could be a black widow or something."

"What?" I take a long pull from my chocolate shake. Gott's Roadside Diner does a hell of a business, and today is no exception. The sun throws down some serious heat, but the picnic tables behind the diner itself have umbrellas, so at least we're in the shade. After visiting a few wineries, we ended up here for some sustenance. Or as Logan so eloquently put it, some grease to soak up some alcohol so we can go back for more.

When I was in my early twenties, I was a firm believer. Drink up. Party on. Yada yada yada. It's different now. We have real jobs, and we're not hanging out underage where we shouldn't be and running from the cops when they get called. Cheap beer or whiskey was great for drinking to get drunk, but it's not about that for me anymore.

The diner is another of our favorite stops when we're on the Napa side of wine country. Logan inhales cheeseburgers like they're snack foods. Chases them with beer. Jasmine and I usually hit the milkshakes, but then for the rest of the day, she complains that she shouldn't have had one because they're fattening.

Is there anything more boring than a girl who constantly worries about her weight and what she eats? FYI? Jasmine *might be* a size six. And even if she were a size twelve? Who cares?

Life's too short. Drink the milkshake. Kiss the girl.

"What if she's got a string of dead exes?"

Josh's question is so ridiculous, I know he's being purposefully stupid. Still, we both have to laugh.

"Okay, well, what if she's got a boyfriend back home?"

"She had one. And he dumped her the night before she flew out here."

"Dick move," Josh mumbles, and I nod my agreement. "What if things are hot and heavy with you guys, but she gets back with the dick when she gets home?"

"What if she does?" I look at him boldly and shrug. "Life's short, Josh. We have a connection."

"I get that." He wads up his napkin, eyes on Jasmine and Kree as they cross back over the grass from the restroom to the table. "I don't know. It's just…"

"I haven't felt like this in a long, damned time—"

"I know." Josh nods again. "I also know the last time you might have felt like this, the girl swore off marriage, and then left you for school and got married."

I flinch at his words. For one thing, even if it was years ago and I've gotten over that whole shitshow, I could do without having it thrown in my face. Second? While I was really into Adrienne, it was different. It was that good friends, long slow slide into something more but never enough kind of thing.

With Cait? It's like there's a current of electricity humming between us, and any time she so much as turns her head, I feel it under my skin. She makes me laugh, and that's sexy as hell. She knows how to talk nerdy—which apparently is sexy, because she sure got my attention yesterday in Sonoma Square talking about the Sebastiani Theatre. The way she looks at me makes my heart stutter and trip around like a drunk stumbling around, high on his surroundings. In my case, of course, that's Cait and her eyes and her smile.

"It's not like that," I mumble.

Josh eyes me with suspicion for a few seconds and finally gives me a knowing grin.

"So, this is a vacation fling?" He raises his eyebrows, and I don't know what it is, if it's a fling or if we could possibly figure out long-distance dating. But I shrug and let him think what he wants.

Kissing Cait yesterday made me want a lot of things last night when I finally crashed. I had tried to be a gentleman and not let my mind go there. After we all said goodnight at the B and B, I went to my room, turned on the TV, and watched a couple of hours of mindless television. But even then, when I turned the TV off, my mind—and every other body part—went straight to thoughts of Cait.

Kissing her.

Holding her hand.

The feel of her warm body pressed up against mine as we walked around the square in Windsor.

The thought of her hands on me.

My mouth on her.

"Race you to the parking lot!"

I look up in time to see Cait's eyes on me, an ornery grin on her face. Teagan and Derrick are a few steps behind her. Before I can move, Cait's running full tilt—sandals and all—across the grass lot, dodging a family pushing a kid in a stroller.

"Dude!" Josh nudges me. "Seriously. She can't beat you!"

I jump up, nearly trip over the leg of the table, and take off behind her. I break my stride for a second to toss my empty milkshake cup in the trash, and then I run after her in earnest.

"You had a head start!" I call to her as I gain on the distance between us.

"I have sandals on, too!" She looks over her shoulder and squeals when she sees how close I am.

"What do I get if I win?"

"When I win, I get to call no Foxtrot or Tango."

I push a bit harder and catch her around the waist with my hand as we near the Escalade they're driving. I bite my lip before I can say something about tangoing in the sheets with her, but my dick's in the race, now, and I'm pretty sure if Cait gets close to me right now, she's going to know it.

"I won," I tell her, and we're laughing, and I still have my hand on her waist, and Cait turns into me, pressing against my chest, and no way she's going to miss the hard-on now.

"You did not!"

"I did," I argue, pulling her closer and sliding my hands down to rest on her hips.

"Well, what do you get if you win?"

She aims that smile and those big eyes up at me, and my heart explodes in my chest. Okay, so no matter what goes on here this weekend—and I won't pressure her for anything, because it's not my style—if we go home and start texting and I find out she's back with her dickhead ex, it's going to suck.

Not like I could really be pissed at her.

But the more time I spend with her, the more I like her. The more I want to get to know her.

It would hurt.

Not exactly the Adrienne thing all over, but yeah, it would hurt.

"I did win." I tip my head at her. "And I get to do this…."

"What?" Her eyes go wide, but when I lower my face to hers, to kiss her, they close slowly, and I notice the curl of her long lashes on her face. She kisses me back, simple, soft presses of her lips to mine. Nothing sexy right now. It's all sweet and playful, and my heart is all swelled up inside my chest. I feel like a stupid cartoon character.

"Well, I'm not sure that counts," she whispers. Instead of pulling away from me, she kisses the corner of my mouth and then nuzzles my cheek with hers. I wonder if she likes the beard scruff or if she wishes I would shave. Not a good thought, because that leads me to wonder if she'd like the feeling of my beard scruff over her breasts and belly, as I kissed my way down to taste her.

"Why wouldn't it count?"

She smells so sweet and feminine, and she kisses my cheek, her breath warm on my skin. I duck my head enough to nip her earlobe.

"Because I've been waiting for you to do that all day." She tips her head back to look at me. "Is that a win for you if I wanted it, too?"

Her confession sends my body into overdrive. My pulse is sky high now, and all the blood in my body just gushed south. I dig my fingers into the soft curves of her sweet, little ass as she moves her mouth back to mine for another kiss.

There's nothing sweet about this kiss. Cait parts her lips, and the soft, little moan in the back of her throat as I flick my tongue inside her hot, wet mouth drives me crazy. Her hands move up over my arms, slowing to cup my biceps and then finally, she rests them on my shoulders for a second. She circles her tongue around mine, with a sexy, needy moan again, and she scrapes her fingernails up the back of my neck. Her touch makes me shiver. I want more. I need the warmth of her skin under my hands, my mouth on her neck.

That sexy moan when she kissed me put all kinds of dirty thoughts in my head. What sounds does she make when a man drives her wild with pleasure? I want to know those sounds by heart. I want to see her face when she's thrashing in the sheets, begging for more, when she finally loses control and lets go to bask in pleasure.

Jasmine's voice invades the dirty thoughts in my head. As much as I want to ease Cait back against the side of the

SUV and dip my head low enough to sample the skin in the warm, sexy nook between her cheek and her shoulder, I don't want to put on a show for our friends.

Backing away from her is so damned hard, it hurts. But by the time the rest of both gangs appear in front of the SUV, Cait and I have moved apart, and we're talking about sweet potato fries versus French fries. I'm pretending I wasn't a minute away from dry-humping her and embarrassing myself, and judging from the look in her eyes, she's playing a similar game in her head.

"Where to next?" Logan stretches his arms over his head and then yanks his ballcap off, bends the bill again, and slaps the hat back on his head.

Teagan glances at her watch and then looks at Cait.

"We should probably head over to Divine." She sounds hesitant, like she doesn't want to break up the fun.

"Definitely should," Cait agrees. "The rehearsal isn't until five, but it's after three. And we should probably...hang out with the bride for a while."

"Absolutely." I nod, because they should. But my heart feels all shriveled up and dry like a stone now.

Cait clears her throat, swings her gaze around the group, and then turns those eyes back to me. If she asks me to go fetch her the moon, I'm on the first rocket out.

"So. Um." She presses her lips together. Thankfully, everyone else starts talking at once, so no one hears the conversation between us. "I know you're here with friends. But um..."

"Yes."

"What?" She looks startled.

"Well, I mean. I'm your plus one for the wedding." I shrug one shoulder. "And most of the time, the wedding plus one is along for the rehearsal stuff, too, right?"

One corner of her mouth curves up, but she only nods.

"So, are you asking me to go with you now? To be your plus one tonight?"

"Um." Her frown is an arrow in my little stone heart. Did I read her wrong? Has she changed her mind? Or did her ex call her last night? But, she just let me kiss her. No, take that back. She *kissed me back*. She pawed those delicate hands up over my arms and shoulders and pressed those delicious curves against me, and there's no way she couldn't tell what she was doing to me. I like her, but I don't want to play games. Not like this.

"No?"

"Plus one sounds so…impersonal." She nibbles on her lower lip again and then gives me a small smile. "I'd rather you go with me as my date."

CHAPTER 18

CAIT

"Is this crazy?" I whisper to Teagan. We're back at Divine. Derrick and Isaac are with Adam and Shane in the barrel room with someone from the winery. I doubt they're doing a tasting, though, since it's almost time for the rehearsal, and Brynna might throw Adam in the pool if he has too much to drink before the festivities get started. Brynna's still in the house with the rest of the ladies, so Teagan and I have a few minutes to ourselves.

We both changed into sun dresses; Teagan pulls off pink like a boss, but mine is pastel blue. When we got here, and we all piled out of the Escalade, I was relieved to see Adam and Shane in khaki shorts. Not that I care if Isaac wears shorts to the rehearsal, but I figured their casual attire might make him feel more comfortable. Adam and Shane didn't bat an eye when he walked up with Derrick, as if they didn't question that he's my date for the weekend.

But now that we're here, I'm a little worried about what Brynna will say. And by a little worried, I mean, my stomach is twisted in knots. The sweet potato fries are just kind of stuck in there, tied up with the worry, and I'm wishing I would have passed at Gott's Roadside Diner.

"What?" Teagan leans her elbows on the wooden railing around the patio and sighs. "Bringing a total stranger as your date to Brynn's wedding?"

Her words make me flinch. I'm not sorry I asked Isaac to be my date. It's just that I'm feeling a little guilty for keeping Brynna in the dark about what happened with Ryan. She'll forgive me; I know that without a doubt, but on the other hand, I handled it wrong. Even knowing that, though, part of me thinks I did the right thing. I didn't want Brynna to be upset for me this week.

"Is it that bad?"

"No." Teagan shrugs. She's not looking at me, though. Her gaze is fixed on the view—the rolling vivid greens and vineyards with a sky so thick and blue it looks like you could scoop it up like ice cream; it's even topped with fluffy white marshmallow clouds.

"Would you be upset? If it was your wedding?"

Now she swings her head around to look at me. "No. Cait, no. And Brynna's not gonna be mad. She'll just be upset that you didn't tell her about Ryan."

I nod. The knot in my stomach tightens.

"But you get why I didn't tell her."

"I do." Teagan nods. "I've got your back, Cait."

Eyes locked with hers, I wait, because I have the feeling she's going to say more.

"But?" I prompt her when she remains quiet.

"If I were you," she says quietly, "I would just tell her."

"Tonight?" I yelp. Teagan looks over her shoulder to make sure no one's around to hear us, but at the moment we're alone on the patio.

"Right now." She tips her head and arches her eyebrows at me, like she's really trying to drive home the point.

"But doesn't that defeat the purpose? She's getting married tomorrow." I groan and lean sideways on the railing. "I don't want her to be worried about me the night before her wedding."

Teagan's right. I have to tell Brynn now, if for no other reason than it's going to be obvious something is up when she sees me with Isaac. When she sees that Ryan is still not here. But I still don't want to tell her. It feels like I'll be raining on her parade, which is the last thing I would ever do to her or Teagan.

"She'll have a moment," Teagan agrees. She gives me a small smile. "But that's what we love about Brynna, right? That ridiculously romantic heart?"

Damn. Another point to Teagan. I answer with a begrudging nod.

"She'll be fine."

Still not convinced, I drop my head back and roll my shoulders.

"And the reason I know she'll be fine..." Teagan draws the words out slowly, waiting until I look at her before she finishes her thought. "Is because you're fine. You certainly don't look like you're wallowing over Ryan. In fact, Cait, you're glowing."

"Probably all that wine I've had already today."

Teag sort of snorts a soft laugh, but she shakes her head. "Or maybe it's that gorgeous guy who looks completely smitten with you."

"Smitten?" I laugh. "Did you say *smitten*? I don't think I've ever heard that word used in an actual conversation."

"I said it, and I meant it. He likes you."

Little tremors of excitement tingle through me. I feel like I could point my fingers and shoot lightening from them. I want Isaac to like me, because I think it's getting dangerous how much I like him. But I also know that after tomorrow, it'll be different. Even if we text or do phone calls sometimes, there's no denying there's just something magical about being with him this weekend.

"Teag." I dip my head and press my fingers to the bridge of my nose. I don't need help with this crush. I need Teagan and Brynna to keep me grounded, not strap me onto cloud nine and send me soaring.

"And besides," she continues before I can argue that Isaac and I will only ever be just friends. "She's not going to obsess over you and Ryan. Not right now. She's getting married tomorrow. I promise you she's got a million other things on her mind."

Wow, okay, Teagan's right again. Of course, Brynna has a million things on her mind that are more important than me and my latest breakup. It's not that I think I need to be in the center ring, I just want her wedding to be everything she's ever dreamt of.

"You guys!!" Brynna's voice rings out behind us in a delighted shriek. Teagan and I turn to watch her hurry out the back door and down the wooden steps to join us. A nasty shiver quakes its way up my spine, imagining her taking a spill there, but she's all grace as she crosses the patio and throws her arms around us. "I'm getting married tomorrow!"

We dance around in a group hug, laughing, and she's still gushing about how happy she is. She's wearing a sleeveless ivory dress, casual, but dressier than either Teagan or me. Her hair is swept up in a loose chignon, with loose curls already tumbled out to frame her face. A touch of blush and lip gloss and I'm guessing a swipe or two of mascara are the only makeup she wears, but it's all she needs. Brynna is radiant.

"I can't wait to be his wife," she whispers, and for a second, we're all borderline weepy. "Loving him makes me so happy."

"Stop it!" Teagan orders her as all three of us dab at our eyes.

"Know what else I can't wait for?" Brynna says quietly as if she's about to spill a secret. Teagan and I shake our heads. "Wedding night sex. There's something special about it, right? Like our moms' moms told them waiting for the wedding night was what made it special, but that's not true, right, Teag?"

"Oh, hell no." Teagan rolls her eyes. "Derrick outdid himself on our wedding night." She nibbles on her lip for a second, a dreamy look on her face. "Well, but then, he outdid that on the second night of the honeymoon."

Brynna and I exchange a look and a laugh. "Are we talking new positions? Super stretches? Or number of orgasms delivered?"

"All of the above," Teagan answers immediately. "And also, quality."

"Quality of orgasms?" I ask her. "Is that a thing?"

"Of course it's a thing."

"Like how?"

"Like don't you feel the difference when you get yourself off and when Ry—when you're with a guy? Like it's more powerful?"

That was close. No need to bring up Ryan's name right now.

"Yeah. I guess so." I keep my eyes on Teagan, though, just in case Brynna caught that near-miss.

"Haven't you ever had meh sex with the same guy who can knock it out of the park sometimes?" Brynna asks me.

"Yeah, yeah, I got it." I nod and throw up a silent, desperate prayer that my cheeks don't look as fire engine red as they feel. I haven't had knock-it-out-of-the-park sex in ages; pretty much never with Ryan. Like, sadly, my last truly incredible orgasm was a late-night date with my vibrator, but I don't want to share that right now. Maybe if it weren't the night before Brynna's wedding, and we were another bottle or a few sips of High West Double Rye in, I'd confess.

"Speaking of which," Brynna twists around to eyeball the patio and beyond. She's looking for another car. Something Ryan would have rented and driven here today to be with me for her wedding. Teagan shoots me a look. TELL HER! Her eyes are screaming it. My stomach drops—sweet potato fries and all—to the patio at our feet, and I give her a tiny little headshake as Brynna whips back around to look at me. "Where's Ryan? Please tell me he's gonna be here."

I swallow a surge of guilt. What if—? Damn, it never occurred to me that Brynna would feel close to Ryan and want him here just as her and Adam's friend. Completely separate from what he is to me. Then again, Ryan dumped me. It's not like I ditched him to hook up with some movie poster dream guy for a fun vacation fling.

There's that flush again. I feel it rolling up my body like an ocean wave. Hook up? Did I seriously just put those two words together in the same thought about Isaac? Good grief. The guy is smokin' hot, and that kiss earlier revved up serious heat in a lot of personal places; in fact, the embarrassed flush I was feeling a second ago now feels more like steam building up from thinking about the kiss.

But that doesn't mean I plan to hook up with him.

Does it?

Do I? Is it a bad thing that I'm even thinking about it? Would that seal it for him? Sexy vacation fling in wine country, but would that make me a girl not worthy of relationship status?

"Cait?" Brynna's fingers circle my wrist. "What're you thinking? Where's Ryan?"

Her concerned tone crashes me back to reality. I'm not back in the parking lot at Gott's, mouth to mouth with a sexy-stranger-turned-friend. I'm not in my cute little room at the Inn at Sonoma, pressed up against the door with that sexy-stranger-turned-friend's slow hands making moves that I suddenly decide I need. Nope. I'm standing on the patio at Divine Vineyards with my two best friends, and one of them stares at me like Ryan's plane crashed en route, and I should be wearing black. The other one just raises her eyebrows as if to say *I told you so.*

"He'snotcoming." I say it all together, really fast, like a child wishing to get away with something after a forced confession. "What time's the rehearsal start? Where is everybody?"

"Wait." Brynna grips my arm tighter. "What?"

Boy does a glass of wine sound good right now.

Or even a shot of tequila.

Or two.

"We broke up."

I'm looking at Brynna, but from the corner of my eye, I see Teagan's frown. Okay, do I have to tell Brynna that he dumped me? That he totally bailed on me the night before we were supposed to fly out here for her wedding? Isn't it enough that she knows we broke up? That I'm okay. We can get into the details later. Like, after her honeymoon.

"You what?" Brynna now white knuckles my wrist. "You —? You broke up?"

"Mm-hmm."

"Since when?"

My hand feels numb, kind of like when I was in the delivery room with my sister and she mistook my hand for a particular part of my brother-in-law's body that she apparently blamed for the labor pain.

"The other day."

"I talked to you Wednesday. You told me he was meeting you at the airport yesterday. That you guys were going to get a rental car together." Brynna turns slightly and waves her hand at Teagan. She looks back at me and opens her mouth to continue, but just as quickly, she snaps it shut and turns her whole body to Teagan. "You don't look surprised. Why? Why are you standing there all calm and collected about this? About Cait and Ryan breaking up?"

Teagan's eyes dart to me over Brynna's shoulder. When her lips part, I shake my head. I can't let her fib for me, nor do I want her to be the one to tell Brynna what happened. That's my job.

"Cait?" Brynna glances back at me.

"I'm gonna go grab us a drink," Teagan announces and scurries back to the house. Brynna's family stocked the house with food and drinks, so no telling what Teagan, the rat, is going after. Okay, a drink might be good, might be necessary right now. But I can't believe she just waltzed away, leaving me to do this alone.

I suck in a quick breath.

"Teagan knew?"

The hurt in Brynna's voice is hard to miss.

"Why did you tell her? When did you break up?"

"He called me at midnight. And just announced out of the blue that he didn't want to come to the wedding. That he was just—that we were over."

"Midnight? Last night?"

"The night before we flew out."

Guilt weighs on my shoulders, and it's doing a number on the sweet potato fries that have made a vicious comeback in my stomach, too. Brynna's eyes widen in disbelief.

"And you told Teagan?"

"She knows."

"When?"

"Yesterday."

"That's what you guys were whispering about?"

Where is Teagan with our drinks? Where're the guys? I need a rescue.

"Were you gonna tell me?"

The tiny note of hope in Brynna's voice squeezes my heart painfully hard.

"Of course, I was, Brynn. Just not yet."

"Why? Why would you keep it from me?"

"Because you're getting married tomorrow! This week is all about you!"

"Do you really think I'm that selfish?"

"I don't think you have a selfish bone in your body, Brynn! Which is why I wanted to wait to tell you. You don't need to worry about me."

"But I do." She shrugs. "I can't help it. Why would he do that to you?"

I toss my hands up helplessly. "I don't know. But Brynna, I'm fine."

"But you were together forever."

"Six months," I correct her. "It's okay. I was pissed more than anything. Leaving me without a plus one for your big day."

"But, do you love him, Cait?"

"No." I shake my head.

"Here we go ladies!" Teagan explodes out of the door and hustles down the stairs and over the patio. "Let's toast." One hand is empty, the other holds a bottle of tequila.

"Umm." I tip my head. "How do we do that?"

"Couldn't find any shot glasses, so we'll have to drink from the bottle." She flashes me a grin.

"Wait." Brynna holds her hands up now to stop the conversation. "You're really okay? Six months together, and he just up and ends it, and you're really okay?"

"Ryan and I were just…it was fun, but it never felt serious. It never felt…."

"What?"

I almost said it never felt like it does with Isaac, but I know how ridiculous that'll sound, since I just met him. Still, there's something to be said for that little spark of attraction that grows and ignites the more you're around someone, right? Never felt the tingly warm flutter in my belly for Ryan that I do for Isaac.

"Right. Like, no zing. No feelings, Brynna. We were friends."

"With benefits," she clarifies and then she tips her head at me.

"Yes."

"Okay, let's toast," she says with a shrug. She reaches for the tequila and nods her head at me. Apparently, we're going for some sort of Three Musketeers hurrah for a toast. I'm in, because no matter what else happens in life, these girls will always be part of it.

When the three of us lay hands on the bottle, Brynna winks at me.

"To finding Cait's one true love!"

"I'll drink to that," Teagan agrees and twists the top off the bottle.

"How about we drink to the bride?" I suggest. The door of the winery building opens, and the guys all shuffle out.

"Is that the guy you met here yesterday?" Brynna sounds a little stunned and a little excited. Neither of them agrees that we should drink to the bride, but Teagan does pass the bottle to Brynna for the first swallow. Brynna tips her head back and takes a big drink. Adam laughs as he pushes the patio gate open to join us. Brynna wipes the back of her hand over her mouth and passes the bottle to Teagan.

"Is it?" Brynna asks me breathlessly. Adam slides his arm around her waist.

"Yes."

Teagan takes a swig and passes the bottle over to me.

"Meeting of the minds?" Derrick leans around her to kiss her cheek.

"Just a girls' powwow," Brynna answers. I tip the bottle up and swallow a mouthful of cold, smooth tequila.

"You ready to practice marrying me?" Adam nuzzles Brynna's neck. But she looks at me and then shifts her gaze to Isaac. She studies him with interest and then laughs and winds her arm back around Adam's head.

"Let's do this."

She might be talking to Adam, but she's looking right at me. The bride's in matchmaker mode already.

CHAPTER 19

Isaac

Since finding the girls out on the patio earlier, knocking back shots of tequila, I haven't had a minute alone with Cait. I'm curious what the girls' powwow was about, but then, they were all smiling when we joined them, including the bride. I take it from the smiles and the fact that Brynna the bride has looked me over several times that she now knows the truth about Ryan the dickhead ex and why I'm here. And apparently, I've been approved for the guest list.

The patio fills up quickly. The bride's family comes outside, and Cait leads me through more introductions. The insane thing is meeting all of these people and not meeting Cait's family. Then again, it's way too early for that. They all seem nice enough, and it's obvious watching them all interact that they're close family and friends. I think that's part of why I'm perfectly at ease out here with virtual strangers. They remind me of my family, of my friends, the way they bounce off each other and trade smiles and laughter.

More people show up near five, one of them obviously a minister. He wears the black clothes and white clerical collar of a Roman Catholic priest. My parents are Catholic, but I'm not too faithful about going to mass, and when Brynna introduces me to Father Kelley, guilt streaks through me and leaves me a little tongue-tied. The guy seems pretty cool, though. Friendly enough. He makes a bit of small talk with me and Derrick and then moves on to inspire fear and guilt in other hearts.

"You look like you saw a ghost." Cait appears at my side and stands on her tiptoes to whisper to me. I side-eye the priest and then look at her.

"Catholic guilt."

She snorts. "Lapsed Catholic, huh?"

"Eh." I shrug. "Convenient Catholic?"

"Oh, a C and E." She nods.

"Not necessarily," I argue, because I do make it to mass a little more often than twice a year. Sometimes. "What about you?"

The grin on her face says it all. "Probably about like you."

"Catholic?" I tip my head, not sure why I'm surprised, other than the fact that it's kind of fun learning things we have in common.

"Yep. Catholic grade school. My mom made me go to religion classes after I started high school. You?"

"Catholic high school," I answer.

"Oh. Did you have scary nuns as teachers?"

"Two nuns. One was scary, and the other was so much fun, it was hard for us guys to believe she was a nun."

A whistle pierces the air, and conversations across the patio die instantly.

"Okay. Let's get down to business."

I think the guy talking is Brynna's dad, but I wouldn't swear to it on a test. Cait sidles up close to me and slips her arm around my waist. Something tugs at my back, and I realize she hooked her finger through my belt loop. Whoever would have thought a woman hooking her finger through my belt loop would make me hard? But there it is. Which is not good. There're parents and best friends and a priest out here with us, and I've got serious wood knowing Cait's hand is two seconds from sliding into the back of my shorts.

If she wanted to.

She wouldn't, Isaac. Get over it.

"So, what exactly does that mean?" she asks so quietly that I know I'm the only one who heard her. The guy is talking again, and now I'm sure it's Brynna's dad. He's saying how we're going to go over the ceremony just so the attendants and groomsmen know what they're doing, and the readers know when they're up. Makes sense, and even though that will mean Cait'll have to let go of my belt loop, it also means I get to sit and ogle her with a legitimate reason to do so.

"What does what mean?" I turn my head and brush my chin over her hair. My heart thumps a little erratically at the worry that she read my mind about her hand in my shorts.

She leans into me, and my brain stalls at the feeling of her soft but firm little body aligned just so with mine. From her breasts down to her smooth legs, she's touching me, and I'm seeing fireworks.

"What kind of fun was this nun?" She giggles. I laugh, but then she moves her hand the slightest bit, the one with the finger stuck through my belt loop. Her fingers smooth down over my lower back, but that's a technicality, and no, she didn't put her hand *inside* my shorts, but her hand is pretty much on my ass, and I'm pretty much dying.

"Get your mind out of the gutter, Cait Pendleton!" I press my lips to her hair to stifle the laugh, but she smells so good, I want to bury my nose in her curls and nibble on her neck.

Teagan shoots us a dirty look, like we're causing a scene, so Cait and I stand up straight and behave. When the wedding party—minus Adam, since he's standing at the far side of the pool with the priest—heads off to the front of the winery to line up, I realize Derrick and I are hanging out at the patio railing. Derrick's looking out at the vineyards, and yeah, I would normally agree it's a pretty view. But I stand with my back turned that way, because the prettiest part of this weekend is about to walk through the patio gate to stand for her best friend.

Adam's parents come in first, and we're assured by the winery rep—her name is Clarissa, if I'm not mistaken—that they will put out the exact number of folding chairs early tomorrow before the ceremony. Next is the bride's brother walking their mom down to the patio. They're all smiles, and again, it makes me think of my mom and dad, and I wonder if this moment will ever happen for me. The attendants are next, first Bailey, who is involved with the bride's brother. Look at me, remembering the whole cast of characters. Then Teagan, walking with some dude who's tight with the groom. So, maybe that's my part if Josh and Kree tie the knot. Which is a really weird thought, and I have to shake my head to knock it loose.

Finally, I see Cait. God, she's gorgeous. Her flowy blue sundress kind of billows around her legs as she walks. She's smiling, and while I watch, she and the guy escorting her (also a friend of the groom's) lean together to whisper and laugh at something. A surge of jealousy rips through me, and I dig my knuckles into my chest to massage the ache there. I get that I can't be her escort, but damn, I hate that she has her arm looped through that guy's. But as they round the pool and part to stand and wait for the bride, Cait glances at me and flashes me a smile that kind of poleaxes me. I think I must grunt or gasp or sigh or something, because Derrick shoots me a knowing look. Our eyes meet, and he actually laughs. But then he shrugs and wags his eyebrows like he's laughing with me instead of at me. Come to think of it, he and Teagan have been pretty lovey-dovey all day, so maybe they're still in the newlywed phase, and maybe he doesn't love some other guy's hands on his wife.

Last—before the bride—comes a couple of little kids that arrived just a while ago with the small influx of new people. Cait told me they're Adam's cousins. Five-year-old twins. Adorable, but I'm guessing also hell-on-wheels. They're the flower girl and ring bearer, and all the girls here do that soft, wistful sigh thing as they watch the kids enter through the gate and round the pool. The little girl eyes the pool longingly, and the mom, who's sitting at a four-top table behind Adam and Father Kelley, quietly says her name as a warning, and the little girl looks away quickly. Derrick looks at me again.

"Teagan wants twins." His smile is half excitement, half terror.

"I didn't know you could order them."

Derrick chuckles. "Her mom has twins on her side of the family."

"I don't know if I'm supposed to offer my encouragement or condolences."

As the words come out, it hits me that I'm kidding. And I'm picturing myself and Cait suddenly, not just at this makeshift altar exchanging vows, not just burning up the sheets, but parenting. Five-year-old twins.

Way too damned early to be entertaining those thoughts.

"Wouldn't be so bad." Derrick gives me a sheepish grin, and then the music on the iPad playing changes. I guess Brynna's cousin will be here tomorrow to play the guitar for the ceremony but for now, they're using some canned wedding music. Brynna and her dad appear, and they're doing some crazy dance steps, but they're completely in sync, and they're laughing. I don't even know them, and it makes me feel sort of emotional. I take another look at Cait, and she's laughing but she's also dabbing at her eyes, like she's trying not to cry.

These are good people, and that woman is so intriguing, and damned if I want this weekend to end. Teagan swipes at her eyes, too, and then the girls reach for each other and link fingers. Brynna's mom throws her arms around her after her dad kisses her cheek and places her hand in Adam's. Even Father Kelley has to laugh, but suddenly, the music stops, and then Father Kelley runs them all through what will happen tomorrow.

It doesn't take that long, but I'm still glad when they're done, and I get Cait back at my side. Caterers show up to set up a taco bar. There are a few winery reps out here now, including the girl named Clarissa. They open several bottles of wine, and Brynna's uncle carries a cooler stocked with soda and beer to the patio. The music playing now kind of sounds like yacht rock, but it works. Cait and I sit with Teagan and Derrick. We're all drinking beer from a local brewery with our tacos, and now and then Cait finds a reason to touch my arm or rest her hand on my leg.

Brynna and Adam make their way around the tables and talk to everyone. I was worried that Brynna would be angry with Cait, but it seems like maybe that girls' powwow thing took care of everything. Still, when the engaged couple makes their way to our table, I see the way Brynna watches me and hold my breath.

"Ladies." Brynna doles out two small packages wrapped in white paper. She and Adam sit down with us. Brynna watches Cait let go of my hand to open her gift, but I'm watching Cait and Teagan. They eye each other, pacing themselves so they open the boxes together. Cait gasps softly, and Teagan sort of groans and then bites her lip as they lift silver chains from the boxes. Both have tiny pendants on them, but I can't see what they are.

Cait looks up at Brynna and swipes at her eyes again. How do girls keep their makeup looking so good when they get all weepy all the time?

"Thank you."

At the whisper, Brynna lurches out of her seat and hurries around the table to hug Cait. I study her hands on Brynna's back. The way her ringless fingers are spread wide to hold as much of her friend as she can. Cait's eyes are closed, but she's smiling and whispering, and then she nods, and they're laughing.

When Brynna moves to hug Teagan, Cait turns to me and holds out the necklace. The pendant is a tiny wine bottle with a small emerald green stone in it.

"We come out here a lot," Cait explains, "and the stone is for May." She licks her lips, and I realize then that she's crying, and even though I know they're happy tears, they hit me square in the heart.

I am *fucked.*

This girl is everything to me, and I've known her all of thirty hours.

"Will you put it on me?"

"Of course." I stand and take the necklace as she turns her back to me and lifts her curls from her neck. I unhook the chain and lift it over her head, but when I hook it, the back of my fingers touch her skin, drawing my eyes to her long, elegant neck.

"Did you get it?" She turns her head to look at me. With a painful swallow, I drag my eyes from her neck and meet her gaze. Her eyes are heated, like she knows what I'm thinking, like she knows I want to kiss her there. To sample the taste and texture of her skin. Like *she* wants to know what my mouth would feel like, pressed open on her skin.

I croak out a yes, and she drops her silky hair to brush over my hands as I pull them away. She turns to me then, and this time I break my gaze from hers to admire the necklace on her skin, nestled between her breasts. For a second, I imagine kissing that spot, just under the necklace. I can almost feel the heat of her skin and the swell of her breasts.

Someone clears her throat, and I look up to find Brynna watching us.

"Cait." She nudges her. "Your parents are here."

Her parents? Her parents are here? Did I conjure them up earlier with all that crazy fastball thinking? This cannot be happening. Can it? How did being a fun wedding plus one translate to meeting parents already? How's she going to explain me? How am I going to hold her close tomorrow when we're dancing and steal kisses if her parents are here?

The heat in Cait's eyes—even her cheeks are flushed like she read my mind a second ago—cools instantly. She blinks at me, and then mildly panicked, she turns to Brynna.

"Oh damn!" She giggles and eyes me again. "Isaac, I'm so sorry. I didn't even think about them flying in for the wedding."

CHAPTER 20

Cait

Oh my god! How did I not think about the fact that my parents would be here for the wedding? They know about Ryan, about what happened. I called my sister early the morning we flew out, just to rant about how angry I was. And yes, she called my mom, so it wasn't long before Mom called me. So okay, they knew I was heading out here to wine country with no date for my best friend's wedding.

But what're they going to think about Isaac?

Okay, let's break it down.

I'm an adult. I've been living under my own roof for several years, and I've done quite well for myself, all things considered. Maybe not in the finding love category, but in all other things, I'm proud of what I've accomplished so far. And as a side note to having had my own place for years, my parents know that I have sex.

Well, I mean, no, it's not something I would ever sit down to discuss with my dad over coffee.

But my mom and sister and I have at least talked enough about that stuff that my mom can't possibly imagine I'm still a card-carrying member of the V club.

They liked Ryan okay, but I never got the vibe that they thought he and I were headed to the altar. And Mom was pretty miffed at him for how he bailed on the wedding. They'll like Isaac, because they've only ever disliked one guy I dated. In retrospect, that one's understandable. I was twenty; he was a biker. Clean cut and good-looking, but I found out after we'd dated a month that he did a sideline business to supplement his bartending gig. Not a fan of illegal activities, so when I found out about the drug deals, that was the end of that.

So, see, my parents will like Isaac. My mom's going to melt when she sees him. My dad? Well, if he finds out I followed the guy out of a coffee shop and across the street to Sonoma Square just because I thought he was hot, he might show a little more caution.

But what's Isaac going to think of them? Not my parents as people, but the fact that my *parents* are here. And that if he comes to the wedding as my date, he's going to have to meet them.

"Your parents are here?" he says, and his face is calm. Voice is neutral, and I find myself wanting to just relax and pretend this doesn't have the potential to be a disaster. To be a deal breaker.

"I told you Brynna and I are close," I remind him.

He nods and looks around the people milling about on the patio.

"How did you forget to mention that?"

Crap. He still doesn't sound *angry*, but he doesn't seem excited to meet them, either. When he looks back at me, his eyes pin me in place and demand an answer. The truth is going to sound like a line, but it's...the truth. And besides, I've got nothing else.

"I got so caught up..." I tilt my head aware of Brynna still standing close enough that we look like a threesome making plans for later. I cut a quick look her way, and she turns her back to us, but still stands close. She's trying to be a wall, to protect us from the moment my parents see me and rush over to say hello. The trouble with that is, she's the bride-to-be, so all eyes go to her immediately this weekend.

"Brynna!"

I flinch when I hear my mom squeal.

"You look beautiful!"

"That's my mom," I whisper and step even closer to Isaac, nudging him gently so he'll take a few steps away from Brynna. His face now looks comically panicked. If he were wearing a tie, I imagine he would be tugging at it now. "I got so caught up in being with you and the idea of spending the rest of the weekend with you, it totally slipped my mind that they would be here."

Just behind us, my mom is throwing her arms around my bestie. My heart is in my throat, because I don't want

Isaac to change his mind about tomorrow. I desperately want him to be here. I want to dance with him. Who am I kidding? I want more kissing, and yes, kissing when we're dancing, and maybe I'm high on too much wine or just his gorgeous smile, but I might want some more kissing and stuff later.

And stuff.

My heart flips in my chest. Holy shit. I'm thinking about it. I'm seriously considering sleeping with him. Sex. Heat floods my face as I stand there looking up at him, praying he'll stick around and imagining him taking my dress off tomorrow night and kissing me where my necklace lays on my chest.

More than that, though. The thought that this weekend might be it? That come Sunday when Isaac and I say goodbye, this will be over, and it'll have been a fantastic vacation story? My throat's so tight with emotion I can only stare at him now.

"Are you trying to tell me you were having such a good time with me that it completely slipped your mind that your parents would be in attendance at your friend's wedding?" His voice is deep and edgy, and that heat hits me everywhere at once. Whoa. My panties are going to melt. Never have I ever felt like this.

I nibble on my lip and nod, still afraid to speak. Afraid he's angry. Afraid if I try, I'll only be able to squeak something unintelligible because my throat is still squeezed tight with hope and fear.

He flashes me a grin, and I melt into him. He slips his arms around me and dips his head to kiss my cheek.

"I'm gonna follow your lead, Cait. Don't leave me high and dry." The words rush out of him as he drags his lips high over my cheek, and then I hear my mom say my name, and this is it. Isaac might be upset with me, but he's not going to go storming out of here yet.

Yes, I know he has no vehicle to spin out and tear down the long drive, but I'm going to look at the bright side and hope he likes me enough to forgive my crush-brain and stick around.

"Cait!" Mom grabs my arm. She's still a pretty woman in her fifties. She colors her hair, but when she doesn't, she just has a streak of gray that my dad says makes him want to dance with her. My sister and I don't ask, but it is kind of cool that my parents are still happy together and obviously very attracted to each other. "You look beautiful, honey."

"Hey, Mom." I hug her and take just an extra few seconds in her arms, since it's the first time I've seen her since Ryan went AWOL. "Where's Dad?"

"Talking to Michael," Mom answers, and yep, I see him over by the pool talking to Brynna's dad. Mom starts to say something, but afraid she might decide to tease me and say that Dad's taking notes for whenever I get married and more afraid that teasing like that will send Isaac running for Limerick Lane, I interrupt her.

"I want you to meet my friend," I tell her, and she sizes him up so quickly, I know from the smile on her face I'm forgiven for cutting her off. He's just that good-looking. I regret that my parents won't get to know him as well as I have because there's a lot more than a pretty face to Isaac Stratton.

As if knowing a guy for a day and a half is enough time to judge his character.

Isaac clears his throat, reminding me that Mom and I are both staring. Right, Cait. Good grief.

"This is Isaac Stratton." Isaac and I are still standing close enough that if we swayed back and forth, we would appear to be dancing. I touch his forearm now, though, and look at Mom. "And Isaac, this is my mom, Diana Pendleton."

"Well, it's nice to meet you, Isaac."

They offer their hands at the same time, making me think of rock, paper, scissors. I almost laugh out loud, but I manage to control myself.

"It's a pleasure to meet you, Mrs. Pendleton." Isaac looks her square in the eyes. Double points there. I can almost feel the hum of approval rolling off of my mom.

"Isaac is an architect," I tell her, and she chuckles and nods at the same time.

"Wow. Don't let this one get away, Cait." She winks, and I know her well enough to know she's kidding, but all the same, I'm mortified that she said it.

"Mom." I roll my eyes.

"Good-looking, good manners, and he speaks your language."

"Just friends, Mom," I assure her, hoping she lets it go at that.

"Where are you from, Isaac?"

"I'm from Indianapolis."

"Oh." She nods and then looks around for Dad. Isaac shoots me a how-am-I-doing look? while she has her head turned.

I give him an enthusiastic nod. He's knocking it out of the park. Then again, maybe he doesn't want to knock it out of the park. Between my parents and my best friends, they might have us married right after Brynna and Adam tomorrow.

"Cait!" My dad's voice booms over the patio as he approaches us. I feel Isaac stiffen just the slightest bit, and a rush of guilt hits me. What was I thinking? Maybe this was a bad idea. My parents are really fun, laid back people, but he doesn't know that.

"Hey, Daddy." I hug him, wondering if calling him Daddy makes me sound like a spoiled little girl. What if that turns Isaac off? "How was the flight?"

"Pilot did a few rolls, but other than that it was good."

"Dad." I roll my eyes again. "I want you to meet my friend."

All six feet five inches of my dad's body adjust slightly to look at Isaac. The guy's kind of scary looking. Tall and broad shouldered. Thick silver hair and bright blue eyes. He's an accountant, but he carries himself like he's in charge, and maybe that's intimidating to guys like Isaac. That random women hit on and pick up in town squares to fill in as a plus one at destination weddings.

"This is Isaac Stratton."

"Martin Pendleton." Dad stretches his hand out to shake Isaac's. "How're you doing?"

"Good." Isaac nods. "It's nice to meet you, Mr. Pendleton."

"Please." Dad waves the formality away. "If you're a friend of Cait and Brynna's, call me Marty."

Isaac smiles and takes a quick peek at me.

"Did you guys get some tacos?" Brynna appears again and throws her arms around my parents to squeeze them.

"No, but that sounds good. I'm hungry enough to eat a horse."

Brynna giggles and plays along with my dad. "Or even a taco or two."

"We'll talk to you again later, sweetie." Mom pats my upper arm and then sends a goofy smile at Isaac, and I hold my breath as they wander off with Brynna in search of a taco or two. The second my dad starts building his taco, my mom head to head in conversation with Brynna, I grab Isaac's arm and pull him over to the railing.

"I'm so sorry."

When he doesn't say anything, I bite my lip and look up at him. He lifts his hand and brushes my lip with his thumb. The touch makes me a little achy and more than a little confused. My body is still in hypersensitive mode from thinking naughty things about him earlier, and I'm still worried that he's angry and pretending not to be.

"It's okay."

"Are you sure? Because I promise you I did not plan for this to happen."

"You don't always introduce your wine-country flings to your parents a day and a half into said fling?"

Nerves snake through my belly again. For a second, I'm too nervous to speak. But when he grins, I lean and almost crash into him.

"No, I don't, actually." I rest my forehead on his chest for just a second and then curl my fingers around his arm. His skin is warm and soft, but there's solid muscle there, too. A low rumble of laughter climbs from his belly, and I lift my head to meet his eyes. I'm laughing now, too.

He wags his eyebrows at me, and I laugh louder, but I'm shivering now from what he said.

"Wait." I lift a hand as if to stop him. "Wait. Is this a vacation fling?"

"I don't know." His eyes sparkle, like he's amused. "Is it?"

Every part of my body is on high alert right now, but I'm painfully aware of the other thirty-ish people here on the patio with us. Including my parents.

"I don't know," I whisper, but I can't keep my mouth from smiling and some other parts of my body are jumping up and down, waving at Isaac, hollering yes, take me!

"I guess it's whatever we want it to be." He leans forward, and my body is lifting to my tiptoes, not even caring that he's going to kiss me in front of everyone, and at some point in the very near future, my mom is going to ask how Isaac and I met. Hope she doesn't think I'm a floozie, but at the moment, I'm all his. He doesn't kiss me, though. He simply rests his forehead against mine, and dammit all, now my heart's jumping up and down and waving a flag like a parking attendant directing traffic.

Yep, Isaac Stratton, pull right on in here.

CHAPTER 21

ISAAC

The rest of the evening is fun. Even if I just sort of accidentally got thrown into meeting Cait's parents. Then again, we're hanging out. I have to keep reminding myself that for now, this is a temporary fun fling—for lack of a better word—and meeting her parents isn't a big deal. It's not like we're dating. I shouldn't feel pressure about anything. This weekend is about celebrating someone Cait cares about and having fun.

Though there's obviously more wine than all of us together could ever consume, everyone seems to play it cool. I'm thinking tomorrow might be different, but no one wants to show up tomorrow looking or feeling green. Still, there's music and lively conversation spread all over the patio, and I spend as much time talking to Derrick and Adam as I do talking to Cait. She stays at our table, but now and then she jumps up and moseys over to talk to someone else for a minute or two. Even when we're all at the table together, there are times when I'm totally caught up in conversation with the guys, and she's reminiscing and laughing with her friends.

At some point, more people join our table, and Cait introduces me to them as her friend. Which is another reminder that this just a fun, stand-alone weekend that doesn't have to mean anything. After a while, Derrick and I hit the taco bar up again, and then later, I find myself at the table talking to Brynna's brother, Shane. He's a few years younger than Brynna, and after he's had a few beers, he leans in and confesses to me that when he was a kid, he had a crush on Cait.

I don't blame him. I probably would have, too. I watch her through the night, never enough to look creepy or stalkerish. But no matter who I'm talking to, I find myself looking for Cait. I can't get enough of her. Shane seems pretty into his girlfriend, so I'm not too worried about an old crush.

The patio clears after nine. I wait with Teagan and Derrick while Cait walks her parents out to their rental car. Even after the whole evening of preaching to myself that meeting her parents, spending time with her parents, is nothing to panic about, I was relieved to learn they're staying at a bed and breakfast in Windsor. I don't expect Cait to invite me to her room tonight, but I do plan to kiss her again, and it just feels wrong to kiss her when her parents are nearby, waiting for her to go to her room. Alone.

Brynna and Adam walk other guests out, too, but they return to the patio before Cait does. Their parents are still out talking to some of those guests, but they join us at the railing.

"That was perfect," Brynna says with a soft sigh and a happy smile. From everything I've seen of her, she's every bit as nice as Cait said she was. I've heard some brides referred to as bridezillas, but that's definitely not Brynna. She could have been pretty put out with Cait for keeping the breakup from her and then inviting a stranger to be her date for the wedding. I'm guessing the girls talked about all of that, but from the way Brynna and Cait have carried on tonight, and from the way Brynna welcomed me as a guest, I'm thinking it's all okay.

"It was perfect," Teagan agrees with a yawn. She leans on Derrick, whose arm is curled tightly around her waist. "Tomorrow will be, too."

Brynna tips her head to share a smile with Adam.

"So, Cait says you do the Foxtrot." She shoots me a fake suspicious look, quirked eyebrow and all.

"I've taken some dancing lessons."

"I'll give you fifty bucks if you drag her out to Foxtrot or Tango or something tomorrow night."

Well, well. Brynna's a bit ornery, too. We laugh, and I shake my head, but then who knows what will happen tomorrow night?

"I'll give you fifty if you get her to twerk." Teagan jumps into the game. We're all laughing by the time Cait comes back. She studies me for a moment and then eyes her girlfriends suspiciously.

"You all look guilty," she decides.

"Walking away from Brynn and Teag is like leaving your phone unlocked when you go to the bathroom," Adam tells Cait.

"Mmm." Cait shakes her head and closes her eyes, but she's laughing. "Don't remind me."

"We blew up her phone with selfies." Teagan turns to me.

"And stranger pics," Brynna adds. "Remember the guy with the kangaroo?"

"It was a dog." Cait rolls her eyes. "And the most scarring picture was the double shot of cleavage, girls."

Adam and Derrick exchange a glance and shrug. Both of them get elbows in their guts. It all sounds so much like crap my friends say and do to each other that again, I forget that I just met these people.

"Okay." Brynna stretches and covers a yawn with her left hand. Even in the darkness, the diamond on her finger shines. Makes me think of Josh and Kree. They haven't been dating long, but they have a pretty serious vibe going. I wonder if theirs will be the next wedding I attend. The idea of them getting married, of Josh being that happy, makes me feel good. But the idea of being at his wedding someday without Cait leaves me feeling a bit hollow. "We're out. Going to bed."

"You can't sleep together," Teagan reminds them. "Not tonight."

"You think we've been sleeping together?" Brynna tips her head.

"Um. Have I met you?" Teagan snorts. "Yes."

Adam snorts, and Brynna rolls her eyes. "I mean this week. With family in that house. With my parents in there?"

"You napped," Cait reminds Brynna.

"That's different. We snuck a—a nap in during the day. That's different than turning the lights off and crawling into bed with someone at night."

"Right." Teagan nods.

The girls all hug, and I hear them whispering things like *seriously, don't sleep together, don't let him see you in the morning, we'll be here early tomorrow*, and then Brynna and Adam head for the house, and the rest of us cross the patio to go to the SUV.

So, even though Cait's parents are staying in Windsor, we're still going to have an awkward goodnight. I forgot that I don't have my own rental, so Cait and I are at Teagan and Derrick's mercy. Oh well. Maybe a quick goodnight kiss is better for both of us. Clearly, there's something wrong with me if I'm putting this much thought into a girl I just met.

The drive back down Limerick Lane and out to the highway is quiet, but it's the good kind of quiet when everyone's had a good time, but they're totally wiped out. It has been a long day—feels like it's been several days since we parted company with my friends at Gott's. But I wouldn't change my decision to go with Cait.

Josh texted a few times through the evening. The four of them hit a few more wineries for tastings and then found a brewery for dinner. Sounds like they had a good night, even sounds like Logan behaved himself for once.

I direct Derrick to the bed and breakfast where my group is staying to the background tune of an older Imagine Dragons song. Teagan's passed out in the front seat. Once, she snorts a soft little snore and wakes herself up, and she and Derrick look at each other and laugh quietly. Yet another giant finger poke for me. Like a neon sign saying, look what you're missing. Isn't it time you settle down and start a family?

Frustrated with myself, because now I'm not sure if I was really feeling that way before this trip, at the beginning of this trip, or if I've just convinced myself I feel that way because I laid eyes on this gorgeous woman who apparently was attracted to me at first sight, too. Maybe being with Cait, being around all the wedding stuff, seeing Josh with a girlfriend—maybe it's just the power of suggestion. I watch the night roll by—I can't see the vineyards, but in wine country, they're everywhere—out my window as Derrick navigates the last few turns. Cait reaches for my hand when he pulls into the gravel drive of the bed and breakfast. Golden light falls through the first-floor windows, but I'm not sure if that means everyone's up or if they just left a light on for me.

For one crazy second, I consider asking Cait if she wants to come in for a while. There're board games stacked in

the living area of the house, and there's an iPad and a
Bluetooth speaker there, too. We could hang out there
and play Battleship or Monopoly.

But really, I want to kiss her. I'd love to just sit with her
on the porch swing and put my arm around her to tuck
her in tight against me. I could sneak into Josh or Logan's
room and find the keys to our minivan to drive her back
to Sonoma later. Chances are, if I suggest that, everyone
in the SUV will think the worst, and while I would love to
spend the night with Cait, I don't want to give her friends
the wrong impression. I'm not that kind of guy.

"So, since I'm actually your date and not just the plus one,
do I rate getting walked to the door?" I lean across the
space between our seats and whisper to her. She only
flashes me a grin, and then when I open my door, she
piles out with me.

"Be right back." She leans back in to tell Teagan and
Derrick. Both of them wave us away so quickly I'm half
convinced they're going to attempt a driver's seat quickie
while Cait's gone. As Cait slides her fingers into mine, I
give myself a mental shake. No need to waste time
thinking about that with them. Not when I'm holding
Cait's hand, and I'm ninety-nine percent sure I'll get a
kiss. After all the crazy thoughts bouncing around in my
head all day long, the second we're around the corner
from the car and I see the front porch is dark, I turn to
Cait and lean in for a kiss. We're still walking, and it's a
difficult angle, so we're doing more laughing into each
other's mouths than actual kissing.

When we're at the porch, I stop and haul her up close. She moans softly when our mouths connect for real this time. It's been hours since we kissed at Gott's. The little pecks at the rehearsal don't count. Alone, here in the dark with her, this is the real thing, and she tastes so good, it's like a sucker punch to my gut. She wraps her arms around my shoulders and clasps her hands behind my neck, which means full frontal contact again.

Maybe I should have suggested that she stick around for a bit. It's not even like it's late.

Nope. Grow up, Isaac. She's not in wine country to hook up with a stranger. She's here for her best friend's wedding, and we bumped into each other, and I got lucky enough to fill in as her plus one. I have to stop reading this as anything else. It's time to let her go until tomorrow.

"I should go." She rests her forehead on my collar bone. My hands rest on her hips. A minute ago, I'm pretty sure my fingers were sunk hard in her sweet ass so I could keep her pulled tight against me. Now I make a conscious effort to move my hands to somewhere a bit more appropriate. "Teag and Derrick might leave me stranded here."

She tips her head back, and my eyes have adjusted enough to the dark to see her face. She's smiling a little, like maybe she's daring me to say otherwise. As if my dick wasn't already like rock. The possibility that we're both thinking about things we could do to entertain ourselves makes me so crazy my dick might weep.

"And what would be wrong with that?"

She laughs softly.

"You're sure?" she whispers. "About tomorrow?"

"Absolutely."

"Do you want us to come out here and get you?"

We link fingers now, even though we're still standing pressed against each other. Hands at our waists, we hold the eye contact and laugh again, maybe at how crazy this weekend really is.

"No. What time are you going to Divine?"

"Around eleven."

"I'll be at the inn waiting on you when you leave."

She tips her head and studies me silently for a second. "Are you gonna walk?"

"No. I'll have Josh drop me off."

"Feels like we're kids again, having to rely on rides."

Maybe so, but I know damned sure I never packed wood for a woman like this when I was a kid, new to dating.

"Be ready to dance," I warn her. She laughs again, but it sounds forced.

"I can't wait to dance with you, but I'm not entirely sure I trust my best friends with you. What're they planning?'

I drop a kiss on her lips and release her hands, because if I don't do it now, I'm going full caveman on her and throwing her over my shoulder and carrying her up to my room. Never would have thought it possible, but standing here in the dark, laughing with this woman is a huge turn-on.

"Beautiful." I press my finger to the pendant still nestled between her breasts. The way her breath catches, and her shoulders jump, and her eyes fly up to mine make me so hard it hurts.

"Goodnight, Isaac."

I watch her slip away, back around the corner before climbing the steps to the porch. Her whisper still lingers with me as Derrick backs the car out of the drive and pulls onto the deadly quiet country road.

If I sleep tonight, I hope to hell I get to dream about where tonight might have gone.

CHAPTER 22

Cait

Sunny skies and green hills set the scene for Brynna's wedding day. The patio is decorated simply with exquisite ivory and pale lavender, lilac, and wisteria tulle bows. True to the winery rep's word last night, ivory resin folding chairs line the sides of the pool, and each chair on the end bears a small tulle bow. Fairy lights hang around the patio, and more of the tulle and lights are wrapped around a simple white trellis where Father Kelley will stand to do the ceremony. The plans are to move the trellis to the side and set up the tables for sandwiches and the cake in the same spot later. Though the lights are not on now, their twinkle later in the evening as the sun descends in a melee of purple and orange streaks will be magical.

Magical seems to be a good theme for how the week has turned out, even for me. There's no question Brynna has been floating in the clouds for the past week, more so than usual, but even for me—after Ryan ditched me—this has been a great week. And I'm thrilled that today is Brynna's big day. But it puts me that much closer to saying goodbye to Isaac, which could bring me down if I let it. I won't, though. Living for the moment right now.

After that goodnight kiss with Isaac last night, I floated back to the car, a little bit relieved to find Teagan and Derrick involved in an epic battle of tic tac toe. If I had come back to find them making out, I might have combusted right there in the gravel drive outside the bed and breakfast. I have no doubt they had some private fun when we were all back in our rooms a little bit later, but at least then I was alone to curl up in the dark and relive kissing Isaac.

So, he'd told my mom he was from Indianapolis. It's not next door to me, but in the big picture, it's not thousands of miles away, either. Might make a long-distance relationship doable. But maybe not. I've never been too into the idea of being with someone who lives that far away, trying to make a relationship work through phone calls and weekend visits. Trying to meld your daily personal life, your routine into someone else's routine at such a distance is hard work. I get that relationships aren't always rainbows and pounding hearts. Being emotionally involved with someone, especially for the long haul, takes commitment and work. I just think adding a few hundred miles and possible insecurities and temptations makes that sort of relationship seem that much harder.

I gave it a lot of thought before I finally fell asleep last night. As much as I wish we could make it work, it seems pretty unrealistic. Hence, my decision to live in the moment.

My crazy, hopeful heart did a little flip when I found Isaac waiting for me in the lobby this morning. With his head ducked over an open newspaper, I took a few minutes to take in the sight. Which was the best sight I've seen first thing in the morning in ages. Dressed in khaki slacks and a blue button-down shirt, he looked both like a preppy businessman and like a guy dressed for a casual Sonoma County wedding.

He noticed me when he reached for his coffee cup. The look on his face—intense, happy, and only for me—made me rethink the long-distance thing for a second. Hard to plan for leaving, for ending something so new with so much possibility. He folded the paper and tossed it on the small two-top table as he stood.

And Isaac, dressed for a casual Sonoma County wedding, all unfolded and standing before me made my mouth go dry. The flat front khakis loved his thighs, and I suspected (and confirmed when we arrived at the winery and climbed out of the car) his ass. How did this man not have a ton of women knocking down his doors back home? Begging for a date?

Before I could even greet him in the lobby earlier, he eyed me from head to toe and told me I looked adorable. Me. Pre-wedding, and remember, Teagan and I were heading to Divine Vineyards to get ready for the big day with Brynna. No makeup yet. Hair in a messy pile at the back of my head. Cut-off denim shorts and a plain white T-shirt.

Apparently, my face gave away my shock, my amusement at his words, because he reached for me and cupped my elbows in his hands and leaned in to kiss my forehead. Which made me want to swallow all of the overwhelming emotions flashing through me like fireworks. But I couldn't. Because my mouth was dry.

Thankfully, I brushed my teeth before coming down to look for him, because before we headed out, he did steal a quick kiss. That one took my breath away. When I licked my lips and said he tasted like coffee, he offered me a drink of his. Which made me swoon in a silly school-girl way.

"He's cute," Brynna says now. She and I are in the master bathroom right now, both of us leaning over the sinks to apply makeup. Teagan and Bailey finished theirs first, so they're perched on the side of the oversized bathtub, sipping mimosas.

I meet Brynna's eyes in the mirror with a silent warning not to start another round of matchmaker. She raises her eyebrows as if to argue that she simply said he was cute, but she turns her focus back to her eyeliner. The picture of innocence.

"They had a marathon goodnight kiss last night," Teagan announces.

"We did not!" I laugh and shake my head. "And Teag and Derrick were playing tic tac toe when I came back to the car. I would think newlyweds would have better things to do."

"Well, you have no idea what we bet on each game."

I glance at Teagan in the mirror and see her sloppy smile. Bailey and Brynna chuckle, but I roll my eyes.

"It is so unfair that I am the only woman in this room not getting some this weekend."

"Well, you do have a smokin' hot guy out there that might be willing to change that."

This time I turn to look at Teagan.

"What?" Brynna caps her eyeliner and drops it as she turns around, too. She watches me closely as I try to figure out how to ask what's on my mind.

"What's wrong, Cait?" Teagan asks me.

"Is it a bad thing?" I clear my throat. "If I go crazy and sleep with him tonight?"

"Why's that a bad thing?" Brynna tips her head. I glance at her and then look at my wrist, but I'm not wearing a watch.

"Shouldn't you get moving? Get your dress on?"

"Don't try to deflect. What's wrong with having some fun?"

"I don't do that."

"Yes, you do," Teagan reminds me. "You've been doing that since you turned nineteen."

"But not…" I shrug.

"Not with guys whose faces belong on Hollywood movie posters?" Bailey suggests.

"Well." I point at her and grin. "Yeah, there's that."

"Spit it out." Brynna slides her foot over the white tiled floor to nudge mine. I stare at our pedicures—hers a simple French, my toenails lavender—rather than meet her eyes.

"I just met him."

"You did." Teagan sips from her glass and purses her lips. "But I've never seen you so...into a guy. So perfectly matched."

"Right." I nod. "Because my face belongs on movie posters, too."

"Don't sell yourself short," Teagan argues, "but that's not what I meant. You guys clicked instantly. It's like you've known him forever."

"Sort of feels that comfortable," I admit in a small voice.

'So, why not?" Brynna asks.

"Because we'll go back to our real lives after this and probably never see each other again."

"You might." Brynna steps into the closet and unzips a purple vinyl bag to reveal her dress.

"So what?" Teagan stands and sets her glass on the counter. "Maybe you do, maybe you don't. If you're careful, who cares? Have a fling and enjoy the hell out of that guy's body."

"I'm with Teagan." Bailey stands, too. It's time to help the bride get her dress on.

Maybe they're right. If we're careful, Isaac and I can have tonight, right? I'm on the pill, but surely a guy with that face and body carries condoms. And if not, we can always hit a drug store later and get some. None of my girlfriends are going to judge me for a fun, casual hookup. My parents might feel differently, but I don't plan to share the information with them anyway.

My only concern is that while we can use protection for casual sex, it feels bigger than that. And I don't know how to protect my heart if I give my body to Isaac.

"Damn, Brynna." Teagan whistles. Bailey and I follow her into the closet to admire the ivory lace dress. "This is so beautiful."

"Thank you." Brynna's voice hitches, and Teagan and I instantly shake our heads.

"No crying." Bailey reaches for the hanger. "No time to redo the makeup, girlfriend."

"She's right. Let's do this. Take the bra off and let's get your girls situated in this incredible dress."

Fifteen minutes later, we're lined up and ready to head outside, Bailey, then Teagan, and then me. And finally, the kids and then Brynna with her dad. Sleeveless, sweetheart, floor length chiffon dresses—so pretty, elegant but simple, too, so we can repurpose them if we choose to. Bailey's is lavender, Teagan's lilac, and mine is wisteria. The neckline is sweet and modest, while still showing a bit of cleavage. And each of us wears the necklaces Brynna gave us, the pendants nestled in that cleavage. Seeing myself in the mirror before we left the bathroom reminded me of how Isaac had touched the pendant last night. Stirred up a whole lot of longing, again, but I forced myself to put all of that away and focus on Brynna.

Her dress is beautiful. The ivory floor length lace with the scallop hem is both sweet and elegant. The neckline plunges so deep she can't wear a bra, so we had some giggles while we helped her slap her sticky cups on her boobs. Her mom and aunt raided the bathroom and whipped us into shape. Otherwise, we might have all ruined our makeup with the giggling and eventual happy tears that would inevitably have followed.

I follow a few footsteps behind Teagan to the door that leads to the drive. Brynna and her dad are whispering behind me. I wonder if this will ever be my wedding, if my dad will ever walk me down an aisle and put my hand in the only other man on earth that will really love me heart and soul. And then I put that thought away, too.

Our escorts meet us at the door, so when Teagan and Adam's friend Ross head out over the sidewalk to the drive, Matt and I step outside to follow them. Matt's another friend of Adam's. He's nice, and he's fun, but he's not Isaac, and I can't deny every bone in my body wishes he were.

As we round the house and the patio gate comes into sight, I hear an acoustic guitar playing the Jason Mraz song "I Won't Give Up." The delicate sounds drifting around us chase shivers over my skin. When Matt and I go through the gate, I look up hoping to see Isaac. My heart pushes into my throat when our eyes meet, and for a second, I can't breathe. His smile is so perfect, so genuine, it hurts.

Once the wedding party is gathered by the altar with Father Kelley and Adam—the kids now in the chairs with their parents so as to avoid the temptation of the pool— the music changes. My eyes burn when the guitarist picks up a violin and starts playing "Canon in D", and my best friend and her dad walk through the gate.

Of course, I want this.

Not particularly the wedding setting. Not particularly a church setting. The venue doesn't matter. But watching Brynna look at her dad and then turn to look at Adam, watching Adam's throat bob as he swallows when he sees his bride—so touching, so stirring, yes, dammit, I want all of that, too. I want my own happy-ever-after, and it sucks that my boyfriend and I weren't close enough to be here together.

That's the simple, sad fact, though. Ryan and I were never destined for this. Never have I felt the pull to a man that would lead me to an altar and a ring and vows with the words *as long as I shall live*.

When I glance at Isaac again, he's still watching me.

My fragile heart gallops away from me as I watch Adam take Brynna's hand, and they turn to Father Kelley.

CHAPTER 23

ISAAC

I know the bride is the princess at every wedding. It's just the way it is. I get it. A woman in love, in a wedding dress, reciting vows and looking into her groom's eyes as he makes his vows to her, is beautiful. No question.

But Cait, in her long, soft purple dress, is breathtaking. Her hair is clipped loosely at the back of her head. The fancy jeweled clip looks like something a princess would wear. A few long, loose curls have slipped free from the styled knot, and they frame her face and long, elegant neck. Small diamond earrings glitter in her ears.

Watching her dance with the guy who escorted her around the patio for the wedding sucks. And they're just dancing. No grinding. I can see an appropriate amount of space between them. Her hands rest on his shoulders and his on her hips. But it's the way they're talking and laughing that kills me. I'm not some jealous jerk who wants to hit the guy just for the dance, but I want this Adele song to end so I can get her in my arms and hear that laugh up close.

Derrick and I wait it out together. Judging from the look on his face, watching his wife dance and laugh it up with another guy bugs him, too. But we drink our wine and keep our cool. Until the song changes, and we both sort of charge the women to grab them to claim a dance. Teagan and Cait laugh as we spin them around on the patio, but I know as soon as I feel Cait pressed against me I'm not letting go of her for the rest of the night.

"You're the most beautiful woman here," I tell her again. I told her that the second the wedding was over, and the small crowd mingled, and I got my arms around her. The first time I told her that, she argued and shushed me. Told me Brynna's the most beautiful woman here. I put my lips by her ear and whispered that Brynna was pretty, but looking at Cait made my heart hurt.

Made other things hurt, too, but I didn't say that to her.

Evening descends slowly, but on the other hand, it feels like the day flies by. Everyone's happy, and we're drinking wine, of course, and we dance. Cait and I dance all afternoon, into the evening, only parting when Brynna and Adam cut the cake, when Adam slides the garter off Brynna's leg and gives it a pitch over his shoulder. The guy who escorted Teagan to the altar catches it, and even though it's ridiculous, I'm relieved. Just catching a garter thrown at a reception doesn't mean that single guy is going to be the next one married, nor does it mean he would marry the maid of honor or whoever catches the bride's bouquet.

Cait and Teagan give a speech together, because as they put it, they're both honored to be part of Brynna's biggest day. Their speech is simple and cute, but by the time they're done talking, they're all three crying. Adam's best man lightens the mood a bit, ribs Adam about things from when they were kids.

Naturally, Cait catches the bouquet when Brynna gives it a toss over her shoulder. That makes the girls get emotional again.

And then I get Cait back to myself for a while.

"Why didn't you get out there with the single guys?" Cait asks me. I pull her close and hold on tight.

"Felt weird, since I just met Adam." It's true. Plus, that would have meant taking my eyes off Cait, and that's not something I'm willing to do. Even if we stay in contact after this weekend, our time here together's almost over. As much as I wish this was the start of something big and real, I keep reminding myself it's not. It's a simple fun weekend in wine country. At the very least, we'll go home with fun memories and a good vacation story to tell. At most, maybe we'll be friends who text and see each other on occasion.

She eyes me intently for a moment, but she lets it go without further comment. I stay close to her even when the music changes to something more upbeat. Several times Teagan catches my eye and mouths the word *twerk*, but I only shake my head and laugh.

"Ready to Foxtrot?" I ask after a while.

"I thought we threw that off the table with that bet," she reminds me.

"It's not hard," I promise as I take a step back from her. "Just follow my lead. You step back twice. Right foot. Slow. Slow." I nod as she does what I tell her. "And then right foot to the side, quick, quick."

"That's it?"

"That's it."

So, we give it a shot for a song or two. Stop to sip more wine. When Cait dances with her dad, I ask her mom if she'd like to dance. Her happy smile when she says yes is a lot like Cait's smile. I like her. We talk about Cait while we dance, but her mom doesn't question how we met or what we've got going on this weekend. She tells me stories about Cait and her friends and how they've been close like sisters for years. Asks me about my family, which I'm happy to answer.

Later, when it's dark enough that the fairy lights are twinkling around the patio, Cait and I dance again. By now, we've tossed away any semblance of real dancing, and we're pressed together shoulders to middles, barely swaying back and forth. It's perfect. She's perfect for me.

That thought always leads me back to the biggest what-if of all. She's on the rebound here. The breakup with her ex is so fresh, any scabs forming over the hurt right now are easily pulled away. What if she goes home without me? Forgets me? What if her ex calls? Decides he made a mistake? What if he wants her back?

Then what?

"You're quiet." Her whisper touches my neck and draws a quick shiver.

"Just enjoying the moment," I tell her, because the last thing I want to do is ruin the moment by mentioning her ex.

She nods, but says nothing, leaving me to assume she's living in the moment, too.

All the more reason to hold something back.

Brynna and Adam make their way around to say goodnight to their guests. They've packed their bags to head to a secret destination for the next few days, somewhere here in wine country, and then they're heading to Sacramento to fly to Hawaii for the rest of the week. When they're gone, the party slowly breaks up, and though Teagan and Cait insist that they'll help with the cleanup, they're shooed away by Brynna and Adam's parents and a few of the winery employees. Even as we stand there saying our goodnights, a few people from the restaurant that catered the light meal of sandwiches and salads hustle around to begin cleanup and tear down.

When we finally climb into the Escalade to leave the winery, Cait leans close to whisper to me.

"Stay with me tonight?"

My mouth suddenly too dry to speak, I simply meet her eyes and nod. I want nothing more than to spend the rest of my time in wine country with her.

CHAPTER 24

CAIT

We part company with Teag and Derrick in the parking lot at the inn. They stroll off hand in hand for a "romantic walk." But I suspect it was Teagan's way of being discreet, letting Isaac and me walk inside first, alone. After hours of feeling his eyes on me, of noticing the appreciation in his gaze, of dancing plastered middle to middle with him, I want to run and drag him up the steps to my room.

I don't, though. I remind myself to have a little dignity. To be mature. My knees are weak, though, as we round the corner in the hall and stop in front of my room. My hands shake ever so slightly as I tap the keycard to the lock and the light flicks green.

Once inside, I'm a bundle of need and nerves, and I almost open my mouth to ramble. But when the door closes, and we're standing in the dark, he kisses me. It's slow and tender and exactly what I need to calm my nerves.

"We don't have to do this." He trails his hand down my back and lets it rest on my hip. "You don't owe me—"

"I want to do this." The whisper gushes out, and then I hold my breath, hoping he doesn't think I make a habit of *doing this*.

"Me, too."

This time, his kiss is deeper and slower, and his lips linger there at my mouth for several long seconds.

"Tell me you were a Boy Scout," I whisper into his mouth as I wrap my arms around his shoulders and clutch the back of his neck.

"Of course." He laughs and kisses a line from the corner of my mouth to a spot just under my ear. "It's all good."

"Mmm." I drop my head back, but the room is pitch black, and I can't see a thing.

"Cait?"

He moves his hand again. I close my eyes and revel in the feel of his fingers sliding up my side, the brush of his thumb on the undercurve of my breast. When he dips his thumb inside the cup of my dress and touches my skin, a little moan of pleasure, maybe a plea, slip from my lips.

"Hmm?"

"I want to see you." He cups my face in his hands now, and in the dark, I feel his eyes, the way he watched me all day, all evening. I feel beautiful for the first time in my life. I love his thumbs framing my mouth, and the feel of his fingers on my cheekbones makes me lightheaded, but I want his hands on my hips again. I want his thumb stroking the skin inside my dress again. I want him to kiss me where the gifted necklace from Brynna falls and rests between my breasts.

"Me, too." I cover his hands with mine and turn my face to kiss his fingers and the palms of his hands. When we move, I link my fingers with his and lead him further into the room. Another flash of panic hits me when I flip on the lamp beside the bed, but Isaac turns me toward him and loops his arms around my waist. He rests his forehead against mine and offers me a smile.

"Hi."

"Hi."

This time I frame his face with my hands and press up to kiss him.

"Did I tell you that you stole the show today?"

"You did," I whisper.

"Cait?"

"Hmm?"

"Thanks for asking me to be your date."

"Isaac?"

"Hmm?"

"Touch me."

His moves aren't gentle, so much as unhurried. As if he intends to savor what we're doing instead of racing through anything. In the times I imagined being with him, I saw frenzied up-against-the-door sex. Hands everywhere, tugging clothing out of the way and groping, squeezing, in a rush to find the pleasure points.

Being with him in reality is nothing like that. It's languid and beautiful, and Isaac is generous, giving, waiting to hear me say yes, to hear my moans or cries of pleasure before moving to touch me again, to claim me as his.

He allows me to undress him as we move, tangled together in my bed. His shoulders are broad and strong, and my greedy hands sculpt them as he kicks out of the khakis. I break a kiss and push back enough that I see his firm thighs and his perfect ass in the black boxer briefs. When we're both naked, he touches me the way other lovers have touched me, but he brings me pleasure like no one ever has. His hands and mouth worship me, and I'm a quivering mess when he finally rolls on a condom and eases inside me with the same control he's shown all night.

We move together in a tender slow pace, both of us lost in each other. It crosses my mind while he moves inside me that I will never feel this again with another man, but I push the thought away and let myself enjoy his touch. Tomorrow will be soon enough for the worry, the heartache I know will come.

Sex with Ryan was usually fast-paced and good enough. He was generous with touching me, but Isaac is different. It's as if his sole purpose is to stretch the little time we have together into the best night of our lives. He increases the pace, but even then, he moves at just the perfect angle to ensure that I love what he's doing as much as he does. When I'm close, when I whisper chant his name over and over, he slows again and pumps inside me just right, promising me he's got me. When I come, light explodes around me and waves of pleasure slide over me while Isaac picks up the pace again. Wanting him to feel even half as delicious as I do, I lock my legs behind his waist and move with him until his body tenses over me and he calls my name and finally buries his face in my neck.

Long, quiet minutes pass, with only the sound of our labored breathing filling the air. Isaac eases to my side and lays there with his arm thrown over my stomach.

"That was perfect," he says. He kisses my head, his lips brushing in my hair, and that kiss is the perfect thing after the way he just tore me apart making love to me. His gentle hands and his deliberate moves were all the right things to bring me incredible pleasure, but my stomach already hurts. That pit of loss, of loneliness, is already eating away at me, and that kiss is so sweet.

"Incredible." I smooth my hand over the scruff on his face and lose myself in his eyes. He just gave me the world like I've never seen it, but he makes me want more than I ever dreamed possible.

God. I close my eyes. *You sound like Princess Brynna now.*

This is a one-night stand. Might be the best sex you've ever had, but it's just a fling. No good will come of wishing for more than that.

"I am never going to forget the first time I saw you." He rubs his hand low over my stomach as he talks.

"Me neither."

"Our first kiss."

I smile, but I need him to stop, because it already sounds like goodbye.

"Isaac?"

"Hmm?"

"Will you stay? I'm not ready to say goodbye yet."

"I'm a little torn," he says, and I frown, wondering where he's going. "I want to hold you. Watch you sleep."

"But?"

He opens his mouth, but instead of answering me, he kisses me. His lips are soft and yielding, but his tongue is hungry, demanding. I feel his erection press into my side. He laughs when he sees the way I arch my eyebrows hopefully.

"But I don't want to waste a second doing something like sleeping." He slides his thumb under my chin and gently pushes it up so he can nibble on my neck. "So much more I need to do with you."

"I want you to do that with me."

He lifts his head to look me in the eyes, and we start again.

CHAPTER 25

C<small>AIT</small>

When I blink awake in the morning, the shades on the window blocking the sun, I decide it was all yet another dream. But when I stretch, my toes run the length of a hard, muscular calf, and a low masculine moan rumbles against my back and reminds me of the naughty things he did to me last night. The way I writhed and moaned under his hands and mouth.

"Good morning." He throws his leg over mine and nuzzles his face in the back of my neck. He nibbles there, making me jump and laugh. He found the pleasure spots, for sure, but he also found the ticklish spots, and he loves to stroke them all.

"Morning."

Neither of us moves. I don't know about him, but I'm in no hurry to get this day going. I don't want to rush a goodbye.

His hands begin another game of exploring my body, and I close my eyes and lose myself in how good it feels to be with him. We used all of the condoms before finally giving in to sleep sometime after two. So now, when he flips me over and finds other things to do to me, I simply tangle my fingers in his hair and hold on.

Later, after I've showered and dressed in worn, comfy jeans and a T-shirt, Isaac takes a quick shower. I flip through channels on TV, but I'm too consumed by thoughts of that glorious naked body in the next room and his generous soul to concentrate. I hate the thought of walking away from him and not seeing him again.

I believe in love, in everlasting, forever and ever love. But not love at first sight. So, I'm not sure what the desperate feeling is crawling through my veins. I pick up my phone when it buzzes, but I don't answer the call from Teagan.

I'm torn between needing to slip out, away from Isaac now and not having to say goodbye and stripping down to join him in the shower. Finding a way to make this work. His phone buzzes. I glance at it tossed screen-up on the bed. It's a text from Josh, but I don't read it.

Instead, I look back at my phone. Thumb hovering over it. Thinking. He's got my number. He might text. We'll be friends. Maybe now and then we'll bump into each other. Maybe I'll find myself in Indianapolis sometimes and see him. Maybe we'll do some phone calls. I don't do much on social media, but I do have accounts on Facebook and Instagram.

Does Isaac? I could look. But, why bother? If we end up texting, do we need to be connected on social media pages? Not really. Texting and possible phone calls would be more personal, wouldn't they? Still, it would be interesting to get a glimpse of him in his element. Maybe he's got pictures of some of the work he's done. That thought interests me enough to do it. I tap the button to bring my screen to life and then I tap the Facebook icon.

When my page fills the screen, I take a few minutes to scroll through my newsfeed. I find fun posts from friends back home. Prayer requests for friends of friends and families in need. The usual assortment of jokes and sarcastic memes about everything from politics to popular TV shows and movies. I take another minute or two to look at Teagan's latest post. She put up a few pictures from last night, but she was careful not to post any of Brynna and Adam, so she didn't steal their thunder. She and Derrick have a couple of selfies there, and she's got a few pictures of her and I together, and then I'm surprised to find a picture of me and Isaac. Dancing. Oblivious to the crowd. To Teagan and her phone. We're dancing close, my arms around his shoulders and his around my waist, looking only at each other.

My hand shakes a bit as I download and save the picture to my phone. Maybe I'll post it on my wall and tag him if I find him on Facebook. That might be fun. At the very least, I'll text it to him once I get his number. At this point, he has mine, but that's as far as we made it that first day in exchanging numbers. Well, okay, I gave him my number *and* my address.

Okay, if I typed my home address into his phone, then it's not a big deal to look him up on social media and take a peek at Isaac Stratton in his real world. I glance toward the bathroom as the shower shuts off and remind myself it's not a big deal. I'm not snooping. If he has social media accounts, whatever is out there is fair game, right? Unless his page is locked down to friends only. Only one way to find out.

My thumbs fly over the keyboard on my phone as I type his name in. There are two accounts for the name Isaac Stratton. The first of them looks like a burned-out hippy dude in his eighties. The long gray braid and wrinkled face makes me think of Willie Nelson. Definitely not my Isaac.

I click on the other one and up comes a picture of my Isaac's smiling face. His arm is slung around a woman who looks just old enough and just enough like him to assume it's his mom. They're laughing; their smiles so happy, I find myself smiling just because they make me feel good. Looks like a tennis court in the background. I scroll down his page and note things like his 847 friends. His cover photo is the Greek Parthenon, and I want to ask if he's been to Greece. If he took the photo.

Isaac's phone buzzes again. I think it's human nature to glance toward a sound, a buzzing phone, even when you know it's not yours. I look again, and this time I see Logan's name on the screen. But this time I catch the words *kitty* and *last night* followed by what looks to be a dozen question marks and exclamation points. I can't help it; his phone is in my hand before I know I'm going to move. I tap the text. Dread climbs in my throat, making it hard to breathe.

How'd it go? Did you feed the kitty last night???!!! Bettin' that piece of ass was smokin' hot!!

I drop his phone like it's a snake about to strike and cover my mouth with that hand. The hand still holding my phone shakes, and my stomach just drops. I feel a little sick inside. How in the hell did I read this weekend so wrong? First Ryan bailed on me and made me look like an idiot in front of my friends and family, and now this? I thought Isaac was different. I thought the last few days were straight out of a fairytale. My own fairytale finally coming true. I liked—like?—this guy enough that realizing I was just a sleazy fling for him hurts so much more than that midnight phone call from Ryan ever could.

I fight tears as I look back at my screen. At Isaac's Facebook page.

The first six friends in his list are familiar to me, the names, if not the faces. Even Adrienne is there. With a quick glance at the bathroom—he won't be long, he doesn't have any of his belongings so he can't even shave —I tap her picture and study it when it comes up. I hate to admit it, but I look at her through a jealous lover's eyes. This is the one woman who hurt him, even though he's over it by now. She's pretty with a short cap of blond hair and big green eyes. In her picture, she wears a white lab coat. I consider scrolling through her page. That's what we do when we're stalking people, right? Further and further down the rabbit hole we go. I'm irrationally curious about her husband, since she left Isaac for medical school and ended up marrying someone else.

But when I hear the bathroom door open, I scramble to get off her picture. To get out of Isaac's page.

"Looks like I get to do the walk of shame," Isaac calls to me with a touch of humor in his voice. "Haven't done that since college."

I lift my eyes, though I catch more on his profile as I click out of Facebook and drop my phone on the bed. Single. *From Indianapolis.* Currently employed by Goode, Harvey, Cash and Associates. Of St. Louis.

Currently living in St. Louis.

St. Louis, Missouri.

One hundred and eleven miles southeast of Quincy.

Where I live.

Two hours and fifteen minutes from where I live.

And he never bothered to mention that to me.

Well, that fact and Logan's disgusting text make it pretty clear to me that Isaac had no intentions of ever looking me up when this weekend is over. He used me for sex. Guess he thought I owed it to him after all.

I try to blink him into focus when he steps out of the bathroom wearing only the boxer briefs he shimmied out of so quickly last night, but I keep seeing that text and Isaac's profile page.

"Hey." He frowns, as if he senses something is wrong. I've never had much of a poker face, and here I am, feeling the need to lie again, the same as I did at the beginning of this trip. The only difference is now I'm lying to protect myself. "What's wrong?"

"Nothing." Okay, I sound normal. That's a relief. Because what I really want to do is crawl back under the covers, alone, and go back to sleep and wake up and realize last night was a dream. Not gonna happen, though. I stand and resume packing my stuff.

"Yeah? Do you still wanna grab breakfast? Coffee?" He snakes a leg into his pants, eyes still on me. "Do you have time?"

I don't know if I do or not. Yes, of course, I want to drag this out as much as I can. Spend as much time as I can with him before we have to head to the airport. Which is ridiculous. How can I want to be with him now that I know what last night was all about? Does he want to hang out now? Or is he ready to jump ship? Now that he got in my pants, is he ready to ditch me and join his friends again? Maybe let Josh and Logan know how easy I was?

My stomach is such a wreck right now I'm not sure I could eat if I tried.

"Yeah." I nod and take a good look around the room to make sure I have all of my stuff packed and ready to go. I know Teag and Derrick will want to eat something before we leave.

"Good." He fixes that damned smile on me, and my stupid knees go weak, and my belly flutters, and all those private places he kissed last night wake up and remind me how good he is in bed. Okay, I suck at this kind of casual sex. It's not like Ryan and I were involved in some incredibly epic love affair. We were friends, and we slept together because we dated. Or maybe we dated because we were sleeping together.

But this is different. My stomach turns as I realize this is my first one-night stand. Because that's all it was. An incredibly hot hook-up after a fun few days of drinking wine and dancing. If he had wanted more, if the idea of seeing me again had ever crossed his mind, he would have told me he lived in St. Louis. Though it would still be a long-distance relationship, a two-hour drive is completely doable.

I look away as he pulls his shirt on and buttons it. I should check and see if Teagan left me a voicemail. Maybe she called about breakfast and not in a fact-finding mission about how hot my night was.

It was, though. God, it was so damned perfect with him.

I want more of him. More of his hand holding mine. Another walk down Limerick Lane. More kisses. More gazing at buildings and discussing historical landmarks and more making love with him. And he's probably ready to go back home and find his next conquest.

Teagan didn't leave a voicemail, but she did text.

"El Dorado Kitchen okay?" I ask him.

"Sounds good. Care if I ask the gang to join us?"

"Of course not."

"Maybe I can talk Josh into finding a T-shirt or something in my room."

I aim a smile at him, but I don't have the energy to laugh now. Or the desire, really, because even though I have to —what?—man up to accept last night for what it was? Is that it? Maybe that way it won't hurt that he used me? I mean, knowing he lives that close to me and never told me hurts that much worse. Funny. I was okay with thinking he lived in Indianapolis and that we might share a night together and then maybe talk for a while and lose touch. But this changes everything. Instead of a mutual agreement to share a night and walk away, it feels more like he played me with his pretty face and witty charm.

Okay, Cait. Man up. Women can do this, too. Other women might be stronger than you, but you can do this. Get through the next few hours, and you never have to see him again.

CHAPTER 26

Isaac

Waking up with Cait in my arms made me think crazy thoughts probably better left alone. Especially since she's acting weird now. She's all smiles for Teagan and Derrick; she's even talking and laughing with my friends as if she's known them for years. She's just acting a little stiff, a little distant, with me.

I don't get it. The past few days have been the best of my life, and if that's too dramatic for a guy to say, if that puts my man card in threat level, okay, the past few days have been fan-fucking-tastic. Even Logan might approve of that. I loved everything about Cait, and yes, that very much includes last night. Does that make me a dick? A player? Just because I loved her body last night? Worshipped her body?

Because she's acting a little bit like she thinks I'm a dick now. Like she's shy or something. Afraid to meet my eyes.

Jumpy if I touch her, as if I didn't explore every inch of her body last night with my eyes. My fingers. My mouth. Like I wouldn't do it all over again tonight and every night for the rest of our lives.

She's been acting like this since I took a shower earlier. She looked upset when I came out. Her phone was on her bed. When I asked her what was wrong, she said nothing, but obviously something upset her. My guess is that it's something to do with her ex.

What if he's already throwing apologies at her and trying to get her back? Cait said she wasn't interested in getting back with him, that they weren't serious. But what if she said it but didn't mean it? What if she's in love with him, and now he's begging her to take him back? And now she feels guilty for last night? I don't want her to regret what we shared.

I don't want her to regret making love, and I don't want to be her rebound. And from the way she's acting today, I have to assume it's one or the other.

I pick at my omelet, not really hungry. Josh brought me a T-shirt, so I changed quickly before we were seated. But I'm hot, and I'm uncomfortable and feeling grumpy, and all I want is five minutes alone with her to find out what's going on. It's like she can read my mind. Since we walked out of her room at the inn, me trailing her luggage behind us, we haven't had a minute alone.

But I'm out of time. Josh eats the last bite of his bacon, and Jasmine clacks her spoon around her fruit dish. The noise puts me on edge, and when Derrick tosses out his credit card to cover his and Teagan's breakfast, I toss down enough cash again to cover mine and Cait's. It's now or never. I want her alone to find out what the hell is wrong, and I want to hold her again. Kiss her. Because in about five minutes, my girl is going to get in a car and head to the airport and fly out of my life.

Doesn't matter that I have her phone number. If we don't address the awkwardness that's popped up since last night, any texting or phone calls will fizzle out fast, and this will become just another vacation memory. I refuse to let that happen.

"C'mon." I take her hand and tug gently to get her to go with me when I stand. She laughs softly, probably for the benefit of everyone at the table, but she does follow me. We walk to the corner of 1st and West Spain and cross the street without conversation. She holds my hand, but it bugs me that she's not talking.

"What're we doing?" she finally asks when I lead her to a vacant park bench in the square. She looks around before perching nervously on the edge of the bench. "This isn't a very private spot for a goodbye kiss."

Instead of answering her, I cup her face in my hand and study the way she struggles not to look at me. First, she watches something just over my right shoulder. Then she flicks her gaze to the ground. When she does let her eyes fly to mine, I move with her when she tries to look away.

"What's going on, Cait?" I lean to the left when she tries to look over that shoulder.

"Nothing. Why?"

"Nothing? You've been acting strange since we got up this morning."

She doesn't answer me, but her struggle to swallow says a lot.

"What did I do?" My voice is low and edgy, and I kind of don't care that I sound desperate. We have very little time to figure anything out, much less everything I want to nail down before she walks away from me.

"Nothing, Isaac." She blinks her composure back into place. Her eyes aren't so much cold as they are politely disinterested.

Frustrated, I drop my hand to my lap and groan out loud.

"Do you regret what we did?"

She might slap me for asking that. Times have changed. Used to be it was cool for a guy to score a night with a woman as beautiful—as sexy—as Cait, but women who engaged in said activities were looked down upon. Now it's acceptable for women to be free with their sexuality, and Cait strikes me as a strong, independent woman. She might take offense to my question, as if I'm suggesting she made a mistake, but I didn't.

But she looks at me this time. Meets my eyes, and for a second, I see my Cait, the woman I've come to know the last couple of days. Her eyes are sad, and her smile is both sweet and sad, and she leans closer to kiss me. Except that her lips brush the corner of my mouth.

"No. Not at all."

I nod. If she doesn't regret what happened, does that mean something is up with her ex? Because something has definitely changed since earlier this morning.

"Do you…" I search my mind for what could be bothering her. For how to ask her what I want to know. "Do you feel guilty? For what we did? When the breakup with Ryan is so fresh?"

She shakes her head and reaches for my hand. "No. I'm fine, Isaac."

"You don't look fine," I tell her. "You don't look like a woman who was thoroughly worshipped last night or a woman who started her morning off with multiple orgasms."

She laughs softly and lowers her face when a soft pink blush tinges her cheeks.

"I don't like goodbyes," she mumbles.

"Doesn't have to be goodbye-goodbye, does it?" I tip my head and hook my finger under her chin to make her look at me.

"Is this where we promise to call? To text? To meet up in Paris or something?"

"Ever been to Paris?" I arch an eyebrow at her. Her smile makes another quick appearance.

"Nope."

"Me neither." I shake my head and shrug. "I don't need Paris. Just anywhere close to you."

I hate that we're in the middle of Sonoma Square, because I can't kiss her like I want to. I can't pull her into my lap to hold her. I don't need to grope her, to cop a feel. I just want to hold her. Remind her how good we felt together. I don't do that, though. I kiss her. It's long and soft, and it's intense and wet, and I feel her kissing me back with just the same hunger, the same fervency she kissed me with last night.

"At least we'll always have wine country," she whispers when we finally break apart to breathe.

We're getting nowhere but right back to where we were. She claims nothing's wrong, but she doesn't want to look me in the eyes. She kisses me with the same longing that I feel, but she's reluctant to agree to continued contact once she leaves.

And it sounds like she's vetoing any future Paris plans for sure.

The walk back across the street is more of the same quiet. Fingers linked, but she won't look at me. Our friends are all gathered on the sidewalk in front of a row of vehicles parked on the street. This is it. I want to squeeze her hand tighter, but Cait lets go of me and hugs my friends with more enthusiasm than she just showed me. I shake hands with Derrick, and then Teagan hugs me.

"What happened?" she whispers so no one else hears.

"I don't know," I answer. "Everything was good until it wasn't."

"Call her." She squeezes me hard. "Text her. Go after her, Isaac."

Relief unknots my shoulders just the slightest bit. I haven't won Cait over—back? Hell if I know, because I don't know what I did. But at least I have one of her best friends on my side.

"Thanks, Teag."

"Don't give up." She pats my back and then kisses my cheek, and finally, I'm holding Cait. I don't care that we have an audience. I hold her hard and tight, and when I let go a fraction of an inch, it's only to kiss her again.

"Maybe you should hire out as a wedding date." She frames my face in her hands and laughs softly. She looks happy; she's teasing me, but it hurts. Is that what I was to her? Just a fill in? Am I alone with these damned ridiculous feelings? Pussy-whipped. Ready to go to my knees for her? To slink home after her? Ready to say words I've never given thought to?

I fell in love with this woman in the space of days, and she just relegated me back to plus one status. Except I served the purpose so I'm not even that anymore. I'm a fling. I'm a wine country memory.

CHAPTER 27

Cait

Waking up alone in my own bed, in my apartment, back in my town sucks. Sucks even more than the flight home did. Ever flown your body home on a 737 when your heart's still on the ground back by the Pacific Ocean? I don't recommend it.

I took today off, thinking I would be exhausted after a fun weekend. Thinking Ryan and I could spend a lazy day together before swapping vacation mode back to routine. Ryan is the furthest thing from my mind now. I dreamt about Isaac.

Of course, I did. And all of the delicious things I could have dreamt of—laughing with him, that first kiss, dancing with him, the way his hands stroked my body with magic and with love—it was that last goodbye that got me.

Walking me across the street. Making me look at him. Asking me what he did wrong.

Why does he care? If the whole week, if all the time we spent together, getting to know each other and dancing and making love, if none of that matters, why would he ask me what he did to upset me?

Teagan jumped me the second my ass touched the damned seat on the plane. She wanted to know what was wrong, and the feeling I had when she hugged him goodbye—that they held on too long for a regular goodbye—hit me square in the face again. They whispered something to each other.

I put her off for a while. Told her I was tired. Didn't want to talk. She left me alone for a while, and I pretended to sleep. But eventually, Derrick did go to sleep, and she caught me peeking at her through one slitted eye, so she knew I was faking it. When she asked again, my eyes decided it would be a good time to water.

She launched into near lecture mode about how normally she wasn't one to believe in instant sparks or instalove, but that she had seen something special between us. She asked how the night had gone with me and Isaac, and she waved her hands and said no details, but was it okay?

Naturally, that made my stupid eyes burn worse, and then I was crying.

Told her it was prefect.

When we landed and I turned my data back on on my phone, I searched Facebook. Scrolled as we filed off the plane and headed to baggage check and then as we stood waiting for the baggage carousel to spit out our belongings, I showed her what I had seen that morning.

Standing in Lambert International Airport, getting my luggage, so I could take my broken heart home. Two hours from where Isaac Stratton lived.

And he never even mentioned it.

I lie flat on my back now and consider Teagan's face, her words. She had flinched, but on a scale of one to ten, one being smallest, her flinch might have been .75. Like maybe not telling me he lived so close was a very minor, stupid, guy-like thing to do. But not unforgiveable. She had argued that same thing. And she pointed out that if he had my number and since I had been *stupid* enough to give him my address on day one, he probably didn't think it was that important to tell me he was in St. Louis. That he probably planned to contact me once we were both home and back to routine.

I want to believe Teagan. That I'm making too big of a deal over this. But I wanted to believe Isaac. And look where that led me. Then again, I've known Teagan forever. I would trust Teag with my life.

That definitely includes my heart. She wouldn't build me up just so he could let me down.

I didn't tell her about the text, though. The text Logan sent Isaac. That hurt a little too much to share.

What did Isaac say to her when she hugged him goodbye? What if he was just trying to avoid an ugly scene? He knew I was upset, and he knows Teagan and I are close. What if he was afraid she was going to tear him a new one for treating me like I'm disposable?

Did he, though? The way he touched me? After telling me he didn't expect sex. It wasn't cheap. It wasn't casual.

Not for me anyway. But maybe his casual sex is a whole level up from mine.

My phone buzzes and jumps on the nightstand next to my bed. I roll my head on my pillow and then roll over and stretch to grab it. I tug the charger from it and then flop on my back, all without looking at it. Probably Teagan.

If it's Brynna, I'm gonna hurt her. And if she has an inkling something is wrong, I'm gonna hurt Teagan, because she's the only way she would know.

I almost drop the phone when I see the unfamiliar number. I have no idea what his number is, but I'm instantly scared it's him and just as scared that it's not. My stomach feels fizzy, and my hands are tingly with nervous energy. I stare at the screen until the call goes to voicemail.

I put the phone on my bed and toss my arms up over my head.

What the hell, Cait? You can't love that guy. You just met him.

Okay, so maybe it's more than a fling, but it's not going to amount to anything. Say he did just neglect to mention that he lives in St. Louis. What if that wasn't a purposeful omission? We're still a couple hours apart. Who wants to drive two hours to meet someone for dinner or a movie?

And as much as I liked him, I don't want my life to be an occasional date or weekend trip. I don't want a relationship that means weekday phone calls and weekend sex. Missing him in between. Wanting to share big and little things every night, and not by phone. Missing out on the big and small things in his life. Turning down dates because of my boyfriend who lives in St. Louis. Worrying about the pretty women I might spot on his Instagram page. Sounds so college, so temporary.

My phone buzzes. I pick it up, assuming it's a voicemail notification. I find a text instead.

It's Isaac. What're you doing?

I consider ignoring him. Saving his number to my phone. Telling him I'm at work.

Cait? Are you there?

Trying to talk myself into getting up.

You're not working today?

Took the day off to recover from vacation.

So...you could have changed your flight? Like...you could have checked into getting my flight back to St. Louis?

I stare at the screen for a moment, stunned with his suggestion. With his casual throwing out of *St. Louis*.

Would you have wanted me to do that?

I roll my eyes at myself. Two minutes ago I was telling myself having a boyfriend in St. Louis, one I don't see often sounds temporary and immature. And now I'm acting like a pouty brat.

Why wouldn't I want to spend every second possible with you?

I don't answer him. Because you know, pouty brat. Wallowing.

Have you heard from Ryan?

Well, that surprises me enough that I can't ignore it.

No. Why?

Thought maybe he was waiting to grovel when you got home.

No groveling. Nothing to grovel for.

You're saying if he showed up right now and asked you to take him back, you would say no?

That's what I'm saying.

I sit up and glance at the clock. It's after nine, so just after seven where he is.

What time's your flight?

Around eleven or twelve, I think. Packed and waiting on the porch of the b&b. Where I kissed you.

His words, the memory they invoke, leave me breathless.

Do you remember that?

Of course. What did you guys do the rest of yesterday?

Guzzled wine. Argued with Jasmine about. Every. Damned. Thing. In. the. World. Watched Josh and Kree flirt and whisper and kiss.

He follows that up with the green sick face emoji. I'm not sure how to respond to that, because that's pretty much what Isaac and I did all weekend. Why would he have a problem with that? With his friend being happy?

Back to work tomorrow?

Maybe I'm being a coward, but I change the subject. Texting him now after the last few days together, after that last night together, is more awkward than being around Ryan would be now.

Yep. You?

Yeah. Going into the office just to touch base and see what's going on. Obviously no showings or closings scheduled.

And then what? Plans this week? Going out this weekend?

No. Nothing planned. Probably a whole lot of being lazy and recovering from the wedding trip.

Looks like the gang's all here and ready to go.

I'm not sure if that's his way of saying goodbye or what. Technically, he could text me until he boards his plane. But maybe he was just bored waiting for his friends to be ready to leave.

Have a safe flight.

I hold my breath, but I don't know what I want. Maybe I want him to let it go. To leave it alone now. My phone still in my hand, I close my eyes and think about the way he kissed me goodbye there in front of the bed and breakfast. The way he touched me Saturday night, like we had all the time in the world to be together, and he wouldn't waste a second rushing through making love.

I want him to keep texting. I want him to say he wants to see me. That he's free Friday night and he'll drive up to see me. But I won't say that. Because he has a life outside of that wine country fling, even if I don't.

Thanks.

I toss my phone on my bed after that last text, somehow knowing that's it for now. Burying my face in my pillow, I close my eyes again to remember how he made me feel. I miss him now more than if he wouldn't have texted at all.

CHAPTER 28

Isaac

I still don't get it, and I've been stewing over this for days. I don't know what to do with myself, because the only woman ever to come close to wrecking me this way was just a friend who called it quits on a friends-with-benefits relationship before I did. The wrecking thing with Adrienne came when she married someone else after claiming her career was more important to her than a family.

I've dated since Adrienne, even if I haven't been in love, so I can read women. But maybe I read Cait Pendleton wrong. That bothers me, but I'm not moping around wondering how I could be so far off. I'm missing Cait. Wanting to talk to her. Wishing she would text me.

Wondering what the hell I did between making love to her Saturday night and walking out of the shower Sunday to have lost her.

I was angry when I texted her Monday before the flight home. Frustrated. My ego was bruised, but it went so much deeper than that. Logan ribbed me a bit about scoring and walking away, and that really pissed me off. Between that and that text he sent Sunday morning, I wanted to throat punch him. Josh put a hand on my chest and walked me backwards away from him. Logan's not a bad-looking guy, but I don't think having missing teeth is a particularly attractive look.

Texting with Cait left me feeling a little bit worse. She seemed casual, like she was blowing me off. Even when I mentioned kissing her, she was too cool about it. Like maybe it didn't mean half as much to her as it did to me. Which, again, still makes me wonder about her ex.

Or maybe she had her eye on someone else before the ex ditched her. Now that she's back home, maybe she's ready to leave the ex and me—the vacation fling—in the past and go after someone new.

I've told myself that at least five times this week, but it doesn't sit right. She's not that kind of girl. She's not the kind of girl who cares more about the chase or appearances. And as incredible, as hot as the sex was between us, I don't think she's the kind of woman only looking for something physical. Sure we flew through the getting-to-know-you process, but it wasn't hot, meaningless sex. There was something special between us, and it started that morning in Sonoma Square, not the last night in her room at the inn.

And then again, maybe not.

It's been five days since I texted her, and I haven't heard a word out of her since.

I've been avoiding my friends, too. I needed a break; we probably all needed a break after being in such close quarters on vacation. But I need this whole Cait thing to die or change or something before I see Logan again, because if the asshat brings her up again, I'll deck him. Josh has enough tact not to ask, but he's also known me long enough to know I'm wrapped up in her. Without coming right out and asking about the night I stayed with her, he fumbled around enough with words for me to put him out of his misery and nod, and that was that.

He didn't harp on me on the flight home, but I think we were all just beat and needed the quiet. Even Jasmine managed to keep quiet. Josh gave me until Wednesday night before he elbowed his way into my personal life again with a phone call. He asked if I had talked to Cait. Because I didn't want to get dragged into a touchy-feely conversation about my feelings, I blew him off and just said that we had texted. I know he wanted to say more, but he dropped it.

But now it's Friday, and for some ridiculous reason, I agreed to grab a bite with Josh. Which I should know by now means Josh and Kree. And again, nothing in the world against Kree, but I'm not up for having my brain picked by Josh and his girlfriend.

"So. Wait." Kree tips her head at me. Her fingers are curled around the bottom of her pint glass, but she hasn't picked it up yet to drink from it. Josh stabs another messy bite of cheesy fries. I'm torn between wanting to eat them and envisioning a heart attack before I'm gray. "You guys did sleep together?"

I shift my gaze to Josh and send him a mental thank you, but he only shrugs.

"Isaac, c'mon. You stayed over with her at the inn," Kree reminds me. "Josh didn't say a word to me."

I groan and nod and shrug and hook my finger around my longneck beer. I take a long swallow and give myself a few minutes before setting the bottle down and giving her my full attention. Hell, she's a woman, maybe she can help me read between the lines and figure something out.

"Yeah." So much for giving her all of my attention. I don't know Kree well enough to look her in the eyes and think about the way Cait kissed me, the way she straddled me, threw her head back and rode me that night we were together. Instead, I study the label on my bottle.

"And it was—"

"Yep." I cut her off with a nod.

"For her, too?" Kree asks softly.

I shoot her a look and read that she's trying to be sensitive, trying to help. Unlike Logan.

"I think so."

"Like she—"

"Many times." I nod again.

"And things were cool when you woke up?"

I make myself go through that morning again before I answer Kree. Both of them are watching me with concern, and I feel my guard go down a bit. They're not just snooping for gratuitous details. Josh wants to help, so Kree wants to help.

"I woke up before she did," I mumble. "But it was perfect. Just...lying there. Holding her."

My voice kind of cracks, so I clear my throat and avoid looking at either of them.

"When she did wake up, she seemed happy. We messed around again. She took a shower, and then I took a shower. By the time I came out, something had changed."

"Like what?"

I roll my eyes at Josh. "If I knew, I wouldn't be sitting here telling you everything."

He nods to concede my point. As close as we are, we've long outgrown the age of oversharing this kind of stuff.

"Did she have access to your phone?" Kree asks me.

"It was on the bed," I answer. "But I have nothing to hide. Nothing she could possibly have seen would upset her. A stupid text from Logan, but she was around him enough to know how he is."

Kree sips her beer and picks up an outlier fry from the plate, away from the epicenter of cheese and bacon.

"And you're sure she's over the ex?"

"She swears she is. I never once got the vibe that she was broken up about it in the first place. It was more like frustration than hurt."

"We're missing something," Josh mutters. He lifts his pint glass to his mouth and takes a big swig.

"Maybe she just needed to pull back," Kree suggests. "Maybe she feels everything for you that you do for her, and it scares her."

"But why? We're adults. If we want to see each other, we could do it. Hell, we live a hop and a skip away from each other. But even if we're on opposite coasts, we could figure it out if we wanted to."

"Does she know that?"

"What? That we're adults? And we could figure it out if we wanted to?"

Josh throws a wadded-up napkin at me.

"Does she know where you live, dumbass? That you're so close to her?"

I open my mouth to say of course she does, but I'm not sure. I don't remember if I told her that. If it ever came up. I told her I was familiar with Quincy, but did I share that I live two hours away?

"I don't know."

"Because the odds of two people meeting in Sonoma Valley, falling in love, and then finding out they live relatively close in the Midwest are pretty low." Kree shrugs, but she's kind of drilling me with her eyes, as if telling me to straighten up and get in gear.

The waitress chooses that moment to bring our dinners; Kree's got some kind of salad, but Josh and I ordered burgers. We ask for another round, and then it's me back to facing the firing squad.

"So you think that's it? She's just trying to end things because she doesn't realize a long-distance relationship between us wouldn't even be that long-distance?" Rather than look at them—I sound whiney, which pisses me off—I work on my burger, flipping the top bun to the side to add ketchup and mustard and pickles to the top.

"Could be."

"Are you gonna text her?" Kree asks me. She holds a forkful of lettuce and feta cheese over her plate, eyes narrowed on me now like I'm in the principal's office, being sworn to good behavior upon release.

"Yeah, yeah." I nod and wave her off as I jam my bun back on and pick up the burger to take a bite. When I put it back on my plate, mouth full, they're both still looking at me expectantly. "What?" I ask around the burger in my mouth.

"Well?" Josh tips his head.

"Now? You think I should text her now?"

"Why not now?"

"What should I say?"

"Dude." Josh groans. "You've been intimately involved with this woman. Surely you can think of something to text her."

Kree's soft snort of laughter cuts through the tension that's grown again. I think Kree and I are both relieved with how Josh phrased his thoughts. I flip my phone over on the table to find a text on the screen.

From Cait.

CHAPTER 29

<small>Cait</small>

Ross is racing to the airport to catch Rachel and tell her he's in love with her when my phone buzzes on the end table. Half-asleep, I flick my eyes up over my head even though I can't see the phone and then look back at the TV. I made my way through the last year binge-watching *Friends* on Nickelodeon. Why would I change that now?

It's been a long week, just because I'm tired. And sad. Normally, I bounce back quick from vacations. I like my job, my life. I had three showings this week with two different couples. One of them was a farmstead, and even that was good. I'm not big on manure and cows or chickens or cornfields, even, but I won't knock the commissions on those sales. And being outside was nice. It's only late May, so the weather hasn't turned Midwest summer humid and gross just yet.

Brynna and Adam are still on their honeymoon. Which is a good thing, because if she were home, she and Teagan would be double teaming me over the whole Isaac thing.

Isaac!

Dammit.

I scramble to a sitting position and reach for the TV remote, knocking it to the floor in the process. My heart pounds in my ears as I lean over and grab the remote and then turn the TV down. As if I have to have silence to read a text. Tossing the remote down beside me on the couch, I eye my phone.

Just because it buzzed, doesn't mean it's Isaac.

Teagan texted me earlier about going out with her and Derrick for dinner. I begged off, too tired. Too blah, to be honest, but I didn't tell her that. I love Teagan and Derrick to death, but the last thing I want to do is sit and watch them make gaga eyes at each other all night.

It's probably her texting again to check on me. I have no idea what time it is, but I catch myself before I snatch my phone to check. Once I pick it up, I'll know who the text is from. No more holding my breath and fearing and hoping it's him.

Seems like it's been a few hours since I texted him. My heart is still racing, the echo of the erratic beat loud in my ears and my throat. I told myself all week that I was over this. It was a vacation thing, a weekend fling, and it was fun, but I can be an adult and let it go.

The way my heart is trying to explode out of my chest at the possibility that it might be him who answered me says otherwise. Nothing Ryan ever did made my heart beat like this, never made my stomach drop and flutter like it is right now.

I can't believe I caved earlier. I was eating last night's leftover stir-fry, flipping through the channels, and apparently thinking about him again. Isaac. Not Ryan. Ryan has texted me several times this week. Nothing romantic. No groveling. No *take me back*. He asked how the wedding was. If the trip was fun. Who the guy is I'm dancing with in the picture Teagan posted. He didn't sound jealous, but when he asked if it was a friend of Adam's, I simply said *something like that*.

Ryan and I are pretty much status quo. Friends, just no more benefits. I'm fine with that. Pretty sure he is, too. He texted me this morning to tell me he had a date. Asked me what shirt to wear. Sent pictures of a pastel green button-down and a simple gray Henley. Imagining Isaac in both made it a freaking hard choice. Both styles looked made for his wide shoulders and slender waist.

The Henley won out, though. God, the way a man can shove long-sleeves up to his elbows to accentuate his forearms? The sinewy strength. The fine hair there. The golden tan of—well, of *Isaac's* skin. Ryan didn't question me. Gave me a thumbs up.

What if he's texting now? He wouldn't do that, would he? He wouldn't text me during a date for dating advice, would he? Because that's totally not cool. Not to me. But to his date.

Pick the phone up, Cait.

I groan out loud at the voice in my head, but I do lean over and grip the phone. I texted Isaac in the midst of leftover stir-fry and channel surfing. Had the TV stopped on *Halloween* at the time, which made me think about Ryan dumping me and thinking about that in wine country, which made me miss Isaac. Which is probably why I caved and texted.

I figured he was out with friends or out with a date, and that if he answered me and said that, it would put me back in my place and make me resolve to forget about him, about our fling, again.

Having a burger and a beer with Josh and Kree.

Well, as social lives go, that's not massively more exciting than what I could have done tonight.

You?

He fires that text off before I can respond to the first one.

Ross and Rachel. Couch. Stir-fry.

You're watching Friends on a Friday night?

Yep. Livin' the dream here.

Jump in your car. Drive two hours and fifteen minutes southeast and meet us for a beer.

That one hurts. Like it takes my breath away. Funny how he can throw that shit out now, after we've done the deed and said goodbye.

Already have my pajamas on.

Mmm. The sexy little number you wore with me?

Hardly. Old shorts and a Blues T-shirt.

You're a Blues fan?

Not much of a hockey person, but sure.

So, let's revisit the pajama thing.

I feel a rush of heat in my face and my belly and lower yet. How can those simple words do that to me?

Are you wearing a bra?

I laugh out loud and shake my head, even though no one's around to see me.

Nope.

Damn. It's hot in here.

His words make me laugh, but I'm speechless, and all I can do is stare at my phone. My hands are sweating, and my heart is racing for other reasons now. I miss him. But I'm still…what? Hurt? Angry? Confused?

Everything.

I'm still a little bit of everything.

I can still taste you.

That text goes straight to my core, and my skin is hot and tingly.

Are you seriously sexting me right now?

Well, no. I'm at a bar. My best friend is across the booth.

Then stop!

Can't help it. I see your body every time I close my eyes.

I watched the end of Halloween earlier. It made me think of you.

???

What?

I'm talking dirty to you, telling you I would kill to get another taste of you and you're talking slasher films?

Not just any slasher film.

He doesn't answer right away. I hold my breath and wait, eyes on the phone. Finally, I see the floating dots telling me he's typing something. But they flicker and flicker and finally disappear.

"Great, Cait." I toss my phone down and drag my fingers back through my hair.

Way to blow it. I climb to my feet and pace around the small living area wondering if he'll text again. On my flat screen TV, Ross hurries to the gate as Rachel boards her plane. Frustrated—I feel bad enough on my own, don't need help from fictional characters tonight—I charge back to the couch and grab the remote. My phone starts buzzing as I turn the TV off.

It's a not a text.

Heart ready to explode at the base of my throat, I flip it over and see Isaac's name. Because of course I added him to my contacts, even if I was upset Monday when he texted me.

"What?" I barely breathe the word. Because for one, I'm shaking. I'm scared. I can't talk. And because maybe if everything right here and now is said quietly, maybe it won't be real. If it's bad, we can sweep it away and pretend none of it was said.

"Do you think about it?"

His voice. God, his voice. It slides through me like warm honey, all sweet and sticky, and who the hell am I kidding? I want this man. I. Want. Him.

"About what?" I'm not being coy. I'm terrified of what's on the line here for me. I'm in love with the parts of Isaac Stratton I know. I want to know the rest of him. I want to love the rest of him.

I want all of him to love me. Everything I am.

"Making love with me."

"Are you still in the bar?"

Okay, so probably not the answer he was looking for. But the thought of him having this conversation in front of Josh and Kree makes me ill.

"Cait. Really?" He sounds broken. Kind of quiet. Sad.

"Of course, I think about it, Isaac."

"But you're talking slasher films while I'm imagining the taste of your skin."

"I'm scared," I admit.

"Of what? What happened? What did I do?"

I can't bring myself to speak, to say anything.

"Is it Ryan? Are you—? I don't know...are you considering—"

"No." My voice is firm.

"Then what's wrong? You closed up on me after we made love, and I don't know why. Cait, I was ready to plan a repeat trip to wine country with you. Ready to figure out how to be with you for the 4th of July. What we could do to spend Christmas together."

"Isaac." I groan and drop to sit on the couch.

"But you don't want any of that, do you? Was I just a rebound guy?"

"No."

"When your friends were exchanging vows, I actually thought for a minute about standing there with you."

"Why didn't you tell me?'

"Tell you what? That I was having crazy fantasies about our wedding and the babies we could make together?" He laughs sarcastically. "I guess I figured that might be a little extreme for a plus one to mention to the maid of honor."

I swallow hard and tip my head down. A hot tear slides over my nose.

"That you live in St. Louis."

"I didn't—what? Why didn't I—"

"You told my mom you're from Indianapolis. You told me you were familiar with Quincy. You had every opportunity to tell me how close you were to Quincy."

"I don't—I guess I thought I did tell you that. I was born and raised in Indianapolis. Went to Wash U in St. Louis. I loved it. So I stayed here after school."

I hear voices in the background, but it's mostly quiet. I wonder if he stepped outside, or if he's home now. If Josh is standing by him, listening.

"Why does that matter? What's wrong with St. Louis?"

"You never bothered to tell me you were just a couple hours away." My voice is just a thick whisper. "Like maybe you didn't want what we were doing to go anywhere. I mean—" I backtrack, hoping I don't sound clingy. "It's one thing. To do what we did. To have fun together, to sleep together, and have to walk away because long-distance things are hard. But to me, it's something else if you kept it from me to keep me away when the weekend was over."

He clears his throat, and then I hear him take a deep breath. Might as well bring up that text from Logan, too. The one that still makes me sick to think about.

"I saw that text." I can barely make the words come out. Feeling the need to hide, I cover my face with my free hand and squeeze my eyes closed. The shame I felt when I saw Logan's text creeps back up my throat again, and I feel like I'm going to throw up.

"What text?" He sounds baffled, but I doubt he is. Or maybe he gets a lot of those kinds of texts, so he honestly isn't sure which one I'm referring to.

"The one from Logan." I don't want to cry, so I make my voice hard and angry. "It was disgusting, Isaac."

"Seriously?" he finally says, but the word is small, like he's speaking to me through a long tunnel. Like we're trying to bridge the distance between two very different worlds. "God, Cait, I'm sorry. I didn't know you saw it, but you know Logan can be a dick. You were around him enough to know that."

"Did you guys have a bet on that weekend? About sleeping with me? Or was it worse than that? A twenty for every dirty thing we did together?"

"It wasn't like that, Cait," he says softly. "I'm not like that. Besides, I told Logan to fuck off."

"Well, how do I know, Isaac? You're gorgeous, you're charming. How do I know you don't have a string of women lined up to sleep with at home?"

"Because I said I didn't."

That gets me. Because I believed him then. And I want to believe him now.

"Cait, what I feel for you isn't just gonna go away just because you're back in Illinois, and I'm in Missouri. It wasn't just the wine. Wasn't the venue."

"Me, too." The words are so small, so quiet, I'm not sure he heard me.

"What do you need from me? To believe me?"

I rub my eyes and shake my head, my throat still painfully tight.

"I don't know."

"Okay, Kree mentioned a grand gesture earlier this week."

"What?"

"Like sweeping you off your feet and taking you back to Sonoma. Where we started this fall."

I open my mouth to argue. It's May. We were in wine country in the spring, but I shut it when it hits me that's not what he means.

"But Cait?"

"What?" I rub my lips together and hold my breath.

"Here's the thing. We know we love each other in wine country. I want to love you right here. Right where we are."

"How's that gonna work?" I sniffle and swipe at my nose. "You're two hours away from me."

"If I get in my car right now, I could have you in my arms before midnight."

CHAPTER 30

Isaac

Traffic on I-64 isn't terrible this late in the evening, but I still cuss out every car and truck I pass until I finally take the Wentzville exit for Highway 61 to Hannibal. I've driven to Quincy, Illinois more than once. Funny that Cait Pendleton lives there, and I never knew how much she would come to mean to me those times I was in her town.

By the time I roll through Troy and head on toward Eolia, the number of cars on the highway has really died off. I hated to get off the phone, but when Cait laughed softly, when she sort of whispered *really? You want to do that?* I took off for my truck and left the bar without looking back. I talked to Cait for a while on the phone—hands free, of course—but eventually, I got off the phone to pay attention to the drive. I called Josh, not surprised to get his voicemail. Left him a message to let him and Kree know I was heading west.

I did stop at my apartment and run in like the place was on fire and I had to rescue something or someone. I grabbed clothes and shoes and my toothbrush and shaver and shoved all of it into a duffel bag I normally use for the gym. Didn't want to take the time to dig my luggage back out of the closet.

Cait sent a text when I was on 64, asking if I was seriously planning to drive up and see her. I sent her a horrible quality picture of the steering wheel under my right hand and the highway out my windshield. After that she demanded that I put the phone down and be safe.

I'm going to see Cait. My whole body is alive with electric energy. I'm high on adrenaline, pumped up like I'm ready to skydive. The thing is? This is better. Seeing Cait, seeing that smile again, and pulling her into my arms? So much better than any thrill I've ever had.

My foot's heavy from Bowling Green to Hannibal, but I'm careful once I hit Mark Twain's hometown. They have a lot of cameras on their traffic lights. I maintain the speed limit until I'm a few miles from the exit. From Cait's exit.

And then, I take a chance. My speedometer pushes eighty and higher, maybe about even with the way my heart's ready to shoot out of my body and rocket sky high. I meant what I told her. I loved her in Sonoma. It was a few days, and they were so good, and I tried to hold the gushy, touchy-feely stuff back. But I loved everything about being around Cait.

Now I want to know her here. In our backyard. In the Midwest, where it's hot and miserably humid in the summer. Where we get snow, now and then even a foot or more. I want to know Quincy Cait, where she lives, where she works, shops, eats. I want to live all of that with her.

And I want her to love the Midwestern boy in me. I want her to know me when I'm living day to day, not kicked back enjoying vacation. I want her to love that version of me. Won't happen overnight. I get that.

But it'll never happen at all, if we don't get started now.

Siri's robotic voice tells me to take the exit, so I do, and I coast to a stop at Highway 96. No traffic, I take a left and head up 96 into Quincy. Thank God she gave me her address that first day. Siri leads me into the southern end of town, tells me to make a left on Harrison and follow past 36th Street. The light's green at the intersection, so I slide through, knowing I'm getting close.

Her address is part of a newer condominium complex. I make a right turn into the area, notice a few lights on here and there, and finally Siri says I've reached my destination. I don't need Siri to tell me, though. When I slow the truck at the curb, a porch light comes on, the front door bursts open, and my girl runs outside.

She's wearing old shorts and a Blues T-shirt. I climb out of the truck and tear my eyes from the soft sway of her breasts in her shirt and find that smile I've been missing. She's beautiful. Hair in a messy knot, old clothes, and tear-stained face, she's everything.

Cait Pendleton is a freefall skydive, a magnum of library wine, the Hope diamond. She's comfort and giving and sexy and fun.

And I'm here to make sure she's mine.

Forever.

"You're here," she whispers and before I can move, she throws her arms around my neck.

"I'm here." I duck my face into the hollow between her shoulder and neck and kiss her there. Cait tilts her head back and treats me to that laugh. I'm here. And here feels like home.

"I can't believe you're here." She attacks my mouth, kissing me, her hands cup the back of my head and hold me in place. But I break the kiss and tip my head back to look at her.

"I have to ask you something."

"What?"

For a second I get lost in the stars in her eyes.

"Isaac?" She strokes her fingers through my hair and rests her forehead on mine.

"I need a plus one. I want that to be you."

Her laugh is sweet and soft, and I feel it race through my body to my dick.

"For what?"

"For anything. Everything that comes up in the next ten or twenty years."

She purses her lips and tips her head, kissing me back when I can't take it anymore and have to get my mouth on hers.

"I'd rather you call me your date than your plus one."

"What if we said girl?"

"Little old for that."

"Too old to be *my girl?*"

"Mmm." She wraps her arms around me and buries her face in my neck. "I do like that."

EPILOGUE

ONE YEAR LATER

Cait

Clarissa, from Divine Vineyards, splashes Estate Pinot in two glasses and gently slides them over the tasting table. Isaac and I are doing a tasting, even though we know what we like. The barrel room is cool, though it's a beautiful, sunny day outside. We've been together since last year, since that night he drove those two hours and minutes to see me.

To claim me.

We're doing the long-distance thing, but we're close enough that for now, it works. We've talked about the future, what we'll do, but never in specific details. He doesn't want to take me away from family and friends, though I've told him several times, my parents might be happy to get rid of me by now. I think if we're going to consider being together forever—the thought still gives me happy butterflies—I need to go to him. We need to build a life together in St. Louis.

For now, we're on vacation. We talked with our friends. Jasmine, Derrick, and I wanted to go to the beach this year, but everyone else was pulling for a return to Sonoma, especially Brynna. And Isaac. I figure they're both in something like anniversary mode—the wedding, obviously for Brynna, and the start of our *fall* for Isaac.

"You've been here before, right?" Clarissa asks now. The blonde narrows her blue eyes at us and tips her head. "You look really familiar."

"We were here for a wedding last year," I tell her. Isaac, hands flat on the tasting table, gives me a sweet, private smile. The rest of the gang is out on the patio. We started early today, swung into Café Notto in Windsor for coffee, and then headed this way. I was a little surprised Isaac was ready to hit the wine, already. He must have chugged his coffee. Then again, that would explain why he's been bouncing his knee constantly since we came in.

The rest of the gang is probably kicked back on the patio. Still nursing their coffee. Except Teagan. She might be sipping orange juice. Derrick won't let her look at caffeine, and she hasn't been able to keep much down through her first trimester. That's right; Teag and Derrick are having a baby.

Josh and Kree are engaged. Isaac pinned me against the wall of his place when he told me that. Said Josh asked him to be his best man. Asked me to be his date. Kissed me. Got a little naughty with his hands in my dress. He thinks that's what convinced me to say yes.

Jasmine and Logan are probably outside arguing about the proper pronunciation of the word *pecan*. If there's anything I've learned the past year, it's that the two of them will argue over anything. Including who can walk away from an argument and who has to have the last word. By the way, the first is neither of them, and the second answer is both.

"You like the Estate?" Isaac nods at my glass.

"I do."

"Have you ever tried their Aglianico?"

"No." I tip my head and look from Isaac to Clarissa. "Never heard of it."

"Would you like to try it?"

"Please." I nod. She takes a full bottle from the end of the table and opens it with ease. Behind me and Isaac, the door opens, and another employee sticks his head in. Isaac and I glance his way; he asks Clarissa something about a different vintage cab. When I turn back, my glass is half full of Aglianico.

I hope I like it, though I don't say it out loud.

Isaac picks his glass up and nods for me to pick up mine. It isn't until he looks at Clarissa that I realize she has a glass, too.

"Cheers." Isaac taps his glass to mine and then hers. And I play along, loving that my boyfriend is so sentimental. We sip the wine at the same time and when I go to lower my glass, I see a diamond ring on the table in front of me.

"What?" I shake my head, confused by the toast, the ring, the brilliant smile on Clarissa's face.

"Cait." Isaac takes the ring and slowly bends to one knee in front of me. "You're my best friend. My life. My heart." He kisses my fingers. "Will you be my everything?"

"Isaac." My eyes burn. I swipe at them with my free hand and laugh softly.

"Be my wife?"

"Yes."

His fingers move at my whispered answer. They push the ring over my knuckle on my ring finger.

"She said yes!" Isaac shouts as he stands and gathers me in his arms. I throw my arms around him as the door bursts open again, and the friends I thought were chilling on the patio burst inside, all but Teagan with a glass of champagne. Brynna's beaming, and I see her exchange a look with my everything.

"You guys knew about this?" I laugh and cry, and Clarissa's laughing. I throw her a disbelieving look. "You knew, too?"

"We all knew," Jasmine tells me.

"We did," Logan agrees. I look at Isaac, shocked that the two of them agreed on something. "We knew you would say yes, too."

"You need champagne," Brynna announces. She squeezes my hand and then hands me a glass. Adam reaches over to hand Isaac one, too. "Congratulations."

"Did you put him up to this?" I ask her. Isaac tugs me in closer and kisses the top of my head.

"Nope. I just told him to drag you out and make you do the Foxtrot." Brynna's wide-eyed and innocent. "Teag wanted you to twerk."

A flash of heat warms my face. I duck my head to Isaac's chest.

"Let's do a toast," Clarissa suggests.

I pick up the glass of Aglianico, still holding the champagne in my other hand. Brynna wags her eyebrows at my ring. The pear-shaped diamond makes my heart skip and beat fast and hard.

"I've got one," Isaac says with a small private smile for me.

"Let's hear it!" Josh calls.

Isaac lifts his champagne. "To late night phone calls and jackass exes. Without Ryan, I would never have met my everything."

. . .

***

THANK you for reading Plus One. If you enjoyed Cait and Isaac's story, please consider leaving a review on your favorite bookish or retail site.

READ THE FIRST CHAPTER OF GETTIN' HITCHED

Chapter 1

Mercedes Ingalls slowed her car to a stop and leaned forward to squint through the windshield at the big brick home to her right. An ornate wooden front door, flanked on both sides by ornate sidelights, gave the two-story brick house a snooty, aristocratic appearance. But the bike thrown down in the front yard and the soccer goal tipped over near the drive were clearly the mark of kids, and though Mercedes thought Nicholas Moore's kids were too young to ride bikes that size, she pulled her little Corolla over to the curb to park.

She consulted her phone again, where she'd typed the Moore address into her notes app. 4769 Stardust. Her maxi skirt felt all wrong now. If the Moore kids were old enough to ride a bike that size, somehow wearing a maxi skirt to the interview felt wrong. Maybe she should have worn khakis.

"Too late to worry about it now, Cedes," she mumbled as she swung her car door shut. The mailboxes out here were the fancy kind covered in bricks made to look like miniature houses. No numbers visible anywhere, so she couldn't be sure this was 4769. A beat-up pickup truck was parked across the street, and the garage door at that house was open. But there was no one in sight to ask if she was at Nicholas Moore's house, so she would just have to ring the doorbell and find out.

Mercedes eyed the pristine lawn as she made her way up the driveway. The bike and the soccer goal felt terribly out of place with the perfectly trimmed edges of grass and the vividly colored flowers in what appeared to be professionally done landscaping. An electronic beat pounded faintly from deep inside the house as Mercedes stepped up on the porch and lifted her hand to press the doorbell with her thumb.

She drew her hand away from the doorbell and studied the chipped robin's egg blue polish on her thumbnail. If she got this job, she could maybe start doing professional manicures again. Or at least, maybe she could afford a new bottle of nail polish. What she had now was old and chunky.

When no one answered the door—probably hadn't heard the bell with that music blaring inside—she looked over her shoulder and spotted a guy across the street. He appeared to be heading to the truck at the curb. Mercedes shifted her weight on her feet and turned to get a better look at him. Her movement must have caught his eye, because he waved and hollered hello. Deciding she might have better luck asking him about where Nicholas Moore lived, she stepped off the porch and headed back down the drive.

"Hey."

"Hi." She flashed him a smile as she crossed the street. "Any chance you can tell me which house is Nicholas Moore's?"

"This is Nick's house." The guy met her in the middle of the drive. Mercedes eyed the way his longish, brown hair curled at his crew cut shirt collar and the shock of the same curls that fell over his eyebrow. Broad shoulders filled out the faded brown T-shirt—Mercedes thought the letters across the front spelled race, but the letters, too, were faded, and given that the body under the letters appeared to be textbook perfection, she didn't want to stare too hard. Loose board shorts hung on his hips, though he was anything but scrawny. His long lean legs had been kissed by the sun—

Mercedes gave herself a mental shake. She'd been reading too many romance novels. Time to switch gears and read a thriller or a spy novel. Anything but something that talked about sun-kissed skin and finely chiseled lips and the perfect amount of scruff—

"Doorbell doesn't work," the guy told her as he offered her both a friendly smile and a handshake. "Are you here about the babysitting thing?"

"Nanny," she mumbled, wondering if this guy was actually Nick Moore. Could she be that lucky? She nodded when she realized she had barely mumbled the word and the guy was watching her curiously. Not only was his body textbook perfection, so was his face. Classic bone structure, a perfect arch in his thick eyebrows, and eyes the color of the ocean as the sun sank in the west and darkness merged with the lighter blue waters.

"I'm Parker," he told her. "Nick's brother."

Of course, this couldn't be Nicholas.

Mercedes caught herself before a disappointed sigh could slip out. It didn't matter what Nicholas looked like; she was here to score a nanny position, not a date with the dad. Who was probably married, although nowhere in the five-line job description and contact information did it say anything other than Nicholas Moore.

No matter, Mercedes reminded herself. She wasn't interested in finding a date. She wanted a job. Specifically, a job that would give her some nights and weekends off.

"Mercedes."

The guy had a firm grip, and if anything, his smile grew bigger and more inviting, but there was no telltale romance-novel zing. She didn't have a sudden urge to hold tight to his hand or to snuggle up close to him and press her face to his.

"Nick's inside. In the office."

"Okay." She nodded as the guy dropped her hand and backed away slowly. The worn flip-flops that completed his outfit screamed surfer dude, but being that they were standing in midwestern Illinois and nowhere near a coast, she doubted he had a surfboard stashed in the truck bed.

As if she would simply know where the office was once inside the house, the guy turned and headed down the drive to his truck. Mercedes watched him for a second, but she shifted her gaze back to the house and wondered what Nicholas would be like.

Should she just go on in? Parker's words and actions kind of insinuated that she should. Behind her, the truck came to life with a pretty, low rumble, bringing to mind exes who drove monster trucks and motorcycles. Mercedes chuckled as she tapped on the front door. Rather than stand here and wait and hope Nicholas heard her—she was already late—she twisted the knob and when she found it unlocked, she pushed it open just a smidge.

She peeked her head into a neat little entry way. Slate gray tiles on the floor in front of the door butted up against the snowy white carpet of the living room. A black baby grand dominated the far side of the room, though a big screen TV hung on the east wall. Two gray wing-backed chairs faced the piano, a white leather loveseat faced the TV.

Mercedes held her breath as she stepped inside. Kids lived here? And the carpet was still white?

"Mr. Moore?" she called now as she pushed the door closed behind her. "Mr. Moore, it's Mercedes. Your brother said the doorbell doesn't work."

She heard a deep male voice rambling about technology—something about design and protocol, not that she cared.

The voice grew louder to her right. She looked up just as another beautiful man appeared at the end of a hallway on the east side of the house. There was a resemblance between this guy and the brother who had just left. Nicholas Moore had the same eye color; though his hair was a bit lighter, definitely shorter. A little long for business casual, but Mercedes liked the way it curled over the collar of his dress shirt.

When their eyes met, she started to say something, but he gave her a slight shake of his head. He lifted his finger to stop her and spoke again, this time talking about numbers and projections. He turned his head just enough that Mercedes saw he had a Bluetooth earpiece in his right ear. She closed her mouth, prepared to wait him out.

She let her gaze roam to a small formal dining room to her left. The ornate white marble table could seat six. The upright iron chairs covered in dove grey cushions looked pretentious and uncomfortable. Abstract art in shades of grays and golds hung on the southern wall. The longer Mercedes stared at the twisted lines and splashes of color, the more her head hurt. Instead, she turned to look her fill at Nicholas Moore while he was otherwise occupied.

He wore charcoal gray trousers—they were expensive, Mercedes could tell from looking—and a lavender dress shirt. The collar was unbuttoned; his sleeves were rolled up to reveal his forearms. A fancy gold watch decorated his left wrist, but his fingers were bare.

Which, Mercedes reminded herself, didn't mean anything. Some men didn't wear wedding rings.

Not that it mattered one way or another to her.

She noticed he was wearing wingtips and wondered if he always appeared this uptight or if it was simply the hassle of hiring a new nanny. Or…a nanny. Did they have to let someone go? Or maybe their nanny quit or moved away?

"Mercedes?"

She wondered where the kids were now. It was awfully quiet in here for children of any age, and though the description hadn't specifically said *how many* children of *what age*, Mercedes thought there should be some kind of noise.

Poor kids.

She couldn't imagine living in a beautiful, cold house like this when she was younger. She and her brother had been holy terrors when they were kids; thankfully, her parents had given them a lot of freedom to grow up and learn on their own. Some people thought she and Aaron had too much freedom. Mercedes thought some people had too much time on their hands if they needed to worry so much about how she and Aaron were raised.

"Ms. Ingalls?"

She snapped to attention at the use of her last name. Nicholas Moore pulled the Bluetooth piece from his ear and stared at her expectantly now.

"Yes."

"We can talk in the office."

***

If you would like to read more about Mercedes and Nick, you can download the full-length novel—Gettin' Hitched —here:

UBL: https://books2read.com/u/baaykv

ABOUT THE AUTHOR

Tracy is the author of the Lorelei Bluffs women's fiction series, the Williams Legacy, and several stand-alone women's fiction novels. She has recently dabbled in contemporary romance, as well.

Visit Tracy online at www.broemmerbooks.com

ALSO BY TRACY BROEMMER

Women's Fiction Novels:

Luther's Cross (Writing as Therese Kinkaide)

Luther's Cross 10th Anniversary Edition (Tracy Broemmer)

Fairytale (Writing as Therese Kinkaide)

Just Like Them (Writing as Therese Kinkaide)

Small Hours (Writing as Therese Kinkaide)

Picket Fences

Two Story Home

Green-Eyed Girl

Say Everything

Come Home For Christmas

Sketching Litchfield Lake

Ever, Again

Safe as Houses

Damsel

Every Little Thing, Lorelei Bluffs, Book 1

Two A.M., Lorelei Bluffs, Book 2

Blind, Lorelei Bluffs, Book 3

Leaving July, Lorelei Bluffs, Book 4

Hesitation Marks, Lorelei Bluffs, Book 5

Four Letter Words, Lorelei Bluffs, Book 6

See Kate, Lorelei Bluffs, Book 7

Boone's Girl, A Novella, Published in the Aced, Back to School Anthology

(Holdin' On, The H Books, Book 2.5, Published in the Snowed Inn Anthology)

Contemporary Romance Short Stories:

Perfect Pictures, The Wine Tasting Series, Traminette

Coming Home, The Wine Tasting Series, Edelweiss

Save Me Every Dance, The Wine Tasting Series, Rosé

Marry Me, The Wine Tasting Series, Shiraz

Birthday Wishes, The Wine Tasting Series, Muscat

Dad Jeans, The Wine Tasting Series, Vignoles